the
is always
with us

Also by David M Allan

The Empty Throne

Quaestor
Thiever

the magic is always with us

david m allan

Elsewhen Press

The Magic is always with us
First published in Great Britain by Elsewhen Press, 2024
An imprint of Alnpete Limited

Elsewhen Press, PO Box 757, Dartford, Kent DA2 7TQ
www.elsewhen.press

British Library Cataloguing in Publication Data.
A catalogue record for this book is available from the British Library.
ISBN 978-1-915304-42-1 Print edition
ISBN 978-1-915304-52-0 eBook edition

Designed and formatted by Elsewhen Press

For Moira, as Always.

contents

Dramatis Personae

Members of the Group of Eleven

Brangret .... Goblin
Dhugalt .... Fay
Fuormil .... Fay
Klinmerd .... Goblin
Sumethla .... Elf
Tredun.. Goblin
Wardlik .... Fay

In Eideann

Igrainid *Cridhe Eideannach* .... Fay
Trinafar (aka Catriona Farquar) *Daughter of Igrainid* .... Fay
Rhiannis *Trinafar's sister* .... Fay
Saefan *Trinafar's sister* .... Fay
Dunarh *Trinafar's brother* .... Fay
Fergus Monteith............ Human / Shapechanger cross-breed
Misghel *Commander of the Guard* .... Elf
Maedron (aka Max Donaldson) *Son of Misghel* .... Elf
Yuseth *Chronicler* .... Antrop
Kegg'gruk A*mbassador from Cairgon*....................... Dwarf
Seglesh... Troll
Hurilt *Member of Igrainid's council* .... Elf

In Obharden

Peruch *Cridhe Obhardennan*...................................... Goblin
Rulidh *Half-brother of Peruch* .... Fay
Volissen *Ambassador from Eideann* .... Elf
Duncan Kirkpatrick .... Fay / Human cross-breed

Others

Fliorign *Member of the Wild Hunt* .... Elf
Ghara *Cridhe Dundhehann*.. Goblin
Husret *Member of the Wild Hunt*..................................... Elf

meeting

The young woman in the reading room was engrossed in comparing the texts of the two books lying on the elegant rosewood table in front of her. One of the books she was frowning at was a modern transcription of the other, a medieval tome in a particularly difficult court hand. In places the manuscript was faded, stained and torn. Some parts were in such poor condition that they were illegible. She was concentrating so much that she wasn't really aware of the reading room door opening and closing and didn't notice the quiet footsteps of someone coming up behind her.

"Excuse me. Are you Catriona Farquhar?"

The voice that asked that unexpected question was quiet but, in the stillness of the library, it sounded like a shout.

Catriona swivelled her chair round to find herself looking at the belt buckle of a tall man standing close to her. He loomed over her, much closer than she had realised, and she made an involuntary sound of alarm as she pushed her chair back and stood up.

Standing made little difference. At barely over five feet tall, even with the benefit of three-inch heels, she was used to looking up at people, but not often so far up, at least not when the person she was looking at was human. He was at least a foot and a half taller than her and, she thought, perhaps even three or four inches more than that.

He took a step back and said, "Sorry. I didn't mean to startle you."

Catriona also stepped back, managing to avoid stumbling over her chair. She swept long red-gold hair back from her face and looked more closely at the man who had startled her. From a couple of paces away he didn't look quite so intimidating. In fact, for all his height, he was rather slightly built, with a long face, blue eyes and a hint of ginger in his fair hair. A slightly quizzical smile made him look much more benign as he repeated his question, "*Are* you Catriona Farquhar?"

"I am," she replied, relieved to hear her voice was steady.

"Oh, good. You're a difficult person to find."

"Obviously not too difficult since you've succeeded in finding me. Now, kindly tell me why you've been looking for me," said Catriona. *Who is he, and what's he doing here? Is he dangerous?* She slid her left hand into a seam pocket in her long tweed skirt. Through it she could touch the hilt of the shadow-knife tattooed on her thigh. She was relieved when it became solid enough to grip as it was supposed to but she hoped she wouldn't need to use it.

"Well … " He looked around. "This probably isn't the best place for a long explanation. Can we go somewhere else? I'll buy you a cup of coffee."

Catriona glanced around too. Although neither of them had spoken loudly both the only other researcher in the reading room and the librarian were looking disapprovingly in their direction. *Don't think I'll need the knife, at least not immediately. He's not going to do anything with witnesses present, is he?* She removed her hand from her pocket and felt the solidity of the shadow-knife fade.

"Coffee! No thanks, I can't stand the stuff. But there's a decent teashop nearby. We could go there."

"That'll do."

Keeping half an eye on the stranger, she picked up the tweed half-cape matching her skirt from the back of her chair, swirled it over her shoulders and fastened it at the neck with an amethyst brooch. She double checked that she had all of her notes before sliding her notebook and pencils into her shoulder bag. The librarian, sitting in her cubicle by the door, took the books Catriona had been studying, checked them off on her list and looked into the bag to make sure there was nothing belonging to the library in it. Then she smiled, nodded, and pressed a button to release the door lock.

The door opened letting Catriona, and the stranger, into

the main room of the rare books library of Edinburgh University. It was considerably busier there, but it held the same air of concentrated hush that all libraries seem to have. There were no signs to indicate that the small room they'd left was the private reading room of ISIS, the Imperial Society for the Investigation of the Supernatural. It wasn't exactly a secret, but its existence wasn't well known and it certainly wasn't publicised. That anonymity was one of the reasons it had been difficult to get access to it ever since James IX had established the Society in the late Eighteenth century.

"This way," said Catriona, leading the stranger out of the library and into the south-east corner of the Old College Quad. They walked past pillars and arches grimy from hundreds of years of smoke, turned up the hill towards Nicolson Square and into the tangle of narrow streets around it. The streets were busy enough that she had no qualms about being unprotected if the stranger turned out to be dangerous. Just in case he wasn't the only person interested in her she kept an eye out for anyone else following them. There wasn't anybody; at least, there wasn't anybody she could see.

Halfway along one of the streets was a nondescript door. The sign above it said '*The T Shoppe*'. It was painted a dark reddish brown, with brass hinges. She pushed it open. A bell jangled. The two people sitting at a table just inside the door glanced up as they entered, then returned to their conversation.

Panelled in polished dark oak, with a mirror behind the counter running down the left side, the shop was deeper than it was wide. There were eight small tables suitable for two people on the right, and half a dozen larger tables beyond the end of the counter. The proprietor of the teashop, an elderly, slightly stooped man with straggly white hair, came forward from behind the counter and said, "Miss Farquhar, how nice to see you again." He ushered her to one of the larger tables at the back and asked, "Will your guest take tea?"

Catriona turned to the stranger, raised an interrogative

eyebrow and received a nod in return. She said, "Yes," and watched the proprietor bustle off to attend to a kettle while she waved her companion to a chair in a corner behind the table. She took the chair opposite for herself so that she had more freedom of movement than he did. Her shoulder bag went on the floor between them. *It might get in the way enough to be useful if he tries anything.*

She looked across the table at him and said, "Well, Mr … ?"

"Monteith. My name is Fergus Monteith."

"Why were you looking for me?"

"Because I need your help."

"*My* help? Why would you need that?"

Fergus glanced around and, although none of the other customers were close enough to overhear, he leaned towards Catriona and said, very quietly, "Because I need to go to Tirog."

I was afraid of that, thought Catriona. Then she realised he had said 'I', not 'you' and relaxed slightly. *So it's not a summons. Perhaps I can get out of this.* She said nothing as the proprietor returned with a tray holding a pot of tea, two fine porcelain teacups with gold rims on matching saucers and a plate of gingerbread. He filled one of the cups and offered it to her. She took it, sniffed appreciatively, smiled, and took a sip. "Darjeeling," she said and took another sip, "Second Flush, I think. You didn't give me this the last time I was here. Have you had a new delivery?"

"Correct as always, Miss Farquhar. It is a new shipment of Darjeeling. It arrived yesterday, a very satisfactory supply."

"Excellent," said Catriona. "I'll take a quarter pound."

"Certainly, Miss Farquhar." He paused for a moment, his head turning towards her companion. "Will there be anything else?"

"Not at the moment," she said, with a slight shake of her head.

The proprietor poured another cup of the fragrant liquid

from the pot and placed it in front of Fergus before leaving them.

"Wouldn't you prefer coffee?" asked Catriona. "It is available here."

"I would, but I've got the idea that asking for it in this establishment wouldn't be looked on favourably. It might even be considered blasphemous."

"Well said, Mr Monteith," she replied in an amused tone. "You are quite correct. It might well be." She slipped her hand into the skirt pocket again. Reassured by the developing solidity of the shadow-knife, she said, "Now tell me how you know about Tirog, why you want to go there and why you think I can help you."

"I know about it for the same reason you do. Like you, I'm a cross-breed. My father was human and my mother a shapechanger. Dad was killed in an accident when I was eleven and mother went back to Tirog leaving me to be brought up by my father's sister."

Catriona looked at his reflection in the mirror behind the counter. She squinted slightly and saw a faint glimmer of ultraviolet in his hair. It was quite weak and she hadn't noticed it previously, but it confirmed his claim to be part sidhe – the tint was always easier to see in a reflection, particularly when it was weak. She drank some tea and nibbled a small piece of the gingerbread, saying nothing in the hope that her silence would encourage him to carry on talking.

Fergus tried the tea, made a face and pushed it to one side. "Mother used to tell me stories about Tirog and how wonderful it is compared with this world. Her stories have left me wanting – no, it's stronger than that – longing to get there. You could say it's my spiritual home. I've been looking for a way to get to Tirog for the last fifteen years, ever since she left me."

"Didn't your mother take you there?"

"She did a couple of times when I was very young. I have memories of a place that seemed more real, more – vibrant than here. I can remember every moment of every visit. I loved the feel of the place. The sun was brighter, the leaves greener and the air sweeter there. But we never stayed there for more than a day or two. It always seemed there was something missing whenever we came back from Tirog." He paused briefly, shook his head and added, "I don't know why she stopped taking me, she never explained. I was about eight the last time I was in Tirog."

"You can't get there by yourself?"

"No," said Fergus. "Mother told me a few cross-breeds, maybe one in ten or twelve, can open a lacuna and pass through to Tirog without help. She said most can't … " His voice dropped to a whisper and faded out.

"Go on."

He shook his head and sighed before saying, "I'm one of the majority. Although I know where to find the lacuna my mother used it won't open for me. I've tried it many times, at dawn, midnight, noon and sunset, at every phase of the moon and in all sorts of weather. That's why I need your help. For years I've been looking for someone who could take me to Tirog. You're the first one I've managed to find."

"What makes you think I can open a lacuna?"

"Because James Ramsey told me about you and how you had helped him."

Catriona jerked upright, a piece of gingerbread part of the way to her mouth.

Ramsey! That's impossible. She took a firmer grip of the shadow knife's hilt wondering again if she'd have to use it.

"How do you know James Ramsey? Is he a friend of yours?"

"I wouldn't call him a friend," replied Fergus. "Just an acquaintance really. I've met him a few times at meetings of the Convocation of Hermes."

Catriona blinked and said, "That credulous bunch! You're not serious!"

"Yes, I am," replied Monteith, "It might not be a particularly respectable organisation with its focus on extrasensory perception and other strange, weird and unexplained phenomena, but it does at least recognise the existence of the two worlds. Not too many people or organisations do that. Even the Imperial court officially denies that Tirog is real, although I understand a few of the nobles will admit to its existence if pressed. I'm sure many others must know the truth but choose not to acknowledge it.

"I joined the Convocation three years ago because I was desperate to get any help I could from any source. To be honest about it I never really expected to get anything out of my membership, but it paid off a couple of months ago."

"How?"

"Ramsey was one of the volunteer subjects at a demonstration of mesmerism I attended. At the end of the meeting the mesmerist released all the volunteers from his influence. He thanked them for their participation in the demonstration and announced they were free of any and all compulsions."

"Ah! I understand," said Catriona. *Curse that showoff mesmerist!*

"Carry on. Tell me what Ramsey told you."

"In the bar after the meeting he told a small group of us that he had forgotten about the incident, but now remembered he had been the victim of a curse a little more than three years ago. He thought a spell must have compelled him to forget it about it, strange as that seemed to the rest of us. He guessed that the mesmerist had inadvertently released him from that spell.

"He described having got a piece of parchment through the post. He said he had felt a cold shiver down his back when he opened it. It had his name on it, all tangled up in a mass of strange symbols. Afterwards all sorts of things had gone wrong for him. I don't remember everything he told us about but there are some I do. They were an odd mixture of the trivial and the significant. For example; he had dropped his car keys into a drain five minutes before the car park closed for the night; the company that insured his business had gone bust and its failure had cost him thousands; he broke both shoelaces within moments of each other; his fiancée had sent his ring back with no explanation and didn't return his calls; milk turned sour as soon as he poured it; he missed an important business meeting because his train was twice delayed by a signal failure; and so on."

Catriona nodded. "I understand," she said. "Technically it was a hex, not a curse although the distinction isn't important. Ramsey is influential enough that he could – shall we say *persuade* me to go to Tirog on behalf of the ISIS and negotiate with the Synod of the Combined Domains and Realms of Alba to force the magician who cast the hex to rescind it."

"Why was Ramsey forced to forget the incident?"

"His amnesia was part of my price for getting the hex negated. I didn't want to be continually pestered by people asking me to do something magical for them, and I still don't." She sighed. "What a nuisance. Now that Ramsey remembers I suppose I can expect to be bothered by everyone he's told about me, like you."

"No, I don't think you need worry about that," said Fergus. "Ramsey realised he had been compelled to forget the incident. I don't think he was too happy about that, but he still felt grateful for what you did and said he wanted to respect your apparent desire for secrecy. He wouldn't give me your name, or tell me anything about you, until I got him very, very drunk. By that stage I was the only one paying any attention to him. After that it was a matter of tracking you down."

Catriona sighed, sat back in her chair and said, "Well, you did manage that. What now?"

"As I said, I need to go to Tirog. Please take me there."

"Why should I?"

"Because that's where I belong."

"You might think that. Oh, I accept it's where you want to belong, but it's not as simple as that. The Domains and Realms can be dangerous if you don't fit in, and there's no guarantee you will. I'm sure some of your mother's stories and some of your childhood experiences in Tirog have involved magic and what can be done with it. She may have, quite literally, entranced you with her tales. Being a cross-breed means there is a possibility you will have some talent for magic in Tirog, but it doesn't guarantee it. If it turns out you don't – and I've got to warn you most cross-breeds don't – then you'll have no status there."

"I'll take that chance."

Catriona sighed again. "I suppose it was Ramsey who got you access to the ISIS library where you found me."

"Yes."

"I want to keep using that library. It's important to my research and I can't take the risk of being denied entry to it. I don't know if you're the kind of person who will resort to blackmail but I'm not going to gamble on it." She paused briefly before saying, "Very well Mr Monteith – I agree to take you to Tirog and try to get you permission to stay."

Catriona saw Fergus's face light up when he said, "Thank you."

"I'll also give you a word of warning. My magic is quite weak and there are many more powerful than me in Tirog. If one of them forbids it you won't be allowed to stay." Catriona paused. "Are you sure you still want to go?"

"Yes! I'll take the chance."

"Right," said Catriona with a shrug. "There's also the possibility you won't be allowed to leave once there even if you want to. You could even end up as an ensorcelled servant. It all depends on the impression you make and who, if anyone, sponsors you. If you are set on going I'll meet you at midday tomorrow at the Tron. I presume you know where that is?"

"Of course I do. I might have been born out in the country near Inverness but I'm not a yokel. I've lived in Edinburgh ever since I came to university here."

"Good. Any questions?"

"What can I bring with me?"

"Anything you can carry."

"No restrictions? What about iron, or salt, or garlic?"

Catriona laughed. "Didn't your mother tell you that a lot of the stories you hear about the sidhe are inaccurate at best and often positively misleading? It is true that some sidhe have particular vulnerabilities but by no means all of them do. Those things won't necessarily provide protection, if that's why you want them. Iron might cancel a spell or prevent one taking effect, but you'd be foolish to rely on that. Salt will, at most, irritate dryads and a few of the other races of Tirog who might take that irritation out on you. As for the idea that garlic is protective, that is complete and utter nonsense. Personally, I wouldn't advise bringing any of them, but you can if you want to. Now leave me to drink my tea in peace."

She watched Fergus leave, let the shadow-knife fade into insubstantiality again, then beckoned the proprietor of the teashop over and said to him, "Did you overhear us?"

"Yes, my lady. I fear he may be a problem."

"He already is."

"Would you have me – take care of him – my lady?"

"No … No, I don't think so," said Catriona. "It's a tempting thought, but I can always leave him stranded if necessary or have someone take insult from him and issue a challenge."

"As you wish."

"Give me another pound of the Darjeeling. It will make a suitable gift for my mother."

"Certainly, my lady. Would you be kind enough to mention to her that you obtained it from me?"

"Of course I will. I owe you that much at least for your work here."

The proprietor disappeared behind the counter and quickly returned with the tea Catriona had requested. Then he bowed as he held the door open for her to leave.

elsewhere

The-place-that-doesn't-exist wasn't dark or light, hot or cold. In fact it had no physical attributes of any type. The most that can be said of it was that it was defined by the presence of the Group of Eleven.

The Eleven who gave it significance were all magi; very powerful magic users who were their own Sources and didn't have to depend on others to supply them with the power they needed for their magic.

As they appeared within the non-space they greeted each other with words and gestures which were carefully chosen and didn't imply any ranking among them. They were quite prepared to accept each other as of equal status both in the real world and in this non-space knowing, as they did, that any sign of weakness could easily be fatal.

Although the membership of the Eleven had been unchanged for almost seventy years there were always other potential members observing a meeting from just beyond the limits of the quasi-space. Each of the observers was a magus, potentially just as strong as any of the Eleven. They lingered nearby, on the margins of the place-that-was-not. All of these observers were ready to replace any of the existing members of the Eleven if they faltered; hoping to be able to pounce on some perceived weakness or error; prepared, under the right circumstances, to risk attempting to oust an incumbent in the same way each of the present members had replaced their predecessors. However, they were all aware that an ill-judged attack on an established member of the Eleven was risky and could easily result in obliteration. Membership of the Eleven conferred long life as well as increased magical ability and political power in return for the relatively minor duties imposed by their peers. Knowing this, all of the magi, whether one of the Eleven or not, felt that trying to gain or hold a place in the Group could be worth the risk.

Each of the Eleven had once been part of the cloud of observers and knew what it was like to linger hopefully on the periphery, waiting for an opportunity. Many of them were, or had been, members of the Synod of the Combined Domains and Realms of Alba. That body apparently ruled Alba, but in fact the Group of Eleven was more powerful.

Members of the Eleven didn't always agree but they all knew each of them was vulnerable to replacement and, on the whole, they did tend to support each other against attacks by the hopeful.

One of the elvish members of the Eleven, called Dhugalt, manifested in the place-that-was-not a moment before any of the others – assuming that a moment, or any other measure of time, had any significance in that place. By custom that made him the leader of the Eleven for the duration of the meeting.

The meeting, one of those arranged to match the phases of the moon, had no fixed agenda. Dhugalt simply asked for questions. He wasn't surprised when Wardlik, one of the fay members of the Group, asked if there was any news about the Failed Source. It was a subject Wardlik had pursued every year for seventeen years, ever since the woman in question had become old enough to generate latency.

"The situation is unchanged," said Dhugalt. "The pedigree of the Failed Source has been confirmed and there is no doubt that she should be a Source. However, she is now twenty-four years old and shows no more evidence of being able to generate latency than she did at seven."

As was usually the case when this topic was raised, Kragum, the only dwarf among the Eleven, criticized Wardlik for wasting their time with that question when he already knew the answer to it.

This censure, although quite mild, provoked some interest among the magi on the periphery of the quasi-space. The permanent feeling of mild pressure within it increased a little. The proximity of several of the hopeful became evident with them manifesting as disturbances in the ambient space, like minivortices hovering on the edge of perception as they prepared to push themselves forward should that become possible.

The feeling of pressure from the halo of observers continued to increase until Dhugalt pointed out that instances of anomalous Source inheritance had been discussed by the Group of Eleven many times without them gaining any understanding of the phenomenon.

Two other members of the Group agreed with Dhugalt. They emphasised how rare an occurrence the anomaly was. Neither of them had been members of the Eleven for long enough to have experienced the last time it happened.

The support the two provided was enough to ease the tension. The awareness of the hopeful faded into the background with a suggestion of chagrin and frustration over lost opportunities.

All that can be said of time in that non-space is that it passed. When Dhugalt brought the meeting to an end some felt that hours had elapsed while others thought it had lasted only seconds. It made no difference. The Group of Eleven left the meeting space to return to their places in the real world.

The place-that-didn't-exist shed whatever cohesion it had and, very quickly, it wasn't there again.

το τιroς

Catriona wasn't the least bit surprised to find Fergus waiting for her when she walked up the steep street to the Tron Square shortly before noon the next day. She sighed to herself. She had wondered if he might change his mind, but had known it wasn't a realistic hope; his mother's stories and his own childhood memories of Tirog had clearly enthralled him. *I expect he's been waiting for a couple of hours at least, or even longer. At least he's dressed well enough for the trip.* He was wearing a sturdy dark-green canvas jacket over a flannel shirt and faded jeans. His hiking boots looked as well used as her own, as did the well stuffed rucksack at his feet.

She saw the moment when he spotted her. He stopped scanning the passers-by and the tension left his stance. He stooped, picked up his rucksack, settled it comfortably on his shoulders and walked to meet her.

"Didn't think I was coming, eh?" she said as she turned back down the street she had just come up.

"I've got to admit I wasn't sure," he replied.

"Well, that's something you'll have to be careful about. I'm sure all the stories you've heard say the sidhe are bound by any promises they make and they will do almost anything to avoid making one."

"Yes."

"You can't believe everything you've heard about Tirog and its peoples but that one at least isn't *too* inaccurate. It's true to say that for some members of some races any agreement, like the one I made to take you to Tirog, might well constitute a binding contract. That's most likely to be true of fay, but bargains can bind other races too."

From the corner of her eye she saw him nod. He was obviously paying attention.

"Then again," she said, "You must be careful about what you say and who you say it to. Some apparent bargains might not be binding because they don't offer anything in return and a bargain has to benefit both parties."

Fergus paused to ease the position of his rucksack, which was quite heavy. The pause to adjust it made him drop behind her. Catriona didn't wait for him. A few long strides soon brought him beside her again.

"The other thing you need to remember is that a few of the most powerful fay can ignore the promises they make without suffering any consequences. They do that by transferring the responsibility for fulfilling a bargain to a subordinate. Such shifted bargains are often on less favourable terms than the original agreements. Sometimes the problem is knowing what level of commitment applies to who."

Catriona saw Fergus frowning and realised she'd have to tell him more.

"It can be difficult," she said. "Be certain you know exactly what is involved in any deal you are offered. Don't accept any offers without understanding what it is you are agreeing to. You should treat anything that might be interpreted as a promise as being one."

She kept walking, confident he would follow her. Near the bottom of the street, before reaching the Cowgate, she turned left into a narrow passage, then left again into a tight, dark space. She produced a torch and shone its beam around. The space was enclosed by, and roofed with, rough, lichen-covered stone. A battered wooden door blocked her way. She felt the slight tingle and the sensation of unreality that always accompanied proximity to a lacuna.

"Isn't this the way to the Vaults?" asked Fergus. "I've heard of them but I've got to admit I've never visited them. They're one of the places around Edinburgh I've always intended to go to but I've never got round to."

"It is, but it's also the way to Tirog."

"You mean it's a lacuna! Right here in the middle of town! Where does it open?"

"In the Domain of Eideann. And that reminds me. Where is the lacuna your mother used?"

"In a sea cave near Elgin."

"What a shame, I was hoping you'd tell me about one that's new to me."

Fergus looked around. "What do we do now?"

"Try to open the door."

Fergus took hold of the doorknob and pulled. The door opened silently and easily on well lubricated hinges to reveal a short passage blocked by a turnstile.

"No," said Catriona, "this is where the Vaults tour starts. I confess I didn't expect it to open for you, but you never know. Some lacunae will open for one person and not another. It was worth a try, but it seems you can't open this lacuna either. Close the door again."

Fergus let the door swing shut.

Catriona reached past him to grasp the doorknob. She pushed. With a squeal of rusty hinges the door opened. This time it revealed a cramped, dark, roughly pyramidal space formed by massive boulders leaning against each other. A glimmer of sunlight was visible ahead. "Go on," she said, "the lacuna will close behind me and leave you here if I go first."

Fergus took one step forward and stopped. Catriona had to push him to get him moving again before she could follow him. She could stand without difficulty in the space but Fergus had to stoop to fit in.

"Keep going," said Catriona, pushing him again.

They walked out into the sunlight where a small copse of trees clustered around the cave that formed the entrance to the lacuna on the Tirog side. The trees were mostly ash and birch just beginning to show autumn colours. Ahead and to the right the ground fell away quite steeply. A grassy path led off to the left and started climbing, gradually narrowing as it did so until it was only wide enough for one person at a time.

Catriona took a few deep breaths, enjoying the fresh, clean smell, so different from the oily, sooty stink of Edinburgh.

Home! She could feel tears filling her eyes and blinked rapidly to stop them from spilling over.

"Where are we?" asked Fergus.

"Exactly where we were but in Eideann instead of Edinburgh," she replied. "Don't you know the geography of Tirog is the same as the world you're used to?"

"Yes, mother did tell me that, but I hadn't really realised it. It looks so different." He looked around, took a few deep breaths and said, "I can hardly believe I'm in Tirog again."

"Believe it. This is Tirog. One reason why it looks different is because man-made things, or sidhe-made for that matter, aren't mirrored in both worlds. This is what Edinburgh would be like if they hadn't drained the Nor Loch and built the Mound and the New Town. You'll find it a confusing mixture of places you almost recognise and those you don't. For example, there is a building that could be described as a castle in the same place in both worlds but they don't look even remotely like each other."

She turned round, examining the small wood with a slight frown. *There's something wrong. There should be a sentry here guarding the lacuna.*

A broken tree stump caught her eye. *I don't remember seeing that before!* She reached into a pocket, pulled out a laser pointer and shone it at a nearby tree. Then she changed her aim, moving the red dot on to the stump. It didn't stop at the bark but illuminated something inches deeper than the apparent surface.

Catriona pointed at the stump and said, "I know where you are. Show yourself."

A multi-coloured shimmering cloud appeared around the stump and quickly condensed into a thin, pale-skinned figure even taller than Fergus, with angular features and amber eyes. Orange and green feathers formed his crest and eyebrows and rimmed his ears. He was wearing a brown and green padded gambeson, was carrying a recurve bow and had a quiver of arrows at his belt. He also had a bronze longsword slung across his back, the hilt protruding above his left shoulder.

"Maedron! What news do you have? Why are you

hiding? And what are *you* doing on guard duty?"

"Lady Trinafar, welcome back to Eideann. It's a pleasure to see you here again," said the elf, going to one knee. "That wand you have is effective. I'm surprised how easily it broke my glamour. Tell me, my lady, who is this you have brought with you?"

"You haven't answered my questions, Maedron, and I asked first."

"True, my lady." Maedron sighed and stood up. "I wasn't hiding from you, merely practicing glamours to relieve the tedium of guard duty."

"That doesn't explain why you, of all people, are here."

"I fear I upset your mother and she condemned me to stand day-guard here for the rest of this moon. Only one more day to go, thank the Starmaker."

"What can you have done to upset her that much?"

"Please, Lady Trinafar, don't ask me that."

"I will find out you know."

"I do, but it will seem less significant if you hear it from other lips than mine."

"I suppose I'll have to accept that as an answer," said Catriona. "Now tell me the news."

"There isn't really an awful lot to tell, my lady. Let me think – Nobody's died, but Lenerish had an accident in the quarry last week and came close to killing himself. He knocked himself unconscious for most of a day and managed to break both bones in his left leg; Lady Rhiannis got back from Uvan six days ago. She's made it clear to everyone who will listen that she didn't enjoy her stay there. I don't think she's stopped grumbling since her return about how provincial a town it is. Hmm, what else? We have a new ambassador from Cairgon, a dwarf called Kegg'gruk who arrived six or seven weeks ago and is boring to tears everyone who will listen to him talk about his home. He's also being very insistent about the correct pronunciation of his name – you know what dwarves can be like about that; The Hunt has been seen twice in the last month but, as far as I know, there were no face-to-face encounters; the weather has been much as you would expect at this time of year, windy and intermittently drizzly. This is the first dry day for a week."

"Rhiannis is home? Thank you for the warning."

"My turn to ask questions, I think," said Maedron. "Who is your companion?"

"He is a cross-breed who asked for my help in penetrating the lacuna."

"A cross-breed!" said Maedron, dropping his bow and drawing his sword as he moved to stand between Fergus and Trinafar.

"Who is your parent?" he asked.

Catriona saw Fergus looking bemused, with his gaze switching back and forth between her and Maedron. He didn't answer the question.

"I ask again," said Maedron. "Who is your parent?"

"You must answer," she told him. "As a sentry he has the right to ask."

With obvious reluctance, Fergus said, "My mother is from Tirog, my father was Brendan Mon …"

"I am not interested in your human parent," snapped Maedron. "I ask for the third time, who is your parent?"

"He has asked three times," said Catriona, "That means he can force you to answer. I suggest you do before he puts a spell on you."

"Her name's Karyia …"

"To which Domain or Realm is her bond?"

"I don't understand."

Catriona took pity on his obvious confusion and said, "He wants to know which Domain or Realm holds her allegiance. Where does she come from?"

"We lived not far from Inverness. I don't remember her mentioning anything about being part of a particular Realm or Domain. We didn't visit Tirog very often and I don't remember the subject ever coming up."

"Well, what *do* you know about her?" asked Maedron.

"She's a shapechanger."

Maedron took a step forward, raising his sword high, ready to strike. "What is her other form? Is she a wolf, or a bear, or a seal, or perhaps a horse? What is she?"

"She's a sea otter. Dad was a fisherman and she would help him by herding fish. That's how they met. He rescued her from a net she was entangled in."

Maedron grunted. "An otter! That's quite unusual. The only lodge of Lutrans I've ever heard of is part of the Realm of Feahranath. They live about thirty miles east of Inbhirnis. The last I heard Eideann and Feahranath were allied." He looked at Fergus.

"Can you shapechange? Did you inherit that from her?"

Fergus shook his head. "No. I got nothing of magic from her. Only stories of how wonderful Tirog is, and how it might be different for me here."

Maedron nodded, then sheathed his sword. "Without creating obligation on either side, I welcome you to the Domain of Eideann, son of an ally."

He turned to Catriona and said, "Lady Trinafar, you should take him to the Towers."

"That's what I was planning on doing, Maedron," she said. "I expect I will see you later." She beckoned to Fergus to follow her and started up the path, saying to Maedron with a laugh, "Meanwhile I'll leave you to practice your glamours in peace."

They climbed up the path until they were well away from the lacuna and out of sight of Maedron, then Fergus stopped and said to her back, "That elf, Maedron. He knelt to you and called you *Lady* Trinafar! And your mother commands guards like him! You can't be a cross-breed. Who are you?"

She stopped too and turned to look at him. "He called me Trinafar because that's my name. Catriona is just a pseudonym I use in the second world. And I never said I was a cross-breed. That was your assumption and I had no duty to correct your error."

"But … You mean you're pureblood sidhe."

"I am."

"What were you doing in Edinburgh?"

"That is none of your business," she said, frowning at Fergus. "Let me give you another piece of advice."

"What will it cost me?"

"Good," she said. "You're learning. In this case it will cost you nothing, I will give you it freely. It's quite simple – don't be too inquisitive. It can be dangerous." She carried on up the path and stopped when it climbed above the level of the treetops and they could look up at the Three Towers.

Trinafar smiled to herself when Fergus gaped at his first sight of Luchairt Eideann. As she had warned him, it looked nothing like the Edinburgh Castle he was used to seeing. The three huge, slightly tapering, circular towers shone white in the early afternoon sunlight. They were interconnected by bridges at various levels, and windows indicated five or six levels in each tower. Single or two-storey buildings filled the gap between two of the towers and the rest was a garden, full of colour.

Many people, some shorter than her and others taller than Maedron, moved along the roads connecting the bases of the towers to each other, to other nearby buildings and along the street which in Edinburgh would be called Castlehill. The majority of them, like Trinafar, were fay, but there were also elves, gnomes, dryads, goblins, and even one troll. She wondered what Fergus made of the mixture of races as he looked first one way then another, clearly trying to see everything at once.

"This way," said Trinafar, leading Fergus towards the base of the western tower. "This is known as the Robhas Tower. It's my mother's base. I'll introduce you to her. Then my obligation to you will be over. If she agrees you can stay you'll be able to go anywhere you want in Eideann."

"But my obligation to you won't be over. You've helped me fulfil my ambition."

"Fool! I thought you were learning. Yes, that debt does exist but I was going to find some trivial service to accept in recompense. Now that you've acknowledged it without suggesting how you might repay it I could ask almost anything of you. For a debt of that magnitude I could make you my slave for life if I wanted to. Fortunately for you I have no need for a slave."

Fergus licked his lips. "How can I repay you?"

"Now that you've freely admitted the existence of the debt the repayment will have to be something significant or there won't be a balancing. I don't have any ideas about what it could be at the moment." Trinafar shook her head. "I'll need to think about it."

"Is there a time limit on repaying the debt?" asked Fergus.

"A year and a day, of course. What else?"

Two elves, dressed in the same style of armour as Maedron, stood guard at the widely open doors of the Robhas Tower. They bowed respectfully as Trinafar led Fergus past them into the building. The space they entered occupied the whole of the ground level of the tower and was floored with multicoloured slate, the subtle colour differences laid to form a spiral pattern of greys, purples, greens and blues. It was big enough that the fifty or so people in it weren't crowded. Most were standing talking to each other in small groups, their voices producing a background hum of conversation but no single voice could be distinguished. The scent of pine dominated, with occasional wafts of other fragrances; lilac, rose, mint and thyme among them.

There were two desks standing against the wall at the opposite side of the room from the entrance. A fay with glittering crystals decorating her dark hair sat at one of them talking to two people who looked very human except for their hooves and the zebra-striped fur covering their heads.

"I expect there will be some races you don't recognise," said Trinafar when she saw Fergus staring at them. "Those are anthrops. That's a generic term for people who look basically human but have some variation such as horns, hooves, fur or scales. Few of them ever visit the second world. From what I've heard, they're not common in most of the other Domains and Realms either so I don't suppose you met any when your mother took you to Feahranath."

Fergus shook his head and continued gaping at the crowd.

A pair of dwarves sat at the other desk, one of them working with fine tools on some delicate-looking mechanical device. The other seemed to be giving him instructions from a large book spread open across the desk. "There's another race I don't think you'll have come across," said Trinafar, pointing at a short figure with deep-red, lustrous, scaly skin who joined the dwarves. "He's a salmad. There's not many of them around and few of them ever go into the second world. They're magical craftsmen of considerable skill and it's well worth making friends with one if you get the chance."

A spiral stair against the wall climbed clockwise to the next level, making one complete circuit before getting there. Directly opposite the base of this stair there was an alcove through which stairs going down could be seen.

Trinafar led Fergus up. The landing at the next level had six doors leading from it. One of them led to another spiral staircase which wound around the tower in the opposite direction to the first. They kept climbing until, at the fifth level, they found the centre door of three was guarded by two elves and four short, thin creatures with gray skin. "You recognise goblins don't you?" Trinafar said, indicating the four guards who were carrying halberds.

Fergus nodded.

"Is my mother present?" Trinafar asked one of the elves. "Is she meeting with anyone?"

The dark skinned elf, who had mottled grey and brown feathers and who seemed to be in charge, told Trinafar that a meeting of the executive council had just ended and her mother was alone.

"Good. Please announce me."

The elf opened the door enough to slip through and closed it behind him.

the three towers

Fergus fidgeted while they waited until Trinafar told him to be still. His pulse sounded loud in his ears. *Will her mother accept me? She's got to.* The idea of being sent away brought a lump to his throat. *She's got to let me stay, doesn't she? I'll find some way of being useful. There's got to be things I can do, or learn, or maybe even teach here.*

After a wait that seemed to Fergus to last hours, the door opened, the guard beckoned them forward and announced, "The Lady Trinafar Chiolet Fion Eideannach – and companion."

Fergus followed her into what he quickly realised was a throne room. *I knew her mother was important but I didn't expect this.*

Not knowing how to behave he watched Catriona carefully – *No! It's Trinafar,* he reminded himself. *Her name's Trinafar, not Catriona.* He was ready to follow her example. She walked forward until she was three paces from the throne and went to her knees. Fergus copied her, then looked up.

Light streaming in through a large window illuminated a silver and ebony throne. The woman seated on it looked startlingly like Trinafar, with jade green eyes, flawless skin the colour of milky coffee and waist-length reddish-gold hair caught up in a thick plait pulled over her left shoulder. He had no trouble believing they were mother and daughter. The only real difference he saw was a slight tension at the corners of the older woman's mouth.

He glanced quickly around the spacious room, which was decorated in silver, cream and pale blue, then returned his attention to the woman on the throne.

The door clicked quietly closed behind them before Trinafar's mother said, "My headstrong daughter! And in the company of a cross-breed! What a surprise to see you here today, Trinafar. I didn't expect you until Samhain."

"I ask for your welcome, mother," said Trinafar.

There was what seemed to Fergus to be a long silence and he grew nervous. His palms started sweating. *What will I do if she rejects me?* His mother had warned him that high-ranking sidhe could be quite arbitrary at times and didn't have to justify their actions – and Trinafar's mother must be as high-ranking as they come.

Fergus waited, trying to stay calm. He was aware that the woman on the throne was studying him. The intensity of that gaze made him look down to avoid making eye-contact.

Eventually Trinafar's mother dipped her head slightly and said, "Be welcome, daughter of mine."

"Thank you, mother," said Trinafar standing up and stepping forward to kiss her mother on both cheeks.

Should I stand? Fergus wondered. *No, I don't think so. Not yet.*

"Tell me of your companion, daughter."

"I ask permission to introduce him and have him tell you his story himself."

The woman on the throne frowned slightly, looked at Fergus again, nodded and said, "Very well."

Trinafar bowed and said, "Mother, may I present to you Fergus Monteith. He is from the second world but has an association with the Realm of Feahranath." Then she looked at Fergus and said, in a formal tone of voice, "This is my mother, Igrainid Luschet Sarel, who is the Heart of the Domain of Eideann."

Fergus stood in response to Trinafar's gesture and bowed.

"He seems courteous enough," said Igrainid to Trinafar, then Fergus saw her attention switch to him. She asked, "What is your association with Feahranath?"

Fergus told her what he had told Trinafar and the guard at the lacuna.

Igrainid listened attentively, nodding occasionally, then asked, "Do you intend to go to Feahranath to find your mother?"

"I don't know if I should, Your Majesty."

"Don't call me that," said Igrainid. "I am not a queen.

The proper form of address is 'Cridhe'."

Fergus bowed again and said, "I apologise, Cridhe. Please excuse my ignorance."

Igrainid bent her head slightly and said, "You are forgiven. Now, answer my question."

"I'm not sure if my mother would want to see me. After all, she abandoned me when my father died and her obligation to him ended."

"You may well be right," said Igrainid after a brief pause. "There are some shapechangers, Selkies and Ursids, who are part of the Domain of Eideann. On the whole, they show very little in the way of familial feelings. This seems to be a characteristic of all shapechangers whatever their alternative form, so I agree your mother's response to your presence in Tirog is uncertain. Without imposing obligation upon you, I suggest you send a message to your mother telling her that you are here and wait to see what her reaction is."

Fergus bowed and said, "Thank you, Cridhe. I appreciate your suggestion."

Igrainid smiled and said, "Fergus Monteith, you are welcome to Eideann. You may walk free in the Luchairt – the palace – and in the town until the next full moon. Then we will reconsider your position within Eideann.

Fergus felt himself breathe more easily. *At least she hasn't thrown me out. I've got just under a month to establish a place here.* He bowed low and thanked her.

"Trinafar," said Igrainid, "take your cross-breed and house him in Caedmon's Tower. Come to eat with me this evening; bring him with you to dinner as a guest of the Domain."

"Yes, mother. Thank you."

#

Fergus followed Trinafar down one level then to one of the bridges between the towers. He was close behind her when she started across it. Then he froze after two steps when he realised the bridge was only about six feet wide and had no guard-rail or balustrade to stop him falling four storeys to the ground. He started shuffling across cautiously, unable to imitate her confident stride. Less than halfway across he met an elf and a goblin going the other way deep in conversation. He had to move closer to one edge to give them enough space to pass. By the time he could move back towards the midline of the bridge he was sweating and gasping for breath.

Trinafar turned when she reached the other tower. She was well ahead of him and gestured to him to hurry up.

He tried, but he couldn't force himself to put one foot more than an inch or two beyond the other.

She walked back to join him, looked up into his eyes and said in an amused tone, "Surely a big strong cross-breed can't be afraid of heights."

"It's not so much the height itself, or the looking down, I can just about cope with that. It's the lack of anything to stop me falling."

"Well you can't just stand there. Let me take your arm."

A feeling of security flooded over him as soon as she grasped his elbow and he walked beside her feeling quite calm until they reached the other tower. Then Trinafar let go and Fergus started shaking.

"It never occurred to me you might have problems with the crossways," said Trinafar. "We'll need to do something about that."

"You used magic on me!"

"Of course I did," she said. "I couldn't very well have left you there, could I?"

"But … You rescued me and I know that rescuing someone establishes a debt to the rescuer. That's why my mother stayed with my father."

"True, a rescue does create an obligation,"

"So my debt to you has increased."

"No," said Trinafar. "There are other aspects you must consider when judging who is indebted to whom and to what extent in any situation. It can sometimes be quite complicated. Firstly, in this case, it was me who put you at risk by not considering the possibility of you being afraid of heights. That balances the rescue; secondly, using magic on someone without permission can establish a debt to either the spellcaster or the bespelled depending on the circumstances and intent. In this case it was to your advantage so, yes, there would be an obligation. However, considering that not easing your fear would make things difficult for you and awkward for me, I can choose to waive that debt and I do. You need not concern yourself about it. Finally, and most importantly, I am under instruction to take you to dine with my mother this evening and that would not be possible if you were frozen in fear on the crossway."

Fergus realised she was making light of the debt and wondered why. He shivered as he looked back at the crossway, "Will we have to cross another one of those?"

"No, we don't have to. We can go down and up again, but it's inconvenient doing that all the time. That's why the crossways exist. Assuming you are going to stay here you need a better long-term solution. If you are willing, I will ask one of our best spellcasters to cure your fear permanently."

"And what debt would that incur?" asked Fergus.

"Nothing. I am sure she will bespell you if I ask because then the onus of repayment would fall on me and she will be pleased to have me owe her."

"Is she an enemy?"

"No, not as such. She's one of my sisters and 'unfriends' would probably be the best description of our relationship."

"Can't you use your magic on me again instead of involving someone else?"

Fergus saw Trinafar shake her head as she started up the stairs.

He followed, wondering why she couldn't. *Or was it wouldn't?*

At the top of the stairs, Trinafar opened one of the doors that lined the landing. She said, "The top two levels of Caedmon's Tower are for the use of guests. I think this room should suit you."

The cosy little room was decorated in shades of cream, brown and russet. It held a bed with a thick quilt, a small table, a couple of bentwood chairs, a wardrobe and an empty set of shelves. There was a small window in the wall opposite the door. "The bathroom is through the middle door at the end of the landing. You share it with everyone else on this floor."

"That's fine."

"I don't know who is in residence at present but it's possible you'll meet some of them. If you do just smile at them and be polite.

"I'll need to leave you now. Stay here until I come back to collect you. Meanwhile I'll send someone with an assortment of suitable clothing for you. Don't worry about being indebted for the clothes. My mother named you a guest of the Domain and, as such, you are entitled to our hospitality, which includes dressing you appropriately."

Trinafar left the room, pulling the door closed behind her and leaving Fergus on his own.

Fergus put his rucksack down beside the bed and went to look out of the window. It faced north, away from the other towers. He was high up but the windowsill between him and the drop let him feel safe. The tower was tall enough to let him see over the densely wooded landscape to water and, beyond that, to a range of hills, blue in the distance. *That must be the Forth, and Fife.* It was with a sense of wonder that he realised again he really was in Tirog. *I've got things I can do, but I'm really here at last. I think I'll just enjoy the feeling for a bit.*

He stood there, revelling in the achievement of his ambition until someone knocked at the door. Two women with purplish, lustrous, scaly skin, who barely reached his waist stood there when he opened the door. He had seen a man like them in the base of the Robhas Tower – *What was it Trinafar called them? – Salmads wasn't it?* He stood there gaping at them and their red eyes with no whites and no pupils until one said, in a voice that sounded like gravel sliding down a hill, "We have clothing for you; gifts of the Cridhe. May we enter?"

Fergus felt himself blush with embarrassment and stammered, "Yes, yes, of course, please do." Then he stood back to let them in. They pulled a small box-on-wheels after them and started taking clothes from it. A stream of muttered comments, "Won't fit him, he's too tall," "That won't do," "Yes, possible," "No, not that colour, sister, not for him," "Better," and so on accompanied the unpacking.

Fergus had trouble believing his eyes when they pulled more and more things from the box. *It must be bigger inside than out!*

Some of the garments were laid aside on the table as they took them from the box, they seemed to be ones the salmads disapproved of. The clothes they did accept were laid on the bed, but some stayed there only briefly before they were replaced by something they seemed to think was better. Others stayed longer until they too were exchanged. Eventually no more changes were being made and the women stepped back. They moved some of the items from the bed on to the shelves and into the wardrobe. Then they started repacking the box, leaving other clothes lying, neatly folded, on the bed.

"Good," growled one of the women.

"Satisfactory. Will not shame the Domain," said the other, who indicated the clothes on the bed and added, "Wear in health."

Fergus realised he wasn't being given a choice of what to wear. *They must know what they're doing. At least I hope so*. He mumbled his thanks and saw them leave.

He looked at the clothes stacked on the shelves and lying on his bed. *Looks like they've given me at least three sets of clothes. I suppose I'd better try them on. The ones on the bed first, I think*. He did so, using the wardrobe mirror to judge their appearance. There was a loose jacket of dark-green velvet, embroidered on the shoulders and sleeves with silver spirals. It went over a spotless, white cambric shirt with a drawstring neck. He thought that looked good on him. The baggy, black-and-

purple striped trousers that tucked into polished black
leather boots were less to his liking, but he reminded
himself that he knew nothing about fashions in Tirog and
had to trust the women who had chosen for him.

#

"You'll do," was Trinafar's comment when he opened
the door to her and asked if he was suitably dressed.

"Are you sure?" he asked, because she had put her hair
up into a complex arrangement of multiple braids and
was wearing an ankle length, satin dress the colour of
fresh cream. It was decorated from neck to waist with
mother-of-pearl buttons in a Celtic knot design and,
draped over her shoulders, she had a finely woven
gossamer shawl with white-on-white embroidery.
"You're dressed for a much more formal occasion than I
am."

She laughed. "This isn't formal, it's ordinary evening
wear. You'll see the difference if you ever get invited to a
Domain Gathering. Are you ready?"

He nodded. "I suppose so."

"Don't worry. It will just be us, mother, my sisters
Rhiannis and Saefan, and three more, I haven't heard
who, to balance the numbers. Both Rhiannis and Saefan
are strong magic users and I'll ask one of them to cure
your fear of heights. Just don't get them mixed up or they
might not cooperate. Rhiannis will be wearing green and
Saefan blue, they always do."

"Rhiannis green, Saefan blue. I'll remember. Do we
have to use one of the crossways to get to wherever?"

"No. I will spare you that. We will take the long way,
down and up again."

#

Fergus entered the dining room and bowed to Igrainid.
He had trouble believing this wasn't a formal occasion
because all the women were wearing dresses similar in

style to Trinafar's. Igrainid's was made of deep purple silk and decorated with crystals. *Or are they diamonds?*

The two other women also closely resembled Trinafar. They were obviously her sisters and looked so much alike that Fergus was glad he knew how to distinguish between them. Rhiannis *was* wearing green, with emeralds, and Saefan blue, with sapphires.

One of the men was an elf who looked like Maedron, the guard he had met at the lacuna. He was a couple of inches shorter than Maedron but his feathers were the same colours. He didn't give his name but identified himself as the Commander of the Domain Guard. Another, describing himself as the Keeper of the Chronicles of Eideann, was an anthrop and looked human except for metallic silver skin. Fergus had trouble not staring at the last of the three, introduced as the ambassador from the Realm of Cairgon. Fergus had met dwarves before when travelling with his mother and this man couldn't be anything else. He was about half Fergus's height with a braided beard almost long enough to trip over. He was wearing many heavy gold necklaces and a soft leather jacket.

Fergus didn't hear the dwarf's name clearly when he was introduced. He was reluctant to ask for it to be repeated and didn't want to insult him by getting it wrong. He remembered from his childhood that dwarves could be touchy about the way their names were pronounced, particularly when there were multiple repeated letters in the name as there often was. *Best if I don't call him anything.*

He admitted, in response to a question from the dwarf, that he was a newcomer to Tirog and wasn't familiar with the Domains and Realms. The dwarf took the opportunity to inform him that the Realm of Cairgon was in the mountains to the east of the Great Glen and proceeded to give Fergus a detailed description of his Realm, its geography, peoples and alliances. Only Igrainid's invitation to sit and eat brought this to a close.

Surprised to find that the seating arrangements had all

the women on one side of the table and all the men on the other, Fergus found himself sitting between the dwarf and the chronicler and opposite Rhiannis. The latter tried to ask him about the second world, but the dwarf kept butting in and dominating the conversation. The meal consisted of four courses and between each of the first three the dwarf dragged the topic of conversation back to the complex interrelationships and the feuds and alliances of the Domains and Realms.

I don't understand a tenth of what he's on about, thought Fergus, *I wish he would shut up and let someone else speak.*

The dwarf started speaking again as the third course was being cleared and the fourth served. Fergus saw Trinafar and Saefan frowning as the dwarf's voice continued to dominate the conversation. Then the dwarf said, "Of course, Lady Trinafar's problem … "

There were gasps from the other side of the table. The servants stopped where they were in mid-service. The feeling in the room was suddenly chilly.

" … is why Eideann and Chrioch are feuding … "

The dwarf's voice cut off abruptly when Igrainid snapped, "Be silent! That is no concern of yours." The expression on her face made Fergus think he wouldn't want that look to be directed at him.

"You have made yourself unwelcome here in Eideann," Igrainid said to the dwarf in a chilly tone of voice. "Leave us, and be outside our bounds within two days."

She looks furious! That dwarf's really put his foot in it. I wonder what Trinafar's 'problem' is.

The dwarf stood, bowed rather stiffly to Igrainid, and left without saying any more. Fergus wondered if he could speak or if Igrainid's command to 'be silent' had been reinforced with magic.

Igrainid looked around the table and said, "I apologise for the disruption of our meal and acknowledge the debt thus incurred. I trust an invitation to one of the High Tables at the next Gathering will be a suitable repayment."

Fergus joined in the murmur of acceptance although he had no idea what he was agreeing to. *If the others are happy with that I'd better be too.*

Igrainid rose and swept out of the room, followed by Saefan, the Guard Commander and the Keeper of the Chronicles.

"Wait, Rhiannis," said Trinafar before her other sister could leave. "I need your help."

Fergus thought Rhiannis sounded really snarky when she said, "My help? You mean there's something you can't do for yourself. How unusual!"

"Please, Rhiannis," said Trinafar, "let's not get into dominance games. We both know you're a lot stronger than me. I ask you, acknowledging that I will owe you, to cure this man's fear of heights so that he can walk the crossways in comfort and safety."

"What! You'll go into debt to benefit a cross-breed! Are you going soft on him?"

"I agreed to bring him to Tirog and get him established here," said Trinafar, sounding tense. "Nothing more than that."

"Come here," said Rhiannis, looking at Fergus.

He walked across the room and stopped about three feet away from her.

She muttered something Fergus couldn't make out, then said, "Allow my touch and the spell is complete."

"Say 'yes', Fergus," said Trinafar when he hesitated.

Fergus nodded and agreed. Rhiannis stepped forward to lay her palm on his forehead. He shivered.

"It is done."

Rhiannis turned to leave, then hesitated at the door and said, "Trinafar, I suggest, at no cost, that you tell him what that dwarf meant by your 'problem' otherwise he might talk his way into trouble."

Fergus saw Rhiannis walk away then he turned to Trinafar and asked, "Is that it?"

"Is what it?"

"Is one touch all that's needed to cast a spell?"

"That depends on the spell and the caster. Many people

find a gesture helps them concentrate on the structure of the spell they're casting but, for most purposes, they aren't actually necessary. A spell that changes someone's attitudes is the exception and always needs a touch to complete it. Tell me, what did you feel?"

"I'm not quite sure how to put it into words. It was weird – a sort of twisting sensation behind my eyes, if that makes any sort of sense. Her hand was cold at first and the coldness spread from it until it felt as if I was turning to ice. Then the twisting feeling reversed and went the opposite way, warmth followed the cold and now I feel fine."

"I told you Rhiannis would be happy to have me in her debt," said Trinafar. "You wouldn't have felt anything if she hadn't actually used magic on you, so I expect she has cured your fear."

Fergus watched Trinafar pacing around the dining room with a scowl on her face. "You don't look happy," he said.

"That last comment she made, about stopping you getting into trouble …"

"Don't worry about it. If you don't want to tell me you don't have to."

Trinafar sighed. "I'm really surprised Rhiannis said that. You must have impressed her. She knows I don't like talking about my 'problem' but she's right. I'm sure everybody in Eideann knows about it. Probably most people visiting from other Domains and Realms do too. They'll all have their own opinions about it and you'd better be aware of them."

Fergus blinked in surprise. *Impressed her! Me impress Rhiannis? She seemed so – so haughty.*

Trinafar stopped pacing, looked around and said, "It's getting late. I'll tell you what you need to know tomorrow. Stay in your room until I come to fetch you for breakfast and I'll tell you after we've eaten."

one-to-one

The place-that-doesn't-exist was a resource available to every member of the Group of Eleven. As well as being their meeting place they could use it individually as a viewing point to keep an eye on the Domains and Realms they visited and as a way to talk to the various Cridhe.

It could also be used as somewhere to have a semi-private meeting on a one-to-one basis with another of the Eleven. The privacy of such meetings was guaranteed by promises between the Eleven which, like all bargains between sidhe, could not be broken without consequences. Such a meeting could never be *fully* private however, as the magi hovering around the boundary of the non-space were all quite capable of penetrating a a privacy spell. The number of potential eavesdroppers was too big to make getting promises from all of them a practical proposition. They tried to listen in to any one-to-one conversations while the members of the Eleven tried to prevent being overheard.

A one-to-one rarely generated the attention a full meeting of the Eleven did, but those magi who did pay attention to them sometimes benefitted from doing so. The topic of discussion at such a meeting was of as much interest to the observers who hoped to gain an advantage by having prior knowledge of what was likely to come up at a full meeting as it was to the Eleven themselves. Dhugalt's membership of the Eleven had come about in just that way when he spotted a disagreement during a one-to-one. Subsequently he had applied pressure at the right moment when the Eleven were all together and succeeded in displacing his predecessor from the Group.

Naturally all of the Eleven were aware of the risks that accompanied a one-to-one and were very careful when involved in one. They were conscious of the observers in the halo but, since physical meetings between them were impossible due to the distances involved, they didn't really have another option.

An elf, called Sumethla, who was the longest serving member of the Group of Eleven, invited Dhugalt to such a meeting. "I know you're interested in the Failed Source," she said. "I've just been informed of a different sort of inheritance anomaly. It's bound to cause some controversy at the next meeting and I wanted to warn you. You see, a sixth child has become a Source."

"Impossible!"

"No, Dhugalt, it's quite possible, but it's very rare. In all the hundred and twenty-two years I've been one of the Eleven it's happened only once before."

"Are you sure there isn't an error in the record?"

"Quite certain," replied Sumethla. "I know the lineage well. The child who has unexpectedly become a Source is my great-great-grand-daughter."

"Well! I've never heard of such a thing before, but I've got to accept you know what you're talking about when it involves your own family."

Dhugalt was puzzled. Why had Sumethla chosen to tell him about this in advance of the next meeting of the Eleven? The two of them were more often allies than antagonists in the politics of the Eleven, but it was still surprising. He thanked her for the information. They left the place-that-doesn't-exist together and it faded into its normal state of non-existence.

pRoblem

Fergus slept poorly that night, his mind full of the excitement of being in Tirog at last, and of speculations about what Trinafar's 'problem' might be.

With his window facing north he didn't see the sunrise but he got up when there was enough light for him to see his way around the room. He put his own clothes on instead of the finery he had been given for the meal with Igrainid and waited for Trinafar to arrive. He thought he was being patient but several times he found himself looking out the window in an attempt to see how the day was progressing.

When she did arrive he was pleased to note she was dressed simply, with none of the elaborate clothing of the previous night's dinner. She was wearing an embroidered blouse and a long dark-green skirt with a knitted shawl over her shoulders. Her hair was pinned back to above her ears and then fell free in a golden cascade behind her.

"Am I ..." He started to ask if he was appropriately dressed but she interrupted him saying, "Good. I forgot to tell you not to wear your outfit from last night. It would be a little pretentious for day-time wear. Come with me to breakfast then we'll go into the garden and I'll tell you what you need to know about my 'problem'."

Breakfast was a communal meal taken in a room occupying most of the third floor of Caedmon's Tower.

The room was busy and noisy. He could understand why she said, "I'm not talking about it here, it's too public."

After they had eaten she took her shawl from the back of her chair, draped it across her shoulders again and said, "Come with me."

Fergus followed Trinafar from the breakfast room, down one level and over a crossway to the Robhas Tower.

Halfway across Fergus realised he wasn't afraid of the drop. He moved closer to the edge and found he could look down without being paralysed by fear. *The magic did work!*

He walked slightly behind Trinafar as she led him down to ground level and through the garden to a small gazebo floored with seashells and furnished with two benches and a small table all made of driftwood. The space had an odd feel to it. He could hear Trinafar's footsteps as she walked around, and occasional faint chirps from birds passing through or perching on the structure. However, every sound from outside was muffled, as if his ears were packed with cotton wool.

"Sit down," said Trinafar, pointing to one of the benches. "This is a Quiet Place. A spell on it prevents anyone outside it hearing anything except the sound of breaking waves if they try to listen to what's said inside.

Fergus sat and waited silently while Trinafar stalked restlessly around for a few minutes.

Eventually she sat on the other bench and asked, "How much did your mother teach you about magic?"

"Very little," he replied. "She didn't have much magic herself apart from shapechanging and the ability to pass a lacuna. She didn't tell me a lot other than that magic is real and it's both commoner and stronger here in Tirog than it is at home. She could lift things with magic here that she wasn't able to move in the second world. I remember her saying almost everyone here has at least some skill with magic but it was quite variable. Some people couldn't do much while others were very strong and could do almost anything they wanted to.

"Were there any other cross-breed children you could learn from?"

"No. We lived in a little village on the coast with only ten houses, and there were no other children my age for me to play with and certainly no cross-breeds."

"How did you learn to read and write?"

"There was a school about two and a half miles away. All the kids from the four villages nearby went there. Most of the other kids in the school were older than me and we didn't mix much. Anyway, mother told me not to talk about magic to them. She said they wouldn't understand."

"Did she tell you anything about the basis of magic? Where the power to do magic comes from?"

"Not much. All she said was it comes from living things."

"That's right. Life of all kinds – people, animals, birds, fish, trees, it doesn't matter what – every form of life contributes to the power that enables people to use magic."

She paused. Fergus nodded and said, "I understand."

"It's not quite as simple as that. Most people can't use the life energy in its raw form. It needs to be transmuted into something that people can use for their spells, cantrips and glamours. That something is known as latent power, or just latency. All pixies and trolls can generate latency but only for themselves. Nobody else can use it. It's just one example of a race specific ability. Many races have some ability others don't. For example, during the expansion phase of the Empire in the mid-nineteenth century, trolls discovered they could translate unknown languages. As you can imagine that made them incredibly useful.

"However, that's not relevant to what we were talking about. Only a relatively small number of people of any race can change life energy into latent power. Don't bother asking them how they do it, they don't know. It's unconscious and instinctive. Those who can do it are known as Sources and are very important to the Domains and Realms. Without them there would be no magic. They are known as the Hearts of their Domains."

"Like your mother!"

"Yes. She is the Heart of Eideann. There is at least one Source in every Domain and Realm of Tirog. Many of them are the rulers of their Domain or Realm because, in return for their allegiance, they allow people to draw on the latent power they produce. They can also shun someone and prevent them from utilising their latency. That's the most severe punishment possible and it's not often used.

"I suppose the Sources are all very strong spellcasters."

"Strangely enough, no. Many of them are, but not all. Mother is among the strongest."

"I understand, I think. But you said 'most people' can't use the life energy directly. Does that mean there are some who can?"

"Well … That's a difficult question to answer. There are tales – rumours of some extremely strong spellcasters who can use life energy in its raw form. The stories call them magi. It's said they don't generate latent power for others to use but they aren't dependent on other peoples' latency either. You might well hear stories about the magi but I wouldn't pay too much attention to stories like that. There's no good evidence that they actually exist. Even if they do you're never likely to meet one, or realise it if you do. All the tales say they are supposed to be very secretive and don't advertise who or what they are."

Fergus felt his head in a spin as he tried to make sense of all this information. He nodded thoughtfully and said, "I think I understand where magic comes from. But I don't know how that relates to your 'problem', whatever that is."

Trinafar sat quietly, with her head bowed, for several minutes, but Fergus noticed her plucking at the fringes of her shawl. *I don't think she realises she's doing that. Or that it shows how upset she is. This must be difficult for her.*

"I've heard that, in the second world," Trinafar began, when she finally broke her silence, "there's a belief that the seventh son of a seventh son will be a magician. I expect you've heard that too."

"Yes. That's quite a widespread superstition. Why?"

"It's not actually a superstition, there is a grain of truth in it. But it's another of those half-true stories you hear about the sidhe in the second world. In reality someone like mother, who can generate latent power, is the seventh child of both their mother *and* their father, at least one of whom must also be a seventh child, although not necessarily a Source."

"That's an unlikely sounding family tree," said Fergus.

"They're always difficult to organise."

"Organise?"

"Yes. Sources are so important to the Domains and Realms that arrangements are made for suitable pairings to make sure as many as possible are born."

"Sounds a bit cold-blooded," said Fergus.

"It's necessary. Otherwise there would be no Sources. You see, it's almost unknown for a sidhe couple, of any race or combination of races, to have more than one child. For some reason nobody understands it seems that a woman can't bear two children to the same man."

"But you have two sisters," said Fergus. "You introduced me to them yesterday."

"No, actually Rhiannis and Saefan are my half-sisters. As well as me, my mother has four daughters and two sons. All seven of us have different fathers, of different races. For example, I'm the youngest and my father's an elf. Saefan is the next youngest of my sisters and her father is a goblin. My brother Dunarh comes between Saefan and me and his father is a fay."

Fergus blinked in surprise. "You mean you're a cross-breed too?"

Trinafar jumped to her feet and shouted, "Don't call me that!"

He flinched from the anger in her voice. Then he saw her take a deep breath and look away from him before saying, "Yes, well, I suppose technically I am, but that's an expression that's only ever applied to people like you with one human and one sidhe parent. It used to be an insult but, nowadays, cross-breeds are accepted and the term no longer has the negative connotations it once had – unless applied to pureblood sidhe, whatever their racial mix is. Using it in that way could get you into all sorts of trouble."

"Sorry. I didn't mean to insult you," said Fergus. "I'll remember that."

He thought about what Trinafar had said, trying to make sense of it. Then he realised something and said,

"You're the youngest of seven! So you should be a Source – no, that's not right. That's only your mother's side of the family. What about your father's?"

Trinafar sighed. "That's the crux of the problem," she said. "After my brother Dunarh was born mother started looking for a suitable partner to have a Source child with. She found him, she thought, in the Realm of Crioch – the closest border of that Realm is ninety miles or so south of here and it overlaps with Eideann for about a mile and a half.

"At the time mother was looking Crioch was very fortunate. It had three Sources. One of them has since died, but that's not relevant. The youngest of the three had six children. He agreed to father me and the treaty his Domain negotiated for his services was very favourable to Crioch."

"Makes it sound as if he's been put out to stud," said Fergus. "Hold on. Your father has six other children too. So I was right when I said you should be a Source – but you've made it clear, without actually saying so, that you're not."

Trinafar started pacing around the gazebo again. Fergus thought he saw tears in her eyes but she turned away from him and he couldn't be sure. What he was sure about was a catch in her voice as she said, "You're right, I am not, although I should be. Everything went as expected until I was seven years old when I should have started generating latency and didn't. Most people in Eideann believe my father lied about the number of children he had in order to get the best deal he could for Crioch. He denies it and insists I'm his seventh child and the fault must lie with mother or me. The whole thing has boiled up into a feud between Eideann and Crioch. The two Domains used to be close trading partners but that's changed and there's now virtually no trade between them.

"My failure to be a Source as I should be is a cause of worry for everyone in the Domain. You see, apart from brief intervals there has never been more than one Source at a time here in Eideann for most of the last two hundred and fifty-odd years. It's almost as if there's a curse on the Domain. Now, with me not being a Source, it seems possible that the line of the Sources in Eideann will end when my mother dies."

"What will happen then?"

Trinafar shook her head and said, "I don't know."

"It must have happened before," said Fergus, "a line becoming extinct I mean."

"Only twice as far as I know."

"And what happened?"

"What would you expect?" asked Trinafar.

"Trouble. Other Domains and Realms fighting over the lands of the failed one."

"Trouble, yes, but not fighting for territory, not in the way wars in the second world are. Here the critical resource is latency. Any place outside the range of a Source's influence is abandoned and desolate. That's what happened to the Realm of Belfeir a bit more than eight hundred years ago and to the Realm of Gertseay almost five hundred years ago. Before their last Source died people in those places had started anticipating their deaths and moving away from the old centres of the Realms into overlap areas where they could tap into the latent power produced by Sources in adjacent Domains. The old Realms of Belfeir and Gertseay don't exist anymore except as ruins because people won't live where they can't have access to latency. There are some places in the north-west of Alba where nobody has ever lived because they are too far away from a Source's base."

"You mentioned overlap areas. Do you mean somebody close enough to two Sources can use the latent power from both? Does that make them stronger?"

"Yes, they can. And no it doesn't. They can draw on only one Source for any particular spellcasting. Close to a Source's base is the most desirable place to live but the overlap areas are popular too because it gives people a feeling of security to have latency available from two Sources. The least favoured areas are places far from the residence of a single Source.

"Everyone, including mother, is worried about my failure to be a Source. We don't want Eideann to end up like Belfeir or Gertseay."

Fergus listened with interest as Trinafar told him this bit of history. He could see how it related to her 'problem' and thought she was forcing herself to be calm and analytical about it. *I wish I could help her in some way.*

"I don't know where these derelict places are," said Fergus, "but I'm surprised that a suitable site would just be abandoned. I can't imagine that happening to Eideann. This is such a great place to live that I'd expect another Source to move in rather than leave it empty."

"That didn't happen in Belfeir and Gertseay because there was only one Source in any of the adjacent Domains and Realms at the time. I believe that it was largely as a result of their failures that arranged liaisons became popular."

"Are there more Sources now because of that? Don't you think some might move from places with two or more into a vacancy?"

"You might be right," said Trinafar after a moment's thought. "I can think of at least five Domains and Realms with two Sources and well developed lineages that will result in more within a dozen years or so. Some of them might be tempted to try that."

"And that could set off a war for possession of Eideann. Now I understand why your mother was so angry when that dwarf referred to your 'problem'. Why did he do that? Was he just being stupid or was he deliberately trying to upset your mother? Or you. Has he got something against you?"

"Not personally, I don't think. I've never met him before. I believe somebody from Cairgon was considered as a possible parent for me but was passed over in favour of my father. I have the impression that Cridhe Glodrin of Cairgon resents that. Or the ambassador might be one of those who thinks that I'm to be avoided because, somehow or other, it's my fault that I'm not a Source."

"That doesn't make sense."

"I know it doesn't," said Trinafar, "Anyway, he's not part of this Domain so I don't have to pay any attention to what he thinks."

"Even so," said Fergus, trying to sound sympathetic, "it must hurt."

"It does. What hurts worse is that particular belief becoming commoner here in Eideann. Sometimes I think perhaps it is my fault after all in some way I don't understand – and I can't bear the idea of being responsible for whatever happens to the Domain. That's one reason why I spend as much of my time as I can in the second world."

"I don't blame you," said Fergus, now certain she was holding back tears.

"Anyway, now you know about my problem," said Trinafar. "Mother has accepted you and you can go where you want in Eideann. She's told me to stay for a few days before I go back to Edinburgh, so I expect I'll see you again."

She turned and hurried away, leaving Fergus sitting alone.

luchaiRt eibeann

"Cridhe, the people you sent for are here," said an elf from his position at the door of the highest room in the Robhas Tower.

The room was Igrainid's private study. Multicoloured rugs were strewn across the tiled floor. Those, and superbly crafted woven wall hangings depicting forest and river scenes, made it a welcoming room, more so than the rather severe decor of the throne room on the floor below. Half a dozen comfortable chairs arranged around a low table waited for the people she had summoned. She put the document she was reading, for what was at least the fifth time, down on the table next to a stack of other documents. A quick glance at the table confirmed that it held a water jug on a silver salver, a compartmented box with a different tea in each section, several perforated metal balls for brewing the teas, a number of tea cups and a plateful of almond pastries.

Yes, everything's ready. She took a deep breath as a gentle breeze swirled into the room through the open window carrying a fresh green smell with it. It made her relax a little as she looked out over the garden and its profusion of colour. Then she turned to look at the doorguard, nodded and told him to announce her visitors.

Unsurprisingly the first in, walking briskly through the door, was Saefan. She barely gave the elf time to announce 'The Lady Saefan Nissel Gronich Eideannach' before she entered. *She's in a hurry*, Igrainid thought, *but then she has been ever since she was born six weeks early.* Dressed in dark blue, as she generally was, Saefan strode across the room to kneel at her mother's feet. Igrainid smiled, told her to rise and leaned forward to receive her kisses.

The next two were announced together as 'Misghel hur Marind hur Yarint of the House of Mochri, Commander of the Domain Guard; and the Noble Dunarh Sinthed

Lubech Eideannach'. They both wore the brown and green uniform of the Guard. Misghel, an elf, towered a good foot and a half over Igrainid's son Dunarh who had been fathered by a fay and, like his sister Trinafar, was barely five feet tall. As they were in uniform they didn't kneel but stayed on their feet to indicate their readiness to protect Igrainid. They saluted her by bowing with hands on hearts.

Igrainid acknowledged them before looking beyond them to the door where Trinafar was hovering on the threshold. She sighed, told herself for the umpteenth time that she shouldn't let her disappointment colour her feelings towards Trinafar. *Whatever else she is, or isn't, she's still my daughter.*

The elf said, 'The Lady Trinafar Chiolet Fion Eideannach,' as Trinafar stepped forward.

Igrainid nodded when Trinafar knelt, gestured for her to rise and accepted her kisses.

The last person to arrive for the meeting was Yuseth, the Keeper of the Chronicles of Eideann. Not being a member of Igrainid's family he didn't salute her with a kiss but crossed his arms over his chest and bowed. His silver skin gleamed in the afternoon sunlight. It reflected the rugs, the wall hangings and the clothing of the people in the room in a confusing swirl of colours that made him difficult to see.

She waited until the doorguard had left the room and closed the door behind him before saying, "Allow me to apologise. I didn't intend this meeting to be so formal as to require your presence to be declared, but I was careless with my words when I told the doorguard to let you in. I told him to announce you rather than just admit you. Having done that I had to let him perform his function."

Her various guests muttered acceptance of her apologies or said they were unnecessary.

Igrainid waved an arm at the chairs and said, "Please relax. Be seated, and help yourselves to tea."

"With your permission, Cridhe, I would … " Misghel, as usual, started to ask for permission to remain standing.

He always said he could be more effective as a bodyguard if he was on his feet and ready to move.

Igrainid interrupted him and said, "You know this is one of the most secure rooms in the Three Towers. You don't need to stand to keep me safe here. Sit down."

Once everyone was seated Igrainid turned to Saefan and said, "Please make sure no one can overhear us."

Saefan nodded. She leaned forward to touch one of the floor tiles, and her magic activated one of the Quiet Place spells built into the room. One such spell would be sufficient but, as an additional precaution, as in the throne room, there were several to choose from. No would-be eavesdropper would know who would be asked to activate one of the spells on any particular day, or which spell they would select, so they wouldn't be able to prepare a counter-spell. Igrainid saw that Saefan had chosen the lightning bolt and knew that anyone trying to listen would be deafened by a continuous peal of thunder.

"I'm a bit worried," said Igrainid. She picked up the document she had been reading before her guests arrived and waved it, saying, "This is from Cridhe Glodrin of Cairgon and it arrived this morning, just a day after I sent his ambassador away."

"That's an amazingly fast response," said Saefan. "How could he possibly get it here so quickly?"

"It's not in reply to the banishment. Glodrin can't even have had the news about that yet," said Igrainid. "This is something else entirely – a request for a liaison between Dunarh and Glodrin's eldest daughter."

Dunarh jerked upright in his seat. "His eldest daughter? I don't think I know anything about her? Does anyone?"

"That's very careless of you, Dunarh, you really should stay aware of every potential mate," said Saefan. She steepled her fingers and added, "Let me see. She's called Slechai and she is Glodrin's third child. I believe she already has three children of her own. She's reputed to be very attractive – by dwarf standards."

"Looks don't matter, Saefan," said Igrainid. "You should know that."

"I do, mother," replied Saefan, "After all nobody, except possibly another goblin, could have called my second child's father handsome."

Saefan paused, frowning slightly.

"Let me think about it," she said. A few moments later she spoke again, "I think it's actually quite a good match from our point of view. Not only would it get Dunarh his third child but it would also establish a link with a not too distant Realm we haven't had a close association with for a long time. I believe my father's second liaison is the last time Eideann and Cairgon were linked. It might be about time to put that right and forge a new connection with Cairgon."

"What bothers me," said Igrainid, "is the timing of this. Did the ambassador deliberately get himself declared unwelcome just before the request arrived in order to disrupt the negotiations?"

"Perhaps he didn't approve of the potential liaison," said Yuseth.

"Exactly what I was thinking," said Igrainid, "If that's why he did it, it leaves me wondering what the general feeling in Cairgon about it is likely to be."

"To do that he'd have to know the offer was coming," said Misghel.

"True, but there's no reason why he shouldn't," said Igrainid. "The information could have been included in any message from Glodrin to the ambassador – and he has received plenty of those since he arrived, as many as one every other day in the last couple of weeks."

"Another possibility," said Trinafar, "is that he was obeying instructions from Glodrin to make it as difficult as possible to reach an agreement?"

"Why would he do that?" asked Dunarh.

"To get some concessions from us, of course," said Saefan. "Cairgon isn't a particularly rich Realm so he'll be looking for some agreement that's more to his advantage than a simple liaison."

"Isn't another link in the lineage of the Cairgon Cridhe enough of an benefit?" asked Igrainid.

"It might be, but I suspect he's looking for more than that, even if all he wants is to give us less of whatever he offers."

"I'm inclined to agree to opening discussions with Cairgon," said Igrainid. "Even if nothing comes of it. What is Glodrin likely to offer us?"

"Sheep," said Yuseth. "Cairgon has plenty of them. We could negotiate for the delivery of a flock of sheep every year until the child Dunarh fathers is seven. All we have to do is decide how big a flock we should ask for."

"Yes, sheep would do," said Misghel. "But do we want to eat that much mutton?"

"Wool might be better," suggested Saefan. "Our weavers would benefit from that."

"Better to have the sheep," said Yuseth. "They can carry on providing wool for years."

Dunarh frowned slightly. "I can't say I'm keen on going to Cairgon. From what I've heard it sounds like a very narrow-minded place. I don't think I'd enjoy living there until Slechai produces a child, but I know my enjoyment or otherwise is irrelevant. I will accept a liaison with Selchai if that's what you want, mother."

"Good," said Igrainid, smiling at her son. "We'll allow his new ambassador to raise the topic when he arrives. Let's see what Glodrin wants and what he's got to offer in return."

Igrainid sat back, looked at the water jug and snapped her fingers. The water in the jug immediately began to boil. She put a spoonful of one of the teas into a tea ball, placed it in a cup and poured water over it. After giving it time to brew she sniffed it, smiled and sipped. "I haven't said thank you for the tea yet, Trinafar, so let me do so now. Getting tea of this quality is as good a reason as any for letting you spend so much time in the second world."

"I am pleased you like it, mother. As always, it is a gift freely given without obligation."

Igrainid inclined her head acknowledging the gift. She studied her daughter over the rim of the teacup as she held it to her nose and sniffed the aroma again. *She's not happy being reminded that she can spend time in the second world only with my permission. I'm sure she's not going to like what I'm going to say next.*

She put the teacup down and said, "You should be thinking about having children too, Trinafar. If it wasn't for the uncertainty about your place in the Cridhe inheritance you would have had at least two by now. I did by the time I was your age."

"But, mother … "

"I know what you're thinking. Who is going to take the risk of fathering a child on someone who upsets the rules of Cridhe inheritance in case that child is also an anomaly and shouldn't be included in a genealogical count. Am I right?"

"Yes, mother."

Igrainid heard the resignation in Trinafar's voice. She looked at her advisers and said, "How do you think Glodrin would react to the offer of a reciprocal liaison, for example one between his youngest son and Trinafar?"

"No!" exclaimed Trinafar. "That might upset the Cairgon lineage too. Glodrin would never forgive us if it did. With respect, mother, you can't take that risk."

"Our line is already compromised by Trinafar not being a Source," said Saefan.

"That's not my fault!"

"I didn't say it was, but you must admit it causes problems."

Trinafar couldn't refute that statement and her head dropped.

Igrainid said, "I called everyone here to discuss the request from Glodrin. I think we've said enough about that for the moment. Does anyone have anything else to add?"

Nobody replied and Igrainid said, "Dunarh and Misghel, you may leave us. The rest of you please stay."

She watched Dunarh and Misghel take their leave, walking backwards for three paces with hands on hearts before turning away.

When the door closed behind them she said, "Help

yourselves to tea," and snapped her fingers to boil the water again.

She turned to the Keeper of the Chronicles, seeing the purple of her dress reflected in the polished silver of his forehead and said, "Yuseth, some time ago I gave you a task – to search all the records you could get access to, from as many of the Domains and Realms as would let you examine their Chronicles. I asked you to look for other examples of people like Trinafar, where the Cridhe inheritance has gone wrong. How is that search going?"

Yuseth sat forward in his chair and said. "Cridhe, so far I have been allowed access to the genealogies of forty-seven of the Domains and Realms. All of the ones I've seen go back at least five hundred years and three of them as far as nine hundred. I have hopes of getting more but there are others, such as Crioch, from whom I don't expect even the courtesy of a reply to my request. Some of the Chronicles I have seen are, I'm sorry to say, poorly maintained and are simply lists of names and their relationships to the Cridhe line. Others are much more comprehensive and include references to second world history which are valuable in establishing the chronology. These might be limited to a record of significant dates or might include more detailed commentaries on history in the wider world."

"What have you found?"

Yuseth opened the folder on his lap and extracted several documents. However, as he gave his report and detailed some of the other Chronicles, Igrainid noticed that he didn't need to refer to them.

He finished by saying, "Cridhe, I have not found any references to someone like Lady Trinafar in any of the Chronicles I feel I can rely on."

Igrainid sighed and turned to the others saying, "I was hoping Yuseth would find another like Trinafar and be able to tell me what happened to that person and that Cridhe line. Unfortunately the idea hasn't worked."

She turned back to Yuseth and asked, "Have you made any progress with the other part of the task?

"On that I can be much more confident," he replied. "There is no doubt that, as we have always believed, it is the number of children in the line that counts and not the racial assortment. The only thing the various lines I have studied have in common is variety, no two have the same mixture of races, and every race in Lady Trinafar's pedigree for the last five generations is found in several other lines."

"You have no recommendation as to what race should provide the father of Trinafar's first child?"

"No, Cridhe."

"Saefan, what do you think?"

"For all I know it might as well be that cross-breed she brought here recently."

Trinafar shouted "No!" as she jumped up from her chair.

"Why not?" asked Saefan. "We don't have any other ideas if you don't fancy a liaison with Glodrin's son. You must have some feeling for the cross-breed. You brought him to Eideann."

"The only feeling I have for him is irritation. He effectively blackmailed me into bringing him because he could easily disrupt my research even if he didn't mean to."

Saefan jumped up from her chair too, glaring at Trinafar. "Oh, yes. Those precious, precious studies! All about the second world. Of no conceivable significance to us. I know all of us who can hold a glamour there have spent some time in the second world as part of our education but we have come back home to help mother run the Domain. It's about time you did too."

"That's enough, Saefan, Trinafar. Sit down, both of you. Remember it's with my permission that Trinafar has been in the second world as long as she has," said Igrainid.

She watched her daughters glowering at each other and waited until they settled back into their chairs. "I hadn't considered the possibility of bringing a cross-breed into the family but the idea has possibilities – no, Trinafar, just keep quiet. I haven't decided anything yet."

She turned to Yuseth saying, "I don't suppose you've found any record of cross-breeds in a Cridhe lineage?"

"No, I haven't."

Igrainid steepled her fingers and brought her fingertips to her mouth. *Perhaps it's time to let Saefan know more. I could wish she was less confrontational but she may have the best brain of all my children.*

"Trinafar, don't pay any attention to Saefan's grumbles about your research. She doesn't know you're following my instructions."

Igrainid saw Saefan pause in the middle of making more tea for herself and look at her, obviously surprised.

Meanwhile Trinafar said, "Yes, mother," in a sullen voice.

"Don't sound so petulant, Trinafar. Tell Saefan about your research."

"Yes, Trin, what *is* it about?" asked Saefan.

"Don't call me that! You know how much I hate it."

"Apologise, Saefan," said Igrainid.

Saefan scowled but did mutter, "Sorry," before asking, "Has your research produced anything useful?"

"You mean apart from Niccolo Machiavelli's *The Prince*? I remember you being fascinated by *that* when I found it among all my 'useless' research."

"Don't squabble," snapped Igrainid before Saefan could reply.

"Yuseth, you said you didn't find anyone like me in any of the Chronicles you can rely on. What about the less dependable ones?"

"None exactly like you, Lady Trinafar. However, there are three where other anomalies are hinted at. In two of them I suspect the apparent anomalies are simply errors with at least one person omitted from the lineage. In both cases people who were not seventh children are listed as Sources. The other anomaly is a pedigree recording the birth of twins in a Cridhe line."

"Twins! Are you sure?" exclaimed Saefan.

"Yes, my lady. That record is from the Chronicles of

Jorvik, one of the more detailed, comprehensive and, I believe, most accurate of the records I've been allowed to see."

"How wonderful."

"Unfortunately, the twins died before they were six years old from a virulent fever that killed about a quarter of the population."

"Oh!" Saefan had tears in her eyes, "Losing one child is so sad. I can't begin to imagine what losing twins must be like."

"Suppose these anomalies you've found are real and not errors in the records," asked Igrainid.

"Then, Cridhe, they are linked to Lost Worlds."

"You're not serious," exclaimed Saefan. "We all outgrew Umbwir's *Tales of the Lost Worlds* years ago. They're fantasies, figments of somebody's imagination with no basis in reality."

"Are they?" said Igrainid. "Yuseth, I think you need to tell Saefan about your discovery."

For the next twenty minutes or so Yuseth told them how he had discovered something strange when recataloguing some of the older records of the Domain. He had found two items which were particularly odd. One was a statuette of a figure in Roman dress and the other a bundle of scrolls. Both of these items were recorded as having been acquired from the second world in the late fourteenth century.

The statuette was of emperor Drusus III, someone who never existed in the history of the second world as they knew it. The scrolls were even stranger as they referred to dates between 2197 and 2236 AUC; dates which just didn't make sense since counting years from the foundation of Rome had gone out of fashion soon after its fall in about 1225 AUC. Assuming they were authentic, and there was no reason to suspect otherwise, they looked as if they had never been read since their acquisition. However, their existence implied that the second world had been Roman when these objects were collected from it.

Since finding those objects Yuseth had found other oddities among the older records and had become convinced that the Lost Worlds were, or had been, real.

"When Yuseth brought this to my attention Trinafar happened to be visiting the second world, as you did when you were her age, Saefan. I asked her to research the Lost Worlds and she has continued to do so."

"Unfortunately," said Yuseth, "I can't maintain a glamour in the second world or I would be doing the research myself. As it is I've found some more abnormalities in the archives."

"Such as?" asked Saefan.

Yuseth told them of other strange things he had found in the archives and Trinafar added what she could from her own work. These were principally about how the history of the second world deviated from what the Chronicles recorded.

She said, "More recently I have found a pamphlet called *The Historie of the Stewards of Alba and Anglaya* in the library I've been using. It purports to be an account of the House of Stuart from its beginning with Robert II in the fourteenth century to its end with the death of Queen Anne at the beginning of the eighteenth."

"Who is she supposed to be? I've never heard of a ruling Queen called Anne."

"According to the pamphlet I'm talking about, she was the last monarch of the House of Stuart and she died without an heir in the early eighteenth century. Supposedly she's the monarch responsible for the Union of Britain."

"Nonsense!" said Saefan. "That was James VI."

"And," said Yuseth, "there's still a Stuart on the throne, isn't there? I'm sure it would be well known if there had been a change of dynasty. Anne, if she ever existed, certainly wasn't the last of the Stuarts."

"Yes, Robert VII is king and emperor and has been for the last thirty-one years. The Stuart line isn't going to die with him either, he has three children and six grandchildren."

"I wish I could read this pamphlet," said Yuseth, "it sounds interesting."

"I can't bring it back with me. There's only one copy and the security in that library is too good to let me sneak it out. Anyway, I wouldn't really recommend it," said Trinafar. "Although the alternate history is ingenious, quite well worked out and does make some sort of sense the book itself is not very well written and it's rather tedious."

"Perhaps so, but tell us more," said Igrainid. "Where does it start to diverge from the real history of the second world we know?"

"With Charles II. He is supposed to have married Catherine of Braganza – whoever she was – died without legitimate children and been succeeded by his brother James VII. I'm sure you know that, in reality, Charles II married Ekaterina of Krakow and had five children. Their son, Gregory I, inherited rulership of large parts of Poland and Lithuania through her, as well as the Union of Britain from Charles II. That was the beginning of the Empire."

"Sounds like your pamphlet is a work of fiction," said Saefan.

"I agree," said Trinafar, "It might be, but it could also be an indication of a Lost World we don't otherwise know."

"That is interesting," said Saefan, "but I don't see any reason to worry about it."

Yuseth disagreed, saying that the three indications he had found of anomalies in Cridhe inheritance were all associated with Lost Worlds. He referred to the Lost World called Jorvekk as an example. It was a favourite setting for swash-buckling tales and they all knew of it. There were two distinct but overlapping Lost Worlds in which Vikings – led by someone called Sven Grimaxe in one world, and Magnus Redbeard in the other – invaded Britain with varying degrees of success. The Chronicles of the Realm of Jorvik documented that one particular lacuna had led from Tirog to a world where Magnus ruled. Suddenly, it didn't go there and opened instead to the world ruled by Sven. The differences between the two worlds were mostly trivial, but it was recorded that anyone who had gone through the lacuna and was in the second world when the change occurred was never seen again.

"That's what my research is all about," said Trinafar. "Yuseth's discovery of a possible link between a change in the second world and something strange in a Cridhe line makes me afraid that my 'problem' may be associated with a risk to Eideann or the second world."

Saefan asked, "Does anybody else know about this? What about the chroniclers in other Domains and Realms?"

"As far as I know," replied Yuseth, "nobody else has done this sort of comparison of Chronicles."

Saefan shook her head, looked at Trinafar and said, "I think you'd better carry on with your research."

#

Dhugalt, like most of the magi, did some delicate juggling of information and memory. It was necessary to allow the Sources he met on his travels to know that he could be contacted for advice. At the same time, he didn't tell them he was a magus. Whatever justification they developed to explain why they would seek advice from a wanderer didn't concern him. It was enough that they did rationalise it in some way and had some means of contacting him when required.

Igrainid's method of contact was a mirror etched with a snake eating its own tail. It hung in a plain blackwood frame in her study. She had used it before the meeting at which she intended to ask Yuseth if he had discovered anything relevant to Trinafar's failure to be a Source.

With the meeting over, she walked across to the mirror, touched the snake's head and asked, "Have you been watching?"

"Yes, I have," said Dhugalt. "I told you I would."

"Thank you, uncle. Can you tell me if there is any substance to Yuseth's belief that there are links between anomalies in the Cridhe inheritance and changes in the second world?"

"Do you want an answer even knowing that I cannot allow you to remember this conversation?"

"Yes, please."

Dhugalt sighed. "Yes," he said, "I am afraid Yuseth is right. There are several other records he hasn't had access to that mention people like Trinafar. I'm impressed that he has developed his theory with so little information to work with."

"What happened to them?"

"To the people themselves, nothing. They lived normal lives … "

Igrainid whispered, "Thank the Starmaker."

"… but, for no obvious reason, at some point the second world they knew disappeared and was replaced by a new one.

"We can see evidence of the approaching change in other Realms and Domains as well as in Eideann. Trinafar's status as a Failed Source is just one indication that a change is coming. Unfortunately, we don't know of any way to predict what the change will be or when it will occur."

"Is there nothing you can do about it – I don't mean you personally but can't the magi work together to prevent it happening?"

Dhugalt shook his head.

"So there's nothing to be done."

"I fear not."

"When are you going to be here next?" asked Igrainid.

"I'll get to Eideann in two or three weeks' time. I'm in Inbhirnis at present and I'm planning on working down the east coast in no particular hurry."

"I'll look forward to seeing you in person again, uncle."

"Although you won't remember details of this conversation, I think I can allow you to feel a bit happier about Trinafar's future – even if you won't remember why you should feel that way."

"Thank you."

"As always, you can also retain enough knowledge to know how to contact me when you need to, Igrainid. Apart from that, this conversation didn't happen."

Igrainid said, "I kno…"

She lifted her hand, turned her head from side to side to examine how her hair was arranged and patted it into place. She made a small adjustment to the position of one of the silver and jet combs holding it and, satisfied with her appearance, went back to her chair.

She picked up another of the documents lying there awaiting her attention. Then she muttered, "I wish the magi were real. They might be able to do something for Trinafar."

She started reading.

Dhugalt let the image of Igrainid's study fade and his awareness returned to his body, sitting at a table outside an inn with a half full beer mug close at hand.

exploring

Fergus returned to his room in Caedmon's Tower with thoughts of Trinafar and her 'problem' rattling around in his head. *Quite apart from my debt to her I'd like to help in some way, but I don't know what I could do. I might as well have a good look around and combine that with the job I've got for Duncan.*

Rummaging in his rucksack he found what he was looking for near the bottom; a dull black box about four inches by five and two inches thick. *What was it his friend Duncan had called it? A NEbox? Now to find out if it works as well as it does back home.* He told himself there was no reason why it shouldn't, but was unable to prevent himself holding his breath as he poked at a recessed button on one edge. There were three quiet clicks and one face of the box started glowing. *Good!*

A small circular opening appeared in the other face revealing a lens. He pointed this at various things around the room and felt relieved when the glowing face showed an image of whatever he pointed the box at. *I suppose the idea that magic and science don't mix is another example of what Trinafar would call a half-truth. I shouldn't really be surprised that it works. There might not be much magic at home, but it does exist there even if I can't use it. Why shouldn't science co-exist with magic here?*

He walked across to the window, raised the box and pressed another button on one edge to record an image of the view to the north. *It's going to take more than one image of the scenery to convince Duncan. It's time to do some exploring.*

With his heart beating faster at the idea of wandering freely around Eideann, Fergus slipped the box into the pocket of his jacket and left his room. He crossed one of the bridges to the Robhas Tower, thinking he must remember to thank Rhiannis for the efficacy of her spell the next time he saw her. He made images of the Three Towers from many angles as he went down through the various levels to the garden, then through it. The majority of the people he saw were elves or fay. Most of the other races were easy enough to identify from his memories of his trips to Tirog with his mother; he recognised gnomes and goblins and remembered her warning him that, although the two races might look similar, both would resent being taken for the other.

He saw a small cloud of pixies and a couple of dryads as he explored the garden, and wondered if the pixies were pollinators and the dryads gardeners.

He realised there were enough people around, particularly at the base of the Robhas Tower, that some of them were bound to appear in the images he was making. However, he tried to avoid including people if he could because he had no idea how they would react. He remembered reading how some primitive tribes had responded to seeing images of themselves during the exploration of some parts of the Empire. Not that he thought the inhabitants of Eideann were primitive. He didn't think they were likely to react that way but he wasn't going to take chances.

He wandered away from the Three Towers and the cluster of buildings in the gaps between them. Heading towards the road leading down the ridge from the Three Towers he couldn't help comparing the scene with what he would see in Edinburgh. His mind insisted on calling the street Castlehill but he was sure it would be called something else here. *I must find out what.*

He saw a few people looking askance at him as he pointed the box back towards the Towers and decided it was time to stop making images. He didn't want to attract too much attention. He put the box back in his pocket.

There was an arch over the road and he thought it must indicate the border of the castle. *No. It's not a castle. Igrainid called it the Luchairt. I think that means palace.* Four armed fay in the green and brown colours of the Domain stood at the arch watching the people moving through it. They were, he guessed, also guarding the top of the path to the lacuna, which went steeply downhill from there. He wandered through the arch and down the hill, seeing solid, stone-built buildings mostly two or three storeys high, a few timber-framed buildings and even, to his surprise, one or two wattle and daub structures. Windows and doors standing open allowed him glimpses of some of the interiors where he could see dwarves working at forges, elves at looms and lace pillows and gnomes at potter's wheels. Other members of various races worked at an assortment of crafts. Among other trades he saw cordwainers, embroiderers and wood carvers working in doorways, under canopies and in stalls lining the street.

The crowd he encountered as he made his way down the street was an assortment of people of different races. He wasn't surprised to see fay were the most common but there were also many elves, goblins and dwarves. A couple of trolls plodding down the street carrying huge boxes on their backs were given plenty of space, although they weren't behaving aggressively. More of the same sort of women who had delivered his clothes, and one or two men of the same race, hurried by. He blinked when he saw a woman dive out of a third storey window and spread membranous wings stretching from her extended arms to her hips. Before she had fallen far she must have caught an up current as she soared away down the hill. *What is she? Mother never told me of a race like that. I wonder if they inspired tales of angels.*

He wandered on. He quickly realised Trinafar had been right to warn him about the similarities and differences between Edinburgh and Eideann. Some of the buildings he passed looked more or less like those occupying the same space in Edinburgh but the majority weren't and some were very different. He soon realised that differences were commoner than similarities. Even the ones he almost recognised were different to some degree. After seeing so many differences he was surprised at first to see how similar the Eideann version of St Giles was to the one he was familiar with. At least the main building looked more or less familiar but, looking more closely, he saw the crown steeple was missing and was replaced by a single octagonal tower. That was different enough to be disorientating. It was even stranger when he realised the dedication was to the Starmaker, a mythical figure he remembered his mother talking about with reverence, rather than to St Giles.

As he went farther from the Towers the stalls lining the streets narrowed them so much that no vehicles other than small two-wheeled carts pulled by goblins, trolls or, in a few cases, fay could pass each other. Even the small carts managed to obstruct the traffic and the rest of the people jostling each other in the street as often as not. It was noisy with the clatter of wheels on the cobbles, arguments about rights-of-way, the shouts of stall-holders advertising their wares and of children of various races playing a chasing game that seemed to require them to scream a lot.

The stalls sold all sorts of things – vegetables, fish, clothes, weapons, fabrics, sweets. The air was fragrant with the smells of garlic, pepper, cinnamon and many other aromatic herbs and spices, some of which he couldn't identify. One stall displayed dozens of small bottles containing coloured liquids. Fergus was puzzled when he saw the stallholder open one of the bottles and wave it in front of himself before corking it up again and doing the same with another. Then he was close enough to the stall to smell lavender, lily-of-the-valley, violets, and realised the stall sold perfumes.

About two hundred yards down the hill the scent of roasting meat and frying onions drew his attention to a cluster of food stalls. The delicious aroma of the grilled venison and hot pickles wrapped up in flatbread being offered at one of the stalls made his mouth water. He was about to ask for one of them when he realised he didn't know if the money he had in his purse would be accepted and he walked away before he made a fool of himself. *Better just go back to my room and take a look at the images. Next time I see Trinafar I'll ask her about money.*

#

Back in his room he called up the images he had made. He was satisfied with some of them but others showed irregular, apparently random, purple-ish fuzzy spots. *What could cause that? I wish Duncan was here. He'd be able to explain it. But then if he was I wouldn't need these to convince him Tirog exists and it's not my imagination.*

He kept flipping between images trying to make sense of them. It was the one of the gazebo Trinafar had described as a Quiet Place that finally gave him a clue. He could see the structure clearly but not the furnishings of the interior. *It's magic! That must be what the box is recording. All these blurs are the people I couldn't avoid including in an image, or places associated with magic.*

He had just put the box back into his rucksack when there was knock at the door. It was repeated, more forcibly, before he could answer it. He opened the door to find Maedron and two other elves waiting outside, swords in hands.

"What are you up to?" growled Maedron stepping forward and forcing Fergus back into the room before he had a chance to say anything.

"Up to? I don't understand what you mean."

"Wandering around pointing some contraption at people. There have been complaints about you. Some people are saying you've been stealing their magic, and others have complained about spells being disrupted."

Fergus couldn't think what to say.

"Come with me," said Maedron. "You've got some explaining to do. I'm taking you into custody until the Cridhe has time to question you herself. Will you come peacefully or do I have to force you?"

He could use magic to make me go with him, so there's no point trying to resist. Not that he wanted to anyway. *I need to find out what this is about. I'd better co-operate or they might throw me out of Tirog before the month is up.* "I'll come with you," he said.

"Where is that – thing you've been pointing at people?"

"I'll get it," said Fergus, "It's in that bag." He took a step toward the rucksack and stopped abruptly when Maedron stepped between him and the bag and raised his sword.

"No!" said Maedron. "Stop right there. You're not getting your hands on whatever it is." He gestured and the rucksack was surrounded by a half-dome of braided blue and silver strands. Maedron waved one of his companions forward and told him to pick it up. As he did so, the shield wrapped completely around the bag and Fergus could see it was actually spherical.

"It's harmless," said Fergus, smiling despite the situation at the careful way the elf carried it to the other side of the room, keeping it as far as possible away from him.

"You would say that whether it is or not, wouldn't you?" said Maedron.

One elf led the way down stairs, followed by Fergus with Maedron behind him and the last elf, with the rucksack, trailing behind them by a dozen or more steps.

Fergus saw several other figures in the brown and green livery watching from various vantage points as they went down to ground level. Some of them carried bows with arrows already nocked. He was escorted across the garden to the Robhas Tower without seeing anyone else. Even the ground floor of the Tower was empty. *They're taking this seriously, aren't they. There must be twenty of them watching me, and they've cleared everybody else out of the way. I must really have them frightened. I hope I can convince Igrainid she doesn't need to worry about me – I must!*

He had noticed an alcove with stairs leading down on his first visit to the Robhas Tower and wasn't surprised when Maedron indicated that direction. *I guess I'm about to find out what a fay dungeon is like.*

Half a dozen doors led from an open area at the bottom of the stairs. Most of them were standing open.

"You don't need to lock me up. I'm not dangerous."

Maedron pointed to one of the doors and said, "I'm not taking chances. In you go."

Fergus was relieved to see it wasn't a dingy, damp, smelly, rat-infested dungeon with chains. It was small but clean and well-lit by a glowing stone set into the wall above the door. A bed, with linen sheets, woollen blankets and a couple of fluffy pillows occupied most of the space. The rest of it was empty. As he crossed the threshold into the cell he felt an irregular humming sensation that was disorientating. *Must be a ward of some sort to disrupt magic.*

A voice called from one of the other cells demanding to know when he was going to be released. "Keep quiet, Yngvi," said Maedron. "You'll get out when the Cridhe says so." He looked at Fergus and said, "Same goes for you." He closed the cell door and Fergus shivered a bit at the solid, resounding thud it made.

Fergus sat on the bed. *How long will I be here, I wonder. I'm sure I won't be high on Igrainid's priority list. She's got to have more things to do than worry about me – unless she thinks I'm a spy from another Domain. She might have me interrogated sooner if she thinks that, or she might keep me locked up with nothing to do in order to soften me up before questioning. Maybe I should have showed her the box and asked her permission before making images.*

He paced back and forth, five steps one way, turn, five steps back, turn, five steps, turn, again and again. It soon became monotonous and he tried push-ups, squats and other exercises to keep himself occupied. Some time later the glowing stone dimmed and he assumed that meant it was night. The darkening and brightening of that stone, and the arrival of food, were the only things that marked the passage of time for the next three days. With nothing to read and no access to writing materials, he quickly became bored.

His mood changed several times, from acceptance that Igrainid might well have a reason for imprisoning him. *After all she doesn't know the box is harmless,* to anger at not being given the chance to explain himself, and back again. Sometimes he thought, *I'm not part of her Domain so I can't really grumble at how she treats me.* And at others it was, *She called me a guest of the Domain but she's not treating me like one.*

Over the next three days he settled into a mindless lethargy of passive resignation.

He roused himself the next time Maedron appeared and begged him for something to read. He didn't expect a response and was pleasantly surprised when Maedron gave him two items the next time he visited.

"It's just a children's book and a map." said Maedron, "Sorry I've nothing else to offer you. It's all I could get my hands on quickly."

"That will do. Thank you."

The map looked familiar to Fergus when he unfolded it. It showed the outline of Alba and a bit of the northern part of Anglaya. Edinburgh, Inverness and other places he knew were marked on it but with different names. He resolved to study it carefully to learn the names.

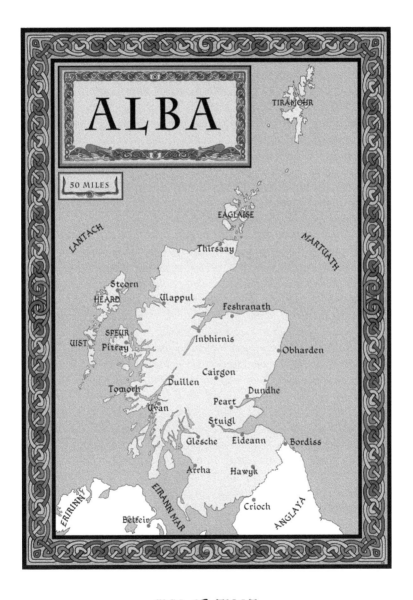

map of tirog

Then he put it aside and picked up the book. It was quite a slim volume with the title:

an introduction to the mythology of tirog

'There are many stories of powerful creatures in Tirog. Some of these are probably no more than that; stories, intended to educate and to frighten children into behaving. However, some of them are undoubtedly true.

Among the truthful are a few tales of kind, helpful beings. Striga, the Little Red Owl is a good example. As any child will tell you, if you can attract Striga and persuade her to perch on your arm she will listen to your questions. Then, in return for milk, freshly baked bread or oatcakes, she will give true answers.

Unfortunately not all of the powerful beings described in legends are benign. Many should be treated with caution and avoided if at all possible. For example, Fenris leads a pack of wild dogs and rampages through the woods striking down anyone foolish enough to try to chain them. In some versions of this story even seeing Fenris is enough to foreshadow death.

Perhaps the most ambivalent of the mythical beings is Cerne, or Herne, the Hunter. He is the leader of the Wild Hunt, a group of people of all races who rejoice in battle. There are, probably, several such Hunts each led by an avatar of Cerne. The Hunt is able to ride the winds and sightings of it are commonly associated with thunderstorms. While terrifying and aggressive, the Riders are also honourable and will bargain for survival or service with those unfortunate enough to encounter them. Any promise made by or to one of Cerne's avatars is binding.'

Fergus stopped reading there, having decided to ration his reading to avoid running out of material. He expected he would have time to read the rest of the book, but he was wrong. Maedron came to collect him the next day saying, "The Cridhe wants to see you."

Fallacy

The next regular meeting of the Eleven started with the unwelcome news that there was a resurgence of the sidhe supremacy fallacy. As Sumethla remarked, and others agreed, suppressing this seemed to be a never-ending task.

The basis of this belief, with which the Eleven vehemently disagreed, was that because the sidhe have skills and abilities humans do not they should rule in the second world as well as in Tirog.

It was a pernicious idea that cropped up every forty or fifty years. It usually started among Sources who felt their importance was not sufficiently recognised. This was often because their Domain or Realm was one of the smaller territories and they wanted to control more. Other sidhe with fairly weak magic were attracted to the idea of ruling people with even less. They were actively recruited by ambitious Sources whenever the fallacy cropped up again.

There was no dissent among the Eleven when they got the news of a new outbreak of the fallacy. There was a well-established way to deal with it, which made use of the magi who clustered around the Eleven. They would investigate how widespread the fallacy had become and report their findings to the next meeting.

All of the Eleven had previous experience of the situation. Most of the magi in the halo had too. They all relished the idea of working together, surely it would benefit them when they finally managed to gain a place in the Group.

The magi's task would be to deliver an ultimatum to the believers with the threat of having their ability to generate or use latency destroyed. This threat was sufficient to stop any attempt to conquer parts of the second world and, as Sumethla said, it had never been necessary in their experience to actually carry out that threat.

With no controversy to keep their attention on the Eleven, the magi dispersed to start their investigations.

The Eleven themselves felt relieved at the lack of pressure from the halo and, more slowly and more relaxed than usual, they took themselves back to Tirog.

#

The Eleven were summoned by one of their number who reported she had found more extensive evidence of plotting by believers in the fallacy. Some of the Eleven were rather dismissive of this news, saying they were easy enough to suppress.

Sumethla's response to this pointed out that the peoples in the territories threatened by the plot would suffer if it was allowed to come to fruition. She said the Eleven had a duty to protect the humans in the threatened lands even if they didn't realise they were at risk.

This sign of dissent among the Eleven was greeted by an increase in the activity of the observers watching from the halo. Those who had provoked Sumethla's response found themselves under pressure to conform to the majority opinion.

Sumethla reiterated the reasoning behind the decision to stop the plot. "The sidhe are outnumbered by humans something like two hundred and fifty to one and the imbalance is getting worse because humans are more fertile than we are. Yes, we have magic and they don't. However, we shouldn't be complacent about that. If it came to a conflict between the worlds then numbers might well win. We can't afford to take that risk."

"There is a well-established way of dealing with the fallacy," said a goblin called Brangret.

"That threat alone has, in the past, been enough to stop any attempts to conquer parts of the second world. It has never been necessary to carry it out," said Sumethla.

Brangret agreed and added, "The ultimatum must be delivered with sufficient conviction to make sure the plotters believe it *will* be carried out."

"Consider what will happen to the people of the Domains and Realms if they lose access to latency because their Source is stripped of the ability to generate it," said one of the Eleven who hadn't expressed an opinion.

Brangret shrugged. "Too bad. We must stop the plot and the best time to do that is before it gets underway."

"We will meet again in three days," said Sumethla, "with the names of every Source who subscribes to the fallacy."

With that the meeting ended and the non-place vanished once again.

ꞅɑꝺꞡꞓ

Igrainid looked up when Trinafar arrived in response to her summons, entered the throne room and went to her knees in front of her.

"I have two questions for you," Igrainid said.

"Yes, mother. I will answer them if I can."

"Good. Get up off your knees and sit down."

Trinafar rose, kissed her mother and took a seat.

"The first question is rather trivial but it intrigues me that you have been trying to find out how Maedron upset me recently. Why are you interested?"

"Because we grew up together and he is my friend. He is devoted to you and I can't imagine what he did to be punished with guard duty. Call it curiosity if you want."

"Is that all? What have you heard?"

"Nothing, mother. Nobody seems willing to talk about it."

Igrainid laughed and said, "Because he has asked for silence on the matter. If you really want to know I will tell you, but you will incur a debt to me. How badly do you want to know?"

Trinafar shuffled in her seat as she thought about it. After a couple of minutes she said, "Please tell me."

"It's ridiculously simple. I suggested it was time he fathered another child and gave him a list of three potential mates – I am *not* going to tell you who they are – but he rejected my advice and refused to breed with any of the three."

"Oh!"

"I told you it was a simple matter."

"Thank you for telling me, mother. What is the other question?"

"How much do you know about this cross-breed you brought here?"

"Only what he told you, mother. Why?"

"He has become something of a nuisance."

"Has he? What has he been doing? I haven't seen him for days."

"Of course you haven't seen him. He's in a cell in the dungeon."

"Why? What has he done?"

"I don't know any details. All I do know is that he's upset a lot of people with suspicious behaviour and Maedron thought it best to imprison him. I don't much like having left him locked up for three days without finding out more but I haven't had time to spend on him until now. I want you here while I question him."

Igrainid rang a bell and sent the gnomish guard who answered it to fetch Saefan, Maedron and Misghel. They had been warned they would be needed so they were expecting the summons and arrived quickly.

Igrainid frowned slightly when she saw Maedron carrying something wrapped up in the shimmering blue and silver braids of a magic shield. Before saying anything she touched one of the painted tiles set into the throne. The one she chose had an image of a bird on it and anyone trying to eavesdrop would hear nothing but the raucous screeches of jackdaws, magpies and seagulls.

"What do you have there, Maedron?"

"Cridhe, it's a bag belonging to the cross-breed. He upset many people by using some device which he says is in it. It's shielded because I don't know what it is or if it's dangerous."

"Are you willing to investigate the contents of that bag knowing nothing about it except who it belongs to?"

"Yes, Cridhe."

"Thank you, Maedron. On behalf of the Domain I acknowledge the debt incurred. We will, of course, take whatever precautions we can to keep you safe."

She turned to Saefan and asked her to establish and hold a shield around Maedron while he examined the contents of the bag.

"Yes, mother," replied Saefan and made a sweeping circular gesture. It left a trail of golden light that flickered across the room and condensed into a shimmering, sparkling dome about twelve feet in diameter. Only Maedron and the rucksack, still wrapped in blue and silver, were inside Saefan's shield.

"Take care, Maedron. Don't touch anything with your hands, handle everything with magic."

Maedron bowed to Igrainid. With a wiping motion he removed the shield around the rucksack, then started unpacking it, removing the contents of the bag one item at a time as he used magic to feel things and lift them. In the various pockets he found a compass; maps of Edinburgh, Aberdeen, Inverness and the Western Isles; a torch; matches; sunglasses; a water bottle; an enamel mug; and two knives, one of them a very good quality double-edged blade about eight inches long in a leather sheath, the other a folding knife with several fold-out tools as well as the three inch blade itself. A purse in one of the pockets contained eighty-seven gold sovereigns and another purse held a mixture of silver shillings and copper pennies to the value of eight sovereigns, three shillings and nine pence.

Inside the main compartment most of the contents were clothes. These Maedron carefully unfolded with his magic and shook out in case they were concealing something. When he found nothing, as was the case with almost all of them, he folded them again and stacked them tidily in a heap. The only incongruous thing he found among the clothes was an oilskin pouch containing a heavy powder. He sniffed it cautiously and shuddered. "Iron filings, Cridhe. More than enough to poison the susceptible."

"Whatever happens he doesn't get that back. Misghel, will you take charge of it and keep it safe."

"Of course, Cridhe."

A metal container when opened revealed a small stove and another was full of slabs of a pungent smelling gelatinous substance. Trinafar identified it as solid fuel for the camping stove.

"Whatever else he has done," said Maedron, "he has come well equipped." He paused briefly, feeling around inside the rucksack with his magic. "There's only one thing left in there. It fits the description of what he was waving around and upsetting people with, but I don't know what it is."

He made a lifting gesture. A black box rose from the rucksack and stayed suspended in mid-air.

Igrainid asked Maedron if he could see any markings on it.

He rotated it and looked at all sides of it from close range. "There's nine or ten dots along one edge and in one corner of the thing there's a bit that's shiny rather than dull. I think it's a symbol of some sort but I don't know what it means. Looks like a semi-circle with a line under it. If I had to guess I'd say it might be the sun on the horizon. And there's an arrow through it, like a compass needle."

"It can't be," exclaimed Trinafar.

"Can't be what?" said Igrainid. "Do you recognise it?"

"Not exactly, mother. I've never seen one, but if the symbol is what I think it is – No, it's not possible. How could Fergus have a – it doesn't make sense."

"Settle down, Trinafar. What do you think it might be?"

"That symbol, it could be the emblem of a company in the second world that makes high technology gadgets. If so, the device might be something called a NEbox. I've read about them. They're very new and very expensive. I don't know how Fergus could have one."

"He's not poor with that amount of gold in his purse," said Maedron.

"We will ask him how he comes to have this thing," said Igrainid. "Misghel, will you get him up here, suitably guarded of course."

"Certainly, Cridhe. It will take about twenty minutes to assemble an escort and get him here." He walked across the room to the door and gave instructions to the guard standing outside before going back to his place beside Igrainid's throne.

"Maedron, you can put that down for now. Carefully, please."

Igrainid could see Maedron become noticeably less

tense after he put the mysterious box down on the floor as far away from them as he could. Then he wrapped a shield around it.

Feeling the need for some relaxation, she said, "I think we will have time for a cup of tea before he gets here."

True to Misghel's estimate, twenty minutes or so later the door opened and Fergus, surrounded by four guards with drawn swords, entered. The glow of a shield enveloped him. Igrainid looked at Misghel who had moved to stand just inside the door and said, "Four, and a shield! Don't you think that's overdoing it a bit for one cross-breed?"

"Cridhe, I'm not taking any chances with your safety."

She looked around again to see Fergus on his knees in front of her, now double shielded.

"I think the shields are enough," she said. "Who is holding them? And what is permitted to him?"

"I'm holding one of them," said Misghel. "He can breathe and talk but can't walk or move his arms to make any gestures."

"And I have the other," said Saefan, "with similar restrictions."

"That's my shield," said Maedron, pointing at the blue and silver mesh wrapped around the mysterious box.

"Good," said Igrainid. "I think that is enough. Misghel you can dismiss the other guards."

Misghel started to object but had to give in when Igrainid insisted there were enough people in the room ready to protect her without needing the guard too.

She gazed at Fergus for a few minutes then she said, "You have disturbed the tranquillity of Eideann."

Fergus looked up and said, "I didn't mean to, Cridhe. I didn't know what I did would have that effect."

"Explain yourself. Give me a reason why I should allow you to stay."

"I … "

"What did you expect to find here? Why did you bring iron filings with you? Who were you planning on poisoning?"

"No, Cridhe – I didn't – I mean – I don't intend it to be a poison – it's just something my mother advised me to have with me any time I came to Tirog."

"Is your mother sensitive to iron?" asked Saefan.

"Yes, she is. I once saw her get a bad burn from touching a fish-hook she didn't know was there in a fish she was gutting. And she never used iron cooking pots or utensils, only bronze or ceramic."

"I think I can understand why she gave you the advice she did," said Misghel, "but you cannot be permitted to carry iron. Steel knives are bad enough but iron filings are intolerable. There are some members of the Domain who would become severely ill, and some might even be killed by breathing that dust. We will confiscate it."

Igrainid nodded in agreement then pointed to the black box and said, "Tell us about that – object. What does it do?"

"Many things, Cridhe. May I demonstrate?"

"Not yet, I think. Tell me about it first. Is it a – what was it you called it, Trinafar, – a NEbox?"

"It is," said Fergus.

"And how did you come by it?"

"It was given to me by a friend."

"Pardon me, mother," said Trinafar. "That doesn't seem likely. I read an article about these things in the *Edinburgh Imperial Gazette* quite recently. It said, and I think I'm quoting it fairly accurately, that 'NEboxes incorporate a new and experimental development of the latest protonic technology' – whatever that is. I didn't understand a lot of what it said so I don't remember any details, but the article was quite lyrical about its possibilities. It said that so far only a dozen or so have been made for testing purposes and NorEast, the company that's developing them, hopes to put them on the market next spring."

"That's right," said Fergus. "This is one of the test batch. They won't go into production until they've been thoroughly tested. My friend is the chief development officer of NorEast. He wanted somebody not involved in the development to try it out independently of the official company testing, so he asked me."

"Why did you bring it here to test it?" asked Igrainid.

"I didn't set out to do that. I've been looking for somebody who could bring me to Tirog for many years. Meeting Lady Trinafar gave me the chance I'd been hoping for. Also, I want to convince my friend that Tirog exists and what I've done with the NEbox will help me do that. We've argued about it for years. He thinks Tirog is a myth or a delusion."

"What does this gadget of yours do that will make him change his mind?" asked Igrainid.

"Well, this one doesn't have all the functions that the production model will have. At home it will be able to link to the far-talker network but obviously it can't do that here in Tirog because there isn't one. Here I can use it to make and store images, and it can also manipulate numbers."

"If they're like the images of Edinburgh Trinafar brought me last Beltane it won't be able to hold many of them. What was it you called them, Trinafar – Daguerograms, or something like that?"

Fergus told Igrainid that the NEbox didn't hold physical images like Daguerograms but stored the information that let it reconstruct the virtual images it had made and display them on the photoscreen of the box. He bewildered her, and the rest of his audience, by talking about protonics, software, thin films, partial conductivity, image persistence and other things they'd never heard of and didn't understand. The more he tried to explain the more confused they became. Eventually he said, "Cridhe, please give me permission to demonstrate."

Igrainid hesitated.

"Forgive me for interrupting, Cridhe, but I feel we need to learn more," said Maedron. "Either we return this man to his cell while you decide his fate, or we allow him to show one of us what that thing does. I offer myself as the one."

"Since he can't pass a lacuna we could banish him from Eideann; send him back to the second world," said Misghel. "That might be the simplest solution."

"No! Cridhe, please let me stay. I promise I don't mean any harm."

Igrainid nodded slowly and, after a short pause, said, "I think you're right, Maedron, we do need to know more about this. I am indebted to you for your willingness to risk yourself. Please be very careful, I don't want to lose you."

All of them, except Maedron and Fergus, moved into one half of the room. Misghel and Saefan moved their shields from around Fergus to set them up as a barrier dividing the room in two, leaving Maedron and Fergus alone in the other half.

Maedron removed the shield around the NEbox and said, "Show me."

Fergus stood up. He stretched and winced.

Igrainid felt a faint twinge of remorse at having kept him kneeling for so long, but not very much. He shouldn't have acted so suspiciously.

Fergus picked up the NEbox, switched it on and held it out so Maedron could see it.

The feathers rimming Maedron's ears rippled from front to back and his crest laid flat against his skull. He took a step backwards.

"What is it?" asked Igrainid.

"Cridhe, it's an image of the view northwards. I think it must be from one of the rooms in Caedmon's Tower."

"My room," said Fergus. He touched a point on one edge of the box saying, "Here's another."

"Now it's what I would see standing on the high crossway from Caedmon's Tower to the Robhas Tower," said Maedron.

"How many of these images do you have?" asked Igrainid.

"I made about seventy."

"And they're all in that box?"

"Not exactly in it," said Fergus. "The box stores the information needed to display the images, not the images themselves. You see … "

"Never mind trying to explain how it works," said Igrainid. "Your earlier description didn't make any sense to me. Show Maedron what else it does."

"Yes, Cridhe," said Fergus, with a bow. He touched a different place on the edge of the box and an array of numbers appeared instead of an image.

"This can be used for reckoning," said Fergus.

"That I can understand," said Maedron. "I like numbers."

"It doesn't just do simple addition and subtraction. It can do much more complex things than that."

Igrainid waited patiently while Fergus showed Maedron the calculation function of the NEbox, then asked him what he had seen.

"It does what he says, Cridhe. It calculates as fast I can, if not faster. And all the answers it has given have been correct."

"Do you think you can learn to use it?"

"I think so," replied Maedron. He said to Fergus, "Show me an image again, and when Fergus did so, added, "Now show me how to make it change."

Igrainid watched as Maedron handled the NEbox, learning how to switch images, rotate them and even magnify parts of them as easily as Fergus did. She was surprised to find herself wanting to get her fingers on the thing and play with it. "Is it safe?" she asked Maedron ten to fifteen minutes later.

"I believe so, Cridhe. It seems simple enough, unless it has uses he has not shown so far."

"Your pardon, Cridhe," said Fergus. "I swear it isn't dangerous."

"And how do I know what your oath is worth?"

"Can't you use a truth spell?"

Igrainid laughed. "You are showing your ignorance, cross-breed. One person's truth may not be the same as another's. There is no such thing as a spell to compel absolute truth. However, you have given me an idea." She turned to look at Trinafar and said, "Am I right in thinking that he is under obligation to you for having brought him through the lacuna?"

"Yes, mother."

"Have you agreed how he will balance that debt?"

"Not yet."

"Then I will assume your position in that transaction and, in return for allowing the change, you may spend another year in the second world continuing with your research. During that time we will not talk of any potential liaisons. He will repay his debt to you by serving me with complete and utter loyalty for a year and a day."

"As you wish, mother," said Trinafar.

Both Igrainid and Trinafar took a silver knife about two inches long from their belt. They used the ritual knives to cut their thumbs, then pressed their thumbs together to let the blood mix.

Igrainid said, "It is done." She looked at Fergus and asked if he understood that he was now under a geas and what would happen if he didn't serve her faithfully.

"I believe I do, Cridhe. I think it means I will die if I am not loyal to you."

"Yes, that's correct, you will. I am pleased you understand that. Now, do you still maintain this thing of yours is safe?"

"It is."

"In that case, let the shields lapse. Fergus, bring a chair over here and sit beside me. I want you to show me what you showed Maedron." She looked at the others in the room and added, "I suppose the rest of you are as curious as I am, so find somewhere to sit or stand where you can see over my shoulder."

The next half hour was spent teaching Igrainid how to use the NEbox. She found the calculation function interesting and could see its value for someone not as good at reckoning as Maedron. The images fascinated her and she spent most of the time trying to work out exactly where they had been made.

"What's this," she asked, pointing at a blur in the background of one of the images he had made in the garden.

"There are several with blurs like that, Cridhe," said Fergus. "I'm not certain but I think they are people. I did try to avoid including anybody in the images because I didn't know how they would react. However, I didn't always notice they were there until I had already made the image. I didn't intend to upset anyone and I apologise for doing so."

"Look at this one," said Maedron, pointing to one displaying a large blur which partially obscured a group of silver birches. "I know these trees. I was talking to Naod the gardener about them yesterday. She was one of the people who complained about having magic disrupted. A branch of one of the trees was damaged by the strong winds we had last week and she was using her magic to support it when she saw Fergus looking in her direction and pointing something at her. Her magic went wrong and made the damage worse. Now she's really worried about that particular tree."

"A dryad's tree magic went wrong! That's difficult to believe," said Saefan, "Naod is too good to make a mistake like that."

"That's very interesting," said Fergus. "That you can identify one of the blurs as somebody using magic, I mean."

"It does not seem a very effective tool," said Igrainid, "if it shows nothing but blurs instead of people."

"It's not just people. There's big blur in another one of the images. It's not obscuring anybody because there was nobody in the Quiet Place when I made it."

"Show me," said Igrainid, passing the box to Fergus who flipped rapidly through the images and handed it back to her.

"This is the one," he said. "I think the blurring must be a result of how the box sees magic but I don't know how or why it should do that when it works well enough back home."

"You have used it in the second world?"

"Yes, Cridhe, I had to become familiar with it to be able to test it. I made about forty images of Edinburgh before meeting Lady Trinafar."

"Are they still in the box?"

"Yes, Cridhe."

"Show me some of those."

Igrainid passed the box back to Fergus and, showing her what he was doing, he called up a new series of images. Igrainid, Trinafar, Maedron and Saefan were all familiar enough with Edinburgh to identify the scenes. The people included in them weren't blurred.

"Why does magic affect the images?"

Fergus shrugged. "I don't know, Cridhe. My friend Duncan might be able to explain it but I can't."

When Fergus mentioned Duncan's name Igrainid shuddered. She sat up in surprise and gasped because it felt as if ice-cold water was being poured down her back. At the same time she flinched from a short shrill whistle, saw a dazzling, rainbow-coloured flash of light that made her blink, then she sneezed as she smelled wood smoke and felt her mouth pucker from the taste of vinegar.

"What is it, mother?" asked Saefan.

"I've just had a premonition. A full sensory premonition!"

"What! When?"

"It was just as Fergus said his friend's name. It's got to mean that this Duncan will be important to the Domain for some reason."

"But," said Trinafar, "Fergus said Duncan doesn't believe in Tirog?"

Igrainid shook her head. "That doesn't matter. I don't understand why he's significant, but the timing was too close to mean anything else."

Fergus looked puzzled and said "I didn't know you were a prophet, Cridhe."

"I am not," replied Igrainid. "There's no such thing. The future cannot be known until it happens. A premonition is not a prophecy. Sometimes people, usually Cridhe, get warnings – indications that whatever or whoever provokes the feeling will be important to the well-being or otherwise of their Domain or Realm. They are very rare. Nobody in Eideann has had one for over ninety years."

"But …"

"Nobody knows how or why they happen, Fergus. Some have speculated that a premonition is the result of unconscious evaluation of some problem by their recipients."

"How can Duncan be important to Eideann?" asked Fergus.

"I can't answer that," said Igrainid. "All I can say is that the premonition came as soon as you named him as someone who might sort out whatever is causing those blurs. I think that has to mean he – and possibly this NEbox – are crucial factors in resolving some issue that will threaten, or at least in some way affect, the Domain."

Saefan started to say something but stopped, frowning at Fergus when Igrainid said,

"Tell me more about Duncan, Fergus. Who is he?"

"Like I said, he's a good friend of mine. He has been since we were at university together in Edinburgh. We met on the first day of classes when we ended up sitting next to each other. I thought he looked a bit lost and he said I did too. He told me he was from Aberdeen and it was the first time he'd been so far away from home. When I told him I was from even farther away he relaxed.

"He went back to Aberdeen after we graduated and I mostly stayed in Edinburgh. We don't see each other all that often, maybe just a couple of times a year, sometimes in Edinburgh and sometimes in Aberdeen. We've kept in touch and stayed friends. He's much cleverer than me, a real innovator, and his family is quite rich. That's how he comes to have his own high-tech company. Perhaps I should go to Aberdeen to see him and find out more about the NEbox."

"Yes," said Igrainid. "That sounds like a good idea. Trinafar can go with you. She has more experience in the second world than anyone else in Eideann." She turned to Trinafar and said, "You will have to be very careful. We don't have good relations with the Realm of Obharden at present."

"We won't go into Obharden," said Trinafar. "We'll stay in the second world."

"And what happens if somebody from Obharden is in that world and recognises you? No, you can't go with only Fergus for company. I think you need somebody else as well. Maedron, you would be a good choice. You can maintain a seeming in the second world can't you?"

"Yes, Cridhe. I have been there many times and used a glamour without difficulty. However, I must warn you I have never been to Aberdeen and I know very little about it."

"I would like you to go with Trinafar and Fergus to protect them."

"Of course, Cridhe. I am honoured to be asked to protect Lady Trinafar. I waive obligation for this service."

Igrainid inclined her head in thanks and said, "You can leave tomorrow."

"Pardon me, Cridhe," said Fergus. "I don't understand how Maedron will be able to do magic there. There is nobody in the second world to supply the latency he needs for a glamour."

"That is not an issue," said Igrainid. "There is always some leakage of latent power through the lacunae into the other world. That's why magic is possible there at all. It is weaker there, but it is available. Maedron's glamour could fail if he moved into a part of the other world that corresponds with a latency-free area in Tirog. There are a few places like that, outside the range of any Source, but there aren't any between Edinburgh and Aberdeen. It won't be a problem."

pRemonicion

The place-that-doesn't-exist was always there again when any of the Eleven wanted it to be.

A simultaneous experience of something odd, strange and mysterious was enough to bring them all together without any of them calling for a meeting.

They were all agitated about what they had felt. Each of them provided a different description of the sensation that had startled them and brought them together. These ranged from the, rather grandiose, comment that it was like 'standing on the edge of a vortex of probabilities' to much simpler concepts such as 'it was a ripple in reality' or 'a convulsion in the aether'. The one thing they all agreed on was that it was an event of major significance.

Sumethla, who had been a member of the Eleven for longer than any of the others reported that she had never experienced anything quite like it. However, she also said she had heard of a similar episode, which had occurred twenty-six years before she joined the Eleven. That event had been described to her by the one who, at that time, had been the longest serving member; her informant had been physically present in a Domain in southern Eirinn when the Cridhe experienced a premonition. The description of the accompanying sensations were so similar to what they had all just experienced as to suggest the same had happened again.

One of the others, the one who had called the event 'a convulsion in the aether', decried the idea that it was due to a premonition.

That was a mistake.

The rest of the Eleven supported the idea of a premonition being the source of their experience. The ten to one disagreement among the Eleven was enough to provoke an immediate reaction from a group of the magi hovering in hope of becoming members of the Eleven. They applied pressure to the dissenter, isolated him and forced the isolated one out of the quasi-space like a cork from a bottle of sparkling wine. The ejected member found himself back in the pack of hopefuls, all struggling for position and, more importantly, for survival. He was just strong enough to maintain his integrity and avoid being destroyed, but it was a close thing.

As always when one of the Eleven was ejected there was a battle for supremacy among the potential replacements observing from just beyond the limits of the quasi-space. Signs of the battle spilled over into both Tirog and the second world with severe unseasonal storms, and even a couple of minor earthquakes.

One presence in the pack managed to establish supremacy leaving the others of the hopeful disappointed and disconsolate.

There was a feeling of developing harmony as the new configuration of the Eleven settled down. The new member immediately suggested that it would be important to find whoever had had the premonition and what it was about.

With no dissent the Eleven dispersed, the onlookers went their separate ways and the meeting place returned to its usual state of non-existence.

to aberdeen

"Let's get going," said Trinafar as they gathered outside the Robhas Tower, well wrapped up against the chill on a misty autumn morning. Each of them was carrying a rucksack containing whatever they thought they would need for a four night stay in Aberdeen.

Fergus and Maedron followed her towards what Fergus now knew was called Luchairt Way then they turned left before going under the arch and went down the steep path to the lacuna. The elf on guard duty bowed to them and moved aside to give them access.

"Give me a moment while I change, Lady Trinafar," said Maedron.

He stepped away from the others. A multicoloured haze surrounded him briefly, then it contracted around him and settled into the semblance of a stocky man with curly brown hair and a well-trimmed, short beard several shades darker than his hair.

"That was so smoothly done," said Trinafar, "it must be a seeming you have used before. What name do you use in this guise?"

"Max Donaldson is the one I usually use," replied Maedron after a slight hesitation.

"That's a familiar name," said Trinafar, looking quizzically at him. "Tell me, Maedron, what does Max Donaldson do in the second world?"

She was surprised when Maedron looked down at the ground and wouldn't meet her eyes. He said, in a quiet voice, "He has some small reputation as a writer of romantic fiction."

"You're *that* Max Donaldson! Really! I had no idea," said Trinafar. "Why have you kept it a secret? It's nothing to be ashamed of. I've read most of your books and enjoyed them. I know my mother likes them too."

"I am flattered, Lady Trinafar."

"You'd better not call me that. We have to get used to our second world aliases. Until we return you are Max

Donaldson and I am Catriona Farquhar. Don't either of you call me Trinafar or address me as Lady."

She saw both of them nod. "Max, you go first, then hold the way open for Fergus. I will follow him."

The space on the Edinburgh side of the lacuna resounded to an outbreak of coughing as soon as Fergus entered it. Catriona apologised for not warning him it was likely to happen when he breathed the smoky, oily air of Edinburgh again after getting used to the clean air of Eideann. "It affects almost everybody at first but, if you use the lacuna often enough, you do get used to the change of air sooner or later."

"Now I really understand why Edinburgh is known as Auld Reekie," he said when he finally managed to stop coughing.

Catriona led them uphill to the Tron Square, then past the castle to the railway station at the West End of the New Town. That station, one of two in the city centre, served trains going north and west. An arched girder roof supported glass panels, all dirty from constant exposure to smoke and steam and lent the capacious space a gloomy air. Despite that, or perhaps due to the contrast, the brass and enamel of the motive engines and their strings of carriages gleamed.

"That'll be the one we want," said Fergus, pointing to the largest and most imposing of the engines with its six huge driving wheels and its twelve coaches painted dark-blue and cream. "The Edinburgh to Inverness express service. It runs three times a day and goes through Dundee and Aberdeen. I've often used it going home."

"The broadsheets are full of articles about the latest advances in protonic technology," Catriona said, "including the development of motive engines more powerful than the steam ones. It seems to be the thing of the moment. I'm surprised such a prestigious train is still using steam."

"I think it's because of that status that it does," said Fergus. "People still trust steam more than the new-fangled protonic motive engines. They haven't been around long enough for people to get really used to them. Also, protonics isn't as easy to understand as steam. I'm sure it will all change in the next few years."

They climbed into a coach near the front, and twenty minutes later the train announced its imminent departure with a shrill blast from a steam whistle before it jerked into motion with a loud hiss.

#

Their journey was delayed for a while between the bridges over the Forth and the Tay because the train had to be diverted. An embankment had collapsed the previous evening.

After an otherwise smooth journey with no more delays, the train glided smoothly into Union station in Aberdeen a little over five hours after leaving Edinburgh; almost two hours late.

Shortly before arriving they started seeing buildings made from the attractive silvery-grey granite that gave Aberdeen both its nicknames; the Granite City and the Silver City.

"We can walk from here," said Fergus when Catriona asked him how they would get to Duncan's office. "It's just around the corner."

Close to the centre of the city almost every building was made of granite. The building that housed NorEast was one of them. Fergus identified himself to the receptionist, collected a passkey from her and led them up to the second floor.

"Is Duncan Kirkpatrick available?" asked Fergus of the first person they met there.

"You're Fergus Monteith, aren't you? Yes, I thought I recognised you. Duncan's in his office. He's expecting you, said you're to go right in whenever you get here."

Fergus led them along a short corridor to a door with the NorEast symbol inlaid in gold on a black background. He tapped on it, opened it and walked through without waiting for a response.

"Fergus! Good tae see you, man. Where hae ye been?" said the man seated behind a massive desk strewn with papers and drawings.

The man asking the question wasn't nearly as tall as Fergus but, with his broad shoulders and solid build, probably outweighed him. He looked every bit the rugby forward he used to be. Apart from his nose, which had been broken at least once, the most conspicuous thing about him was his hair, which, despite him being no older than Fergus, was already white.

He stood up and held out his hand for Fergus to shake.

"Hello, Duncan," said Fergus. "I'm sorry if I'm interrupting."

"No. Dinnae worry about it." He turned to the other two people in the room and said, "Will you excuse us? I'm sorry tae break up the meeting but we've made good progress and covered just about everything we can today. I've been waiting for Fergus tae turn up. He's the last o' the testers and I need tae hear what he's got tae tell me. We'll carry on the morn, if that's fine with you."

The man and woman assured Duncan they had got enough from their meeting to keep them occupied and that they'd return the next day to finish the job. They stood up, rummaged through the papers on the desk and picked out a few of them. Then they shook hands with Duncan, nodded towards Fergus and his companions and left.

"Whae's this you've brought tae see me, Fergus?"

Fergus introduced his companions being careful to call them Catriona Farquhar and Max Donaldson. Duncan welcomed them, invited them to sit and offered refreshments, which they declined. As they found seats he looked quizzically at Fergus as if to ask 'why have you brought them?'

"I've got something to show you, Duncan." Fergus took the NEbox from his pocket, switched it on and gave it to Duncan saying, "What do you think of that?"

The image was the first one from Tirog, looking north from Fergus's room in Caedmon's Tower. Duncan looked at it, shrugged and said, "Nice image. Don't recognise it. Where is it?"

"Tirog."

"Come off it, Fergus. Dinnae waste my time with that fantasy." Duncan looked at the image again then added, "Looks like ye've done a nice bit o' image editing. I've got tae admit I didnae ken that function was active on the box I gave ye but it looks as if ye've found it for yerself and worked out how tae use it."

"Try the next image," said Fergus.

Duncan did as Fergus suggested, then he looked startled when the next image showed the Robhas Tower from one of the crossways.

"Still think I've been manipulating the images?" asked Fergus.

"Ye must hae been. That's nowhere I've ever heard o'. Shows a nice bit of imagination. I never thought ye were so creative."

"Duncan, you know you didn't tell me about any image manipulation capability when you showed me how to use this box. If it is available on it I've no idea how to access it. Go on, check for yourself. See if it's loaded and if it's active."

Duncan took the NEbox and examined it. After a couple of minutes of manipulating the controls he sat down heavily, put the box on the desk, shook his head and said, "That function's no there."

"So you have to believe me. Now you've got to admit Tirog is real."

"It's no real," said Duncan, "it cannae be. Anyway ye've aye said ye cannae get tae this mythical land of yours, so how could ye make images there?"

Fergus nodded towards Catriona and said, "I had help."

He saw Duncan's face go pale.

"I think I could dae wi' a drink," said Duncan, standing and going to open a cupboard. It revealed a well-equipped bar. He poured himself a generous measure of whisky. "Are ye sure none o' ye want anything?"

"I'll take whisky too," said Fergus.

This time Catriona accepted a glass of sparkling wine when Duncan apologised for being unable to supply tea. Max just shook his head and said nothing.

Fergus sniffed and sipped his whisky. "What a beautiful dram," he said. "What is it?"

"Eh? Oh, it's Bowmore," said Duncan, "fifteen year old." He looked puzzled and distracted and uneasy.

"Duncan. I'm telling you these images were made in Tirog. How much more evidence do you need to admit it exists?"

Duncan shook his head and swallowed a large mouthful of whisky, an action that convinced Fergus he was worried about the images of Tirog. Duncan was a whisky connoisseur and would normally sip a good whisky rather than gulp it.

"Take a look at more of the images I made in Tirog. You really need to see them anyway. There's something wrong with a lot of them."

"Something's wrong with the images!" said Duncan, sounding alarmed.

Fergus put down his whisky, picked up the box and displayed the image of the Quiet Place in the garden, the most blurred image of them all. "What do you think could cause this?"

Duncan's expression changed when Fergus handed him the box. Suddenly looking very worried, he studied it, flicking rapidly back and forward through all of the images then slowing to examine some of them in more detail and magnifying parts of some of the images. He muttered something about possible light-guide contamination, and immediately said it couldn't be that because it would produce the same defects all the time and the flaws in the images showed too much variation.

"I dinnae ken what's causing it, but I really wish ye could have brought this tae my attention a bit sooner. None o' the other testers has come across anything like it," said Duncan. "We're nearly ready tae start tooling up for production but we'll have tae put that on hold until we sort this out. We canna launch the NEboxes on tae the market with a major fault like that."

When Fergus told him the blurring seemed to be caused by active magic, and none of the other testers had found it because none of them had been to Tirog, Duncan snorted. "I dinnae understand why you keep up this story of yours about Tirog and magic. Ye ken it's nonsense."

"Is it, Mr Kirkpatrick?" asked Catriona. "I think you know better than that. After all you are a sidhe-human cross-breed yourself, like Fergus. Why do you deny your heritage?"

The question produced a stunned silence which lasted for one long moment before Duncan and Fergus spoke over each other; Duncan demanding how she could know, and Fergus asking Duncan if it was true.

Fergus couldn't think of any reason why Catriona should lie and Duncan's reaction convinced him she was right. "Why, Duncan? I thought we were friends. Why tell me, all these years, that you don't believe in Tirog when you know it *is* real?" He took a couple of steps towards Duncan. Startled to find his fists were clenched, he stopped.

Duncan lifted his head to look at Catriona and asked, "Are ye fay?"

She nodded and he said, "Will ye tell everybody the truth about me?"

"Why should I? There's no advantage to me in doing so," she said. "You can keep it a secret if you want, but it's nothing to be ashamed of."

"Aye it is," said Duncan as he slumped into the chair, put his elbows on the desk and took his head in his hands. "At least it is if ye work among scientists and engineers. They find the very idea o' magic intolerable, because they want tae understand the rules that govern the universe. They expect them tae be known, consistent, fixed and reliable. They cannae stand even the idea o' magic because it would mean people could break – or at least ignore – the rules they believe should be immutable. I have tae pretend tae have the same point o' view as them or they'll laugh at me, force me out o' the company and destroy my life. I have tae live a lie. I ken fine magic is real. I've seen my faither use it often enough, but I cannae afford tae come oot an admit it." He paused, then added, "Fergus, we've been friends for a long time. I'm really sorry I've aye disparaged your belief in Tirog when I ken it's real. I hope ye can understand why I had tae do that. Can ye forgive me?"

"I don't know," said Fergus. "I'll need to think about it." Frowning, he unclenched his fists, walked away from Duncan to subside into a chair in a corner, picking up his glass of whisky on the way. He took a mouthful, sat and let his head droop in thought.

Duncan rested his head in his hands again.

There was silence in the room for several minutes, then Fergus looked up and asked Duncan, "Can you get to Tirog?"

"No by myself."

Fergus nodded. That was the answer he hoped for and it made him feel a little better.

"Saying that implies you have been to Tirog, Mr Kirkpatrick, so someone must have taken you," said Catriona.

"Aye, I've been there," said Duncan, lifting his head to look at Fergus. "My faither's taken me a couple of times. I wanted him tae take you as well, Fergus. I pleaded with him because I kent what it would mean tae ye; but he refused."

"Why?"

"I've nae idea, unless it's because I'm no that excited by Tirog. I think he's a wee bit disappointed by that and my lack of any magic. Anyhow, I prefer this world."

"I like this world too, and I spend a lot of time here," said Catriona, "but I can't imagine how you can prefer it to Tirog."

"I didnae mean to offend ye," said Duncan.

"Don't worry. I'm not offended. Your preferences are your own business. From my point of view Tirog is infinitely preferable."

"You asked your father to take me to Tirog?" said Fergus.

"Aye."

"Knowing that does make me feel a bit better," said Fergus, lifting his head to look at Duncan. "But I'm hurt you didn't trust me enough to admit to being a cross-breed like me – didn't you think I'd keep your secret? This completely changes our relationship. I hope we can still be friends, but I'm not sure if we can."

"Mr Kirkpatrick, I think I understand why you didn't tell Fergus," said Catriona. "I expect you were thinking along the lines of what Emperor Karl II said after the Recharan conspiracy was exposed."

Fergus lifted his head to look at Catriona and said, "Do you mean 'a secret may be kept by two or more people if all but one of them are ignorant of it'."

"That's the one," said Catriona.

Fergus snorted, but recognised the quote's validity, and the mood in the room eased a bit. "I'll want to talk this over later, Duncan, but I know you're worried about the NEboxes being seen as faulty. Deal with that first then we can have a long talk."

Duncan picked up the box and scowled at it. "Aye," he said, "I do need tae look into this, but I want tae save our friendship if I can. Just offering tae wait and let me sort oot the NEbox problem makes me think ye'd like tae save it too."

"I do, but that can wait," said Fergus.

"Might take a long time," said Duncan.

"Like I said, I can wait."

"Thank you, Fergus. Leave the NEbox with me and I'll get started on it." Duncan paused then added, "Hae ye got anywhere tae stay?"

"No, we haven't arranged anything."

"Ye'll stay at my hoose. There's plenty room and I'll ken where tae find ye when I've got some answers."

#

Duncan's house was about a mile and a half west of the centre of Aberdeen, in the Rubislaw district, near the quarry that had provided so much of the granite for the city's buildings. Fergus suggested taking a hansom, but Max said he had been cooped up in the train for long enough and would rather walk. Catriona agreed because she had never been to Aberdeen and would like to see more of it. They strolled through the city centre, taking their time and gradually working their way westwards to climb the gentle slope of Rubislaw Hill.

Duncan's house was one of many imposing buildings in the area, all built of the best quality close-grained granite to come out of the quarry. His housekeeper welcomed them, expressing pleasure at meeting Catriona Farquhar and almost speechless with delight when introduced to Max Donaldson.

The next day, after a gargantuan breakfast, Fergus tried to make light of the absence of any news from Duncan; he was sure Duncan was doing all he could because the NEbox was such a big thing for his company.

Despite his words, he did worry. Igrainid's premonition suggested the NEbox was important to Eideann as well. *Tirog has come to mean as much to me as I always thought it would. I hope the significance of the box, whatever it is, doesn't cause a conflict between Igrainid's and Duncan's interest in it.*

He couldn't help being impressed with how calm Catriona seemed to be. She hid any anxiety she felt very well. On the other hand Max was restless and taciturn, responding to attempts to start a conversation with nothing but grunts.

There was some light relief when the housekeeper, rather diffidently, produced copies of all nine of Max's books and begged him to sign them. Fergus laughed at Max when he admitted to being somewhat embarrassed by her reaction and told him it was his own fault for being such a popular writer.

Late that evening, when they were sitting around the fire and beginning to think about going to bed, Duncan arrived. From the grin on his face Fergus could tell he had good news.

"I think I've got it sortit," said Duncan, his accent getting thicker in the way Fergus knew meant he was excited by something. "I'll still need tae test it tae make sure but I think I ken what it's a' aboot."

"Well, don't keep us in suspense," said Fergus.

"Pour me a dram," said Duncan, "and I'll try tae explain."

Fergus did as requested, then sat down again.

He was surprised when Duncan produced two NEboxes from his briefcase.

"One o' them is the one ye had, Fergus. Can ye tell which it is?"

Fergus examined them carefully, one was slightly bigger than the other but he couldn't tell which was which and said so.

"This is it," said Duncan, picking up the larger of the two. "I made a mistake giving ye this one. It should never have left the lab. It's a prototype, no one of the test batch at a'. It's a wee bit thicker because it's got a different image substrate in it – one we rejected. That was partly because we wanted tae keep the production model as wee as we could, but mostly it's because the substrate turned out tae be a wee bit unstable and we chose tae use a mair reliable one. It took me a ridiculously long time tae realise that was the source o' the problem, but I think it has tae be the answer. I need tae make another test tae make sure. So, with your permission Miss Farquhar, and yours, Mr Donaldson, I'd like for Fergus to make images of both of ye with both the boxes and see if there's a difference."

"We are going to be working together," said Catriona, "so I think we could be less formal. I won't be offended if you call me by my first name."

She agreed to the experiment and nodded to Max who also agreed, although she could tell he was reluctant.

"Thank you, Catriona. Please call me Duncan.

He used the smaller NEbox first. The images of

Catriona and Max it produced were perfect, no blurring or other fault at all.

Duncan exhaled noisily and Fergus was sure it was because he was relieved.

Fergus made more images using the larger of the NEboxes. They were very badly blurred, far worse than any of the images from Eideann.

"Why are they like that?" asked Fergus.

"I think I might be able to answer that," said Catriona. "Fergus, make an image of Mr Kirkpatrick with your box. I think you will find it'll have a slight blur."

"Ye're right," exclaimed Duncan when he examined that image. "How did ye ken it would blur like that?"

"Didn't you wonder how I identified you as a cross-breed?" asked Catriona. "It's because fay, and cross-breeds, have an ultraviolet pigment in their skin and hair. Fay see deeper into that end of the spectrum than humans and can recognise the colour."

"Oh! That explains why the other NEbox disnae show the blur. The image substrate it uses has an integral nanofilter that restricts its range tae the visible spectrum – visible tae humans, that is."

"I didn't understand your explanation," said Catriona, "but I'm prepared to believe you know what you're talking about."

"There's one mair thing I'd like tae try," said Duncan, rummaging in his briefcase and producing a miniature tool kit. "I've brought a couple o' plug-ins that might give some interesting results."

Catriona, Fergus and Max watched with interest while Duncan used his tiny tools to open the larger of the NEboxes. He removed a couple of components and replaced them with others that, to their eyes at least, looked the same, then he closed it again. "Try that," he said, passing the box to Fergus. "Let's see if that's made any difference."

"None as far as I can tell," said Fergus after making images of Catriona and Duncan. "Those images are just as blurred as the others."

"Ah weel, that was aye one possibility. Let me try something else." Duncan took the box back and changed some of the components again.

Fergus raised the modified NEbox to point the lens at Max and gasped.

"What is it?"

"Something's gone wrong with the display," said Fergus. "I'm seeing two superimposed images."

"Show me," said Duncan, walking around Fergus to look over his shoulder. He looked at the screen, then at Max, then at the screen again, then back at Max, before saying in a hushed voice, "You're an elf!"

"That thing can penetrate my glamour?" said Max.

Fergus nodded. "Yes. It shows you with and without a glamour at the same time."

"How is that possible?" asked Catriona.

"One o' the components I put in is a polarising filter. I thought it might eliminate the blur, and it has. But it must be resonating wi' some other element and oscillating off and on again. When it's in phase it shows one image, out o' phase and it shows another. I dinnae ken why it's doing that."

"Gobbledegook," snarled Max. "That explanation explains nothing."

"It's no my fault you dinnae understand."

"Calm yourself, Max," said Catriona. "I didn't understand it either, but it's not because he's being difficult, we just don't have the knowledge to know what he means."

Max scowled but said nothing.

"What does it show when it looks at me?" asked Catriona. "Am I still blurred?"

"There are two images," said Fergus after studying the new image of Catriona, "just like with Max. One of them is clear and sharp and obviously you. The other doesn't show you at all. There's a – a darkness? – no, I think an absence is a better way to describe it, where you should be. It's as if you're not there. Except that there's one small patch of iridescence, about the size of a fingernail. It's just between your eyes – or where your eyes would be if the image showed them.

"What can that mean?" asked Catriona, looking at Duncan.

"I've nae idea."

"Have you any more of these bits you want to try?"

"No, I didnae bring ony mair. But now that we ken what happens wi' these I've got some ideas. I'll bring some other bits tomorrow."

evasion

Dhugalt summoned the Eleven to a meeting saying he had news about the supposed premonition.

This was enough to bring them, including the gnome who had filled the latest vacancy, together quickly. The meeting also attracted a lot of attention from the magi around the periphery of the quasi-space. This was inevitable; it was generally believed that a new member took several meetings to get fully established and was potentially vulnerable during that time.

Dhugalt reported that he could confirm the sensation had been due to a premonition experienced by Cridhe Igrainid of Eideann. She had been so startled by it that she had appealed to him for aid. As a result he could report the exact words she had used to describe it. When he repeated those words the Eleven unanimously agreed; it had indeed been a premonition.

He told them the trigger for the premonition was a man's name and that Igrainid was sending an expedition to find this person and discover what he knew. "I will continue to keep an eye on this expedition," he told the Eleven, "and I'll report whatever I find out."

He didn't want to give the Eleven any reason to involve themselves more closely with the affairs of Eideann, so kept to himself the fact that one member of the expedition was the Failed Source they had discussed so many times.

Enough had been said at a previous meeting about the association of an inheritance anomaly and a premonition in the same Domain. It had been considered suspicious by two of the Eleven at the meeting when they had first heard of the premonition. However, they had been unable to suggest what it might mean. Fortunately, none of the others suggested it was anything more than a coincidence.

He also avoided reminding them that he was related to the Failed Source. That knowledge might provoke a reaction from the Eleven, and was certain to cause some excitement among the observers.

Dhugalt knew he was taking a risk by keeping things to himself. It could be dangerous if enough of the others felt he wasn't working in the best interests of the Group. The idea of being on the wrong end of a ten to one confrontation made him shudder. That would make his survival unlikely. Nevertheless, in the interest of protecting Igrainid, and Eideann in general, he thought it worth the risk.

He tried to present a calm, moderate front and got away with it. Hopefully he would have some results to report the next time the subject came up.

in aberdeen

Catriona turned away from the windows and the soggy, grey clouds she could see piling up over Aberdeen. She looked at the row of chafing dishes lined up on the massive oak sideboard on the opposite side of the room, walked over to them and lifted one of the lids. The dish held scrambled eggs. She examined the rest of the array of dishes, finding bacon, sausage, and all the other ingredients necessary for either a good, hearty breakfast or a light one.

She settled down at the end of the table nearest the windows with a bowl of porridge, a smokie and a pot of tea. Max and Fergus arrived soon after her. Bacon, mushrooms, grilled tomatoes, tattie scones, Lorne sausage and black pudding filled their plates and they exclaimed about the quality, and quantity, of the food on offer just as they had the previous day.

"There can't be a spread like this every day," said Catriona. "It must be because of you, Max. The housekeeper's putting on a show for you."

Duncan arrived in time to hear that comment and said, "That's no right, Catriona. She'll dae that onytime we hae guests. She likes tae show off and I dinnae provide much of a challenge because I dinnae often take a cooked breakfast."

Catriona thought Duncan looked pale and exhausted and asked him if he had been up all night.

"Aye, I couldnae sleep. I've got ower many ideas in my heid."

He wanted to start experimenting with his new ideas immediately and Catriona had to persuade him to eat something first.

"Fine," he said, "I'll just have twa rowies, then we can get started."

"Rowies?"

"Aye," said Duncan, pointing to a plateful of flaky looking bread rolls. "They're an Aberdeen specialty, you'll no get them in Edinburgh. Some folk ca' them 'butteries' and say they're like those French croissant things, but that's no right. They're no the same. You need tae try one for yourself. Put a wee bit jam on it."

Catriona did take one. "That is nice," she said, "the texture's really good."

Duncan smiled. "Telt ye!"

After breakfast they moved back to the comfortable sitting room and settled into the sofas and deep armchairs to hear what Duncan had been doing overnight. He told them he had managed to remove the resonance effect and showed them a refinement of the NEbox that let the user choose which image to see, or even see both at the same time superimposed on each other.

Then Duncan said, "I want tae try something new. If I'm right aboot this it might show magic in a mair useful way than the blurs we saw on the other images." He opened up the box and put new components into it, telling them he was fitting a circularly polarised ultraviolet filter and a variable frequency light guide.

"I'm more interested in the results than in the mechanics of what you're doing," said Catriona. "I'm afraid the details mean nothing to me."

Duncan apologised to her for getting carried away by his enthusiasm for anything new. He closed the NEbox up again saying "There, that's ready. Let's see if it works. Miss Farquhar, do ye want tae be the first tae try this new configuration?"

She said, "Yes, I'll try it."

Catriona took the NEbox from him. Duncan and Fergus arranged themselves where they could see over her shoulder. She pointed the tablet at Max and pressed the new button on its side.

The only difference was that the screen showed Maedron sitting at the table rather than Max. It was no different to seeing him directly.

Then Duncan asked Max to move something with magic.

"Didn't you try it yourself, Duncan?" asked Catriona, "No, I forgot, you can't use magic."

"That's right, Catriona. I've nae magic at a'. I ken my faither's disappointed in that but …" Duncan shrugged.

Knowing that Max wouldn't use magic in the second world without her permission, Catriona nodded to him and repeated Duncan's request for him to move something.

She gasped when a multi-stranded braid of violet light appeared on the screen of the box. It zipped rapidly across the space between Max's hand and the vase of chrysanthemums sitting on the low table in front of him. Catriona switched her attention from what she could see to what the screen showed and back again.

On the screen she saw the braid wrap around the vase and lift it into the air but when she looked at it directly all she saw was the vase rising from the table with nothing to explain why it did so.

"Is that enough?" asked Max. "Shall I hold it there, or put it down again?"

Catriona looked at Duncan and raised an eyebrow.

"Hold it, please," said Duncan, "if ye don't mind."

Max shrugged and said holding it was easy.

As they watched, the braid reshaped itself into a cylindrical pedestal under the vase, holding it about a foot off the table. The link between the support and Max's hand faded away leaving the vase of flowers floating in mid-air. To the naked eye nothing was holding it up.

Catriona looked at the display again and saw Max's magical construction supporting the vase. She jumped up in excitement and said, "That's amazing, Duncan, really – well, *astounding*. I can hardly believe it. You've actually got a way to make spells visible to everyone, not just the spellcaster. That's as important a discovery as – as – Oh, I can't think of anything as significant, unless, perhaps, gunpowder in the second world or Neuven's Principles in Tirog."

"Do ye mean ye cannae see Max's magic?" asked Duncan. "Without using the NEbox I mean."

"No, not without looking at the screen. People generally can't see someone else's magic, only their own."

"Really?" said Duncan. He frowned. "That's a bit weird. I'll need tae think about that for a while."

"Are we finished for now?" asked Catriona.

"Aye, I think so," said Duncan. He looked across the table at Max and said, "Thank you for your help. Would you put the vase down again, please."

In the screen of the NEbox they watched violet strands of magic separate themselves from the mass under the vase. Once detached they faded away as if evaporating, allowing the vase to sink slowly and gently and settle back into its original position on the table.

Catriona saw a puzzled expression on Duncan's face. She watched him run his hands through his white hair several times until it looked like the head of a mop. He said nothing for a few minutes.

"I dinnae understand why ye can see your ain magic but naebody else's. It disnae make sense. I'll need tae gie it some thought."

Catriona wasn't surprised when he started asking more questions about magic. He wanted to know what she meant by Neuven's Principles, saying he had never heard his father use the term.

"I know a bit about the theory," said Catriona, "although my magic is too weak for me ever to be invited to join a Neuven's gang. Max, you have been part of one, haven't you?"

She saw him nod and said, "Will you explain it to Duncan, please. I'm sure you'll do a better job of it than I could."

"Neuven was an elf who lived a bit more than two hundred years ago," said Max, standing up to face his audience as if giving a lecture. "He, like many, was frustrated by the failure of most attempts at working magic in combination with others. He realised that the occasional successful attempts had something in common and developed the first of what are now known as Neuven's Principles. Basically, he said that two people could never cooperate well enough because there would always be an imbalance in their strengths and skills and the stronger would tend to dominate. Adding a third person made collaboration easier because the tension between them became dynamic rather than static and control flowed from person to person around the circle."

The look of concentration on Duncan's face told Catriona he was fascinated by hearing more about magic. She was quietly amused, considering his previously dismissive attitude to Tirog and magic.

"The First Principle was a major breakthrough," said Max, "but a few years later, when successful collaborations had become commoner, Neuven went beyond that and produced a more general principle that applies to larger groups. Any gang, as a group working together is now called, must have an odd number of members and all except one must be of the same race. The odd one out is the focus and directs the combined magic of the gang."

"Is that like a conductor directing an orchestra?" asked Fergus and added, "Fascinating," when Max agreed.

Duncan looked thoughtful. "Tell me, how long would that spell, suspending the vase in mid-air, have lasted if you hadnae cancelled it?"

"As long as I wanted it to," said Max.

Catriona added, "The jug would have stayed there indefinitely unless Max had put a time limit on the spell."

"What happens if the spellcaster dies? Do their spells stop working?"

"Why should they?" asked Catriona. "What magic does is impose a change on the world. The world won't change spontaneously and the magical alteration will persist unless someone chooses to change it again."

"If somebody changes a spell is the original spellcaster aware of the change?"

"That's a difficult one," said Max, "It rather depends on how many spells the caster has active. Somebody is bound to notice if their only spell stops working but might not if the one that's cancelled is only one of many."

"Would anybody changing a spell need tae be stronger than the original caster?"

Catriona shook her head. "No, all she has to do is be able to see the magic she wants to change so that she can manipulate it. On the whole, people can see their own magic, often that of close relatives, and sometimes others but the latter seems to be random. That's why I think your discovery is so important. It'll let people see, and possibly modify, magic they couldn't otherwise see or change."

She paused for a moment then said, "Strength in magic is a difficult thing to define. Saying somebody is strong sometimes just means they can visualise the effect they want more clearly. Some people are better at one sort of visualisation than another, so somebody that's strong in one respect might be weak in another. For example, Max is much better at picturing how he wants to appear than I am. He can maintain a convincing glamour that's radically different from his true appearance while I have trouble even changing my hair colour." She waved her hand at the window and said, "On the other hand I could go out in that rain and stay dry while he gets wet."

"That," said Max, "is because you prefer to keep your hair dry. Getting wet doesn't bother me at all. I could stay dry out there if I could be bothered to cast a spell for such a trivial purpose."

Catriona added, "The other aspect of strength is the extent of the change that can be caused. That's why a Neuven's gang is so valuable, it allows more complex spells to be cast with different people in the gang contributing to different aspects of the spell."

Duncan started to ask something else but his question disappeared in a jaw-stretching yawn.

"I think you need to rest," said Catriona.

"Ye might be right," admitted Duncan after another yawn. "I've some mair ideas but they'll need tae wait til later. I'm going tae put my heid doon or I'll no be fit to see faither when he comes tonight."

"You're expecting your father?" said Catriona.

"I'm no certain. He spends most o' his time in Tirog but he often comes tae visit on a Wednesday evening."

"I don't think we want to meet him," said Catriona.

"Why?" asked Duncan.

"Politics," said Catriona. "We're from Eideann."

"What's that got tae dae wi' it?"

"Eideann and Obharden aren't on speaking terms right now."

"Oh! My faither can be a bit aggressive when he gets upset so, if it's likely he'll start an argument with ye, it might be as well if ye're no here when he comes. I'm embarrassed tae ask it but would ye mind moving tae a hotel before he gets here?"

"Don't worry," said Catriona. "We don't want to cause trouble. We'll find a hotel for the night. I remember seeing one near here when we arrived."

"Aye," said Duncan, "there's quite a few around here."

Catriona watched Duncan push himself to his feet and, staggering a bit, leave the room. *He's been pushing himself too hard!*

#

The rain continued all morning and well into the afternoon. They were watching the raindrops trickling down the windows, dripping from the trees in the garden and making circular ripples in the puddles when Duncan found them in the sitting room. He answered Catriona's questions with assurances that he was well rested.

"I'm getting used to you discovering new things about magic," she said, "Have you got anything else to try out?"

"I do hae another idea but I'll need tae get some bits from the lab before I can try it."

Catriona was surprised to find herself feeling sad that Duncan had no more discoveries to offer. "When can you get what you need?"

"No until tomorrow," said Duncan, picking up the NEbox.

They were all clustered around the windows speculating if the small patch of blue sky visible in the distance might mean an end to the rain and commenting on how miserable a day it had been. Nobody noticed the door opening, so everybody was surprised when a new voice said, "I didn't know you had guests, Duncan."

They turned to look at the new arrival, a man about Duncan's height and build wearing a brocade jacket and baggy trousers. He had straight, pale-blond hair worn in a simple bowl cut.

Duncan exclaimed "Faither, ye're earlier than I expected," as Max moved to put himself between Catriona and the newcomer.

Catriona was speechless for a moment. *Rulidh!* She recognised the fay. He was the magus who had hexed James Ramsey and so, in a way, was responsible for her being in Aberdeen. *Rulidh is Duncan's father!* The possibility had never even occurred to her.

"Well, well, well," said Rulidh. "Lady Trinafar Chiolet Fion Eideannach! What a surprise to find you here."

"I'm just as surprised to see you," said Trinafar. "You seemed to be so at home in Gresche when we met there that I thought you must have shifted your allegiance to that Realm."

"One can always be mistaken," said Rulidh. He smiled at her, pointed to Max and said, "I don't know him by name but, despite him hiding behind a very good glamour, I kmow he must be your bodyguard. Please introduce him."

Reluctantly Trinafar said, "Rulidh Trischan Farnist, meet Maedron hur Misghel."

"Maedron himself! Captain of the Cridhe's Cohort of the Eideannach Domain Guard and son of the Commander of that company. I'm honoured to meet you," said Rulidh, inclining his head slightly towards Max. "Your reputation precedes you."

Max dipped his head to exactly the same degree and said nothing.

Trinafar suddenly understood why Duncan was looking puzzled. *He only knows Max and me by our pseudonyms.*

"Duncan, didn't you know you were entertaining important people from Eideann?" said Rulidh.

Duncan shook his head but said nothing.

"Well," commented Rulidh, "two of them are important anyway. I have to admit I don't know who the cross-breed is."

Duncan said, "He's my friend Fergus," at almost the same moment as Fergus said, "My name's Fergus Monteith. I'm the cross-breed you refused to take to Tirog when your son asked you to."

Trinafar heard the anger in Fergus's voice. *He's got to be careful. I hope he doesn't get on the wrong side of Rulidh. He's far too powerful to risk antagonising.*

"Ah! So you're the one," said Rulidh. He turned and glared at his son.

Duncan took a couple of steps back and looked away.

"You know, I think I might change my mind about taking you to Tirog," said Rulidh. "In fact we'll all go together."

"I have no interest in visiting Obharden," said Trinafar.

"Perhaps you haven't. However, I'm sure Cridhe Peruch will be interested in meeting you, and in his dominion his will prevails."

"We are in Aberdeen, not Obharden. This is not part of his territory."

"In his opinion it is," said Rulidh. "It's just that Aberdeen doesn't know it yet."

"Stars above! He wants to control Aberdeen as well as his own Realm? Don't tell me he's fallen for the fallacy."

"You can call it that if you want," said Rulidh, "but it's obvious to anyone who thinks about it that fay, and elves, and other races of Tirog, *are* superior to humans. We have abilities and skills they don't. We should be ruling them."

"Why would any of the sidhe want to rule them?" asked Max. "It's not as if they trouble us. Most of them don't even know we exist, or care. They go their way and we go ours."

"Do you enjoy being denigrated and considered myth because of their ignorance?"

Max shrugged. "Humans may not know of my

existence but there are many fay who haven't heard of me either. I don't feel my sense of identity is threatened by that, so why should the human lack of knowledge of me do otherwise?"

"You know, Maedron, from what I've heard about you I believe you're powerful enough that you could easily ensure everybody does know of you and respect you. I'm certain that if you switched your allegiance from Eideann to Obharden you could end up ruling a large piece of Aberdeen."

"When you say 'respect' what you really mean is 'fear'. I don't think so. That doesn't appeal to me. Cridhe Igrainid has my loyalty, and I don't feel the need to rule anywhere."

"I rather expected you to say that. I'm really sorry to hear it because you would be quite an asset to our cause," said Rulidh. He moved the fingers of his left hand as if they were a pair of scissors and then closed his fist.

Trinafar gasped as Max vanished and Maedron appeared in his place. He was leaning forward slightly as if in mid-step but didn't move. "What have you done?"

"I have cut him off from any source of latent power, so he can't hold his glamour," said Rulidh.

Trinafar's breath caught in her throat.

"I've also immobilised him. He's in stasis."

"What do you propose to do with us?"

"We'll all go to Luchairt Obhardenan. Perhaps Cridhe Peruch can persuade Maedron to change his mind. As for you, I haven't decided what to do with you yet. I'm sure I'll think of something suitable. Or Cridhe Peruch will. You must realise that, after our encounter in Glesche and the coalition you built against me, you're not one of my favourite people. I've got to admit you built an effective alliance. It might have been largely because of your mother's standing in the Synod that you had such success, but I have to admire the skill you demonstrated in putting it together. I couldn't resist the pressure it put on me. And you did it all for the benefit of a human – how demeaning."

"You are perfectly well aware that the Great Agreement between the Imperial Court and the Synod prohibits the sort of interference you indulged in."

"True, it does, but that agreement was made about two hundred years ago … "

"Two hundred and forty-three."

"… and it's no longer relevant."

"That's not for you to decide."

"It isn't? Isn't that a shame! Cridhe Peruch and his allies will be so disappointed to hear that."

"Allies!"

"Oh, yes. He has supporters among the other Cridhe of Alba, and some from Anglaya too. I'm sure you'll forgive me if I don't tell you who they are at the moment." Rulidh paused.

Trinafar said, "No, Fergus," when she saw him take a step towards Rulidh with his fists clenched. "Don't try anything. You're overmatched."

"Sensible," said Rulidh when Fergus stopped where he was. "She's right. A cross-breed with no magic stands no chance against me."

She could see tension in Fergus's stance and realised *that he had to do something he can interpret as serving mother or the geas will kill him.*

"When will you decide what you're going to do with me?" she asked, trying to distract Rulidh's attention from Fergus.

"When we get to Obharden I'll introduce you to Cridhe Peruch. I think what happens after that is fairly obvious," said Rulidh. "Your mother's time in a Synod seat may have expired but she's still respected and she would still be a valuable addition to the alliance. She might not join voluntarily, but with you as a hostage – who knows? Your cross-breed can carry a message to Igrainid telling her where you are."

Trinafar asked, "How are you going to get Maedron to the lacuna in his present state and without a glamour to conceal his appearance?" Then she shook her head, "How foolish of me. You weren't wearing that jacket out there in the rain, were you? You don't need a glamour. The lacuna must be in this house."

"In the basement; but you're right. His appearance won't make a difference but it would be awkward getting him down there while he's in stasis. Once I can guarantee his good behaviour, he can walk downstairs himself."

She backed away from him as he produced a small silver knife from a pocket but she was too slow and ended up trapped against one of the armchairs. Rulidh closed the gap between them, grabbed Trinafar, pulled her towards him and stabbed her left forearm.

"No, Fergus," she called when he responded with a curse and moved towards Rulidh. "The best thing you can do now is carry a message to my mother." She saw Fergus stop where he was and sighed with relief that he wasn't going to get himself killed by attacking Rulidh.

Rulidh released his grip on her after wiping a finger through the blood welling from the stab wound. He walked across the room to a corner cupboard, took a beeswax candle from a drawer and rubbed the blood into the wick. With a snap of his fingers he lit the candle, which burned with a steady, smokeless, blue flame. He put it into a holder, stood that on the table, stepped back and said, "You'd better explain this to your cross-breed."

"Fergus," said Trinafar, staring at the candle in horrified fascination, "that – *thing* is called a life-candle. My blood links it to me and if it goes out my life goes with it. A candle that size will burn for a day, but that doesn't have to be the end of me. If he wants to keep me as a hostage the flame can be transferred from one candle to another as many times as he wants. That will let him keep me alive longer than one candle will last. But it also means he can snuff out my life anytime he wants to, even if we're not in the same place."

"Actually," said Rulidh. "I have changed the spell a little. It's only if the candle gutters out that you die. Snuffing it won't kill you, merely render you unconscious until it's relit."

"Is that supposed to reassure me?"

Rulidh raised a closed fist towards Maedron and opened it. "You're not going to cause any trouble, are you?" he said.

Maedron completed the step he had started before being put in stasis and staggered slightly as he regained his balance. "I'm sorry, my lady," he said, "I fear he caught me by surprise." He glowered at Rulidh but did nothing else and Trinafar realised he had been able to hear their conversation.

"We're going to Obharden now," said Rulidh. He reached into the cupboard again and produced a lantern. He put the candle, in its holder, into the lantern and said, "Follow me."

"Just a minute," said Trinafar. "You want Fergus to take a message to my mother. He will get to her faster if he does the travelling in this world rather than Tirog."

"True. On the other hand, if my son wanted me to take him to Tirog it must mean he can't pass a lacuna himself. So how does he get from Edinburgh to Eideann?"

"Let me worry about that."

Rulidh looked thoughtful, tapping a fingernail against his teeth. "If you have a way to get him into Tirog it would be better than hoping he'd manage to find his way through Dundhe without falling foul of Cridhe Ghara. Certainly it would be safer. Are you aware of what Ghara thinks of cross-breeds? No? He considers them an abomination and persecutes any unlucky enough to be caught in his Domain." Rulidh paused, then said, "Very well, Mr Monteith. It seems I won't be taking you to Tirog after all."

"Fergus," said Trinafar, "do you remember where I took you after we first met?"

"Yes, of course."

"Go there. The owner will recognise you. Call him Armach and he'll know you come from me. He'll get you through the lacuna. Tell my mother what's happened."

"And tell her Lady Trinafar and Maedron are safe with me," said Rulidh, "unless they do something stupid. I will send a messenger to her to discuss what happens next –

tell her she'll hear from me before the next full moon. That will give her time to think." He looked at Trinafar and said, "I hope, for your sake, she's sensible about joining us."

Trinafar scowled at Rulidh. "What he said," she told Fergus.

Rulidh looked over her shoulder and said, "Duncan."

Trinafar was taken aback. She had been so engrossed with confronting Rulidh, and Duncan had been so inconspicuous that she had forgotten he was there until his father spoke to him. She turned to look at him. He had retreated into a corner and she was startled by his hangdog expression.

"Aye, faither."

"We're going off to Luchairt Obhardenan. You make sure this friend of yours gets a train to Edinburgh as soon as possible."

Rulidh turned to face Trinafar, indicated the door and, with a mocking half-bow, said, "After you, my lady."

somewhere

There was a strong feeling of tension and disquiet in the place-that-was-not as the Eleven assembled again. Three of them reported meeting Cridhe who, it seemed, were firm believers in the superiority of the sidhe, but who had not been identified during the previous discussion of the topic.

Recriminations and accusations of laxity, sloppiness and failure to believe in the importance of maintaining the balance between the first and second worlds were thrown around. Some of the Eleven were even accused of not believing in the need to discipline the errant Sources. The inhabitants of the halo of onlookers started pressing closer and most of the Eleven, including Dhugalt, found themselves under severe pressure for not dealing with the conspirators forcibly enough. It was suggested, quite emphatically, that their actions should be scrutinised more closely. The Eleven were in disarray and, unusually, the opinions of the magi on the periphery of the quasi-space were strong enough to be heard, or rather experienced, by the Eleven.

Briefly there was consensus both within and outside the Eleven. A very rare phenomenon, a supergroup of eleven elevens, came into existence. It lasted just long enough to confirm the need to prevent the conspirators succeeding. Then the unstable supergroup broke up. Two of the Eleven were overwhelmed. The ejected ones lost the battle for survival. Their shrieks of anguish tailed off into silence as they vanished.

Feeling that they had been specially selected by the supergroup two new members settled into their rôles with some confidence and without difficulty.

In the moments before the supergroup formed Dhugalt had found himself under severe pressure from three of the Eleven who accused him of weakness in his dealings with the conspirators.

If it hadn't been for the convulsion that followed the

formation and break-up of the supergroup he might have been overwhelmed. As it was, it allowed him to push two of his antagonists outwards to the edge of the reforming Eleven, and over it.

Dhugalt was safe.

As the new configuration of the Group settled down he overheard someone commenting on his part in ejecting the two who were lost. There was no criticism of his actions, any one of the Eleven would have done the same, it was more a warning to the others to be careful.

The inevitable accompaniment of the changes within the Eleven was severe weather, even more so than usual because two changes had occurred, not one. In those areas of the world where the defeated magi had operated there were earthquakes. Dhugalt noted with some relief that the closest of these was in Hisphana and the Domains and Realms of Alba weren't threatened by them.

τo eιδeαnn

Fergus had an odd, hollow feeling in his stomach as he watched Rulidh lead Trinafar and Maedron away. *Is that the geas affecting me? Perhaps I should try to stay close to her.* He started to follow, then changed his mind. *No, like she said, the best thing I can do is get to Eideann as fast as I can. I can't do anything against magic. I wish I could.*

He turned to look at Duncan, who had slumped into one of the armchairs, and said, "I don't think much of your father. He's a bully. Is he always like that? No, don't bother answering that, it's none of my business. I'll just pick up my rucksack and be off."

"I'll come … "

"You don't need to do what your father said and make sure I get on a train, I'm quite capable of doing that myself."

"But I can help!"

The anguish in Duncan's voice made Fergus stop in mid-stride.

"How? And why would you want to? Don't you always do what daddy tells you?"

"No a' the time. I do hae a life o' my ain. He's aye telling me I need tae stand up for myself, but I dinnae think he really means it. Anytime I try he slaps me doon. You saw how he treated me, like I'm insignificant, or a servant. There are times I've argued with him but he just ignores me. Sometimes he's used magic tae force me tae do what he wants. It's just easier for me if I pay as little attention tae him as I can get away with and do what he says."

"Why are you still here if you feel that way?"

"Because he's got the money. I couldnae run the company without it. But I'll get free of him when I get the NEboxes tae market and they start selling as well as I expect."

"Unless he uses magic to bind you closer to him. Even

if you think your business will grow you out from under him it doesn't explain why you'd want to help now."

"Catriona."

Fergus groaned. "Oh, no! I can't believe I'm hearing this. Are you still falling for inappropriate women?"

"What do you mean?"

"It was almost one a term when we were at university. There was Maggie, and Simone, and Geraldine, and … "

"All right, all right, so I've gone overboard a few times in the past, but Catriona's different."

"Yes, she's different all right. She's *fay!*

"Aye, I ken that, but look at the pair o' us. Both crossbreeds. That shows sidhe can have feelings for humans."

Fergus snorted in disbelief. "Feelings of sexual attraction, yes. But love? I don't think so. Maybe your father did care for your mother. I don't know, you've never told me much about her and nothing at all about him, but I know my mother didn't have any real affection for my father. She only stayed with him because she had an obligation to him for rescuing her. She left as soon as she could after he died."

"I'm sure Catriona's no like that."

"Are you? You just met her a couple of days ago and most of the time since then you haven't even been in the same building as her, far less the same room. I've got to admit I've not known her much longer, only for a little over a week, but I can't imagine anybody less likely to have any affection for non-sidhe – unless maybe one of her sisters."

"I *do* know fay can care for humans. Faither did love my mother at first, I'm certain o' it. I remember the care and kindness he aye showed her until about three years ago. Then something happened to him. I dinnae ken what it was, but something changed. He never explained why but we had tae move back here from Glesche. After that he became – different, intolerant of humans and crossbreeds. Mother started arguing with him about it and he'd growl at her, even slap her. Or he'd destroy some prized possession seemingly for no other reason than tae upset her and teach her tae keep quiet and dae what he telt her. Casual cruelty replaced the tenderness he used tae show her. She had a breakdown. He says she's well cared for in a private nursing home but he won't tell me where it is or let me go tae see her – and I dinnae think he ever goes himself."

"Why'd you never tell me this before?"

"What good would that have done? There's nothing you can do tae help her. And neither can I, no until I can escape from his influence. I cannae help my mother, but I'll do what I can for Catriona. I dinnae ken what that might be, but I'm feared o' what he might do tae her and I've got tae try."

"There's nothing you can do for her. That candle thing puts her right under his thumb. There's nothing anybody who can't do magic can do about it."

"But we can *see* the magic. I caught a glimpse o' the spell he used in the NEbox and managed to get an image of it," said Duncan. "Take a look."

Fergus took the NEbox from Duncan and looked at the display. The image showed Rulidh's hand holding the candle. A cage of fine violet lines enclosed the flame. A chain of delicate links ran from the cage to the edge of the image and disappeared off the screen.

"That chain goes round Catriona's neck," said Duncan. "I didnae get an image o' that but I saw it clearly enough. If we can show this tae somebody who can do magic, they'll maybe be able to do something with it."

"Right," said Fergus after pausing for a moment before handing the NEbox back to Duncan, "maybe we have got something useful. It's a long shot but we've got to try. We need to show this to her mother and the only place to do that is Eideann. Let's go."

"We'll go tae the lab first. There's a couple o' things I want tae try with the box, see if I can make it mair useful. I'm going tae need a few more bits and pieces. We've probably got enough time tae get there and still get the last train tonight."

"Won't matter if we miss it. It won't get into

129

Edinburgh until after midnight and I only know where to find the person who can take us through the lacuna during the day."

#

"This is the place," said Fergus, pushing open the teashop door. In mid-morning it was busy, with at least one person at every one of the tables. Fergus looked around in dismay. *How am I going to get a quiet word with the owner?*

The dried-up looking man he remembered from his visit with Catriona came out from behind the counter and said, "Sorry sir, I can't seat you at present."

"We don't mind waiting," said Fergus. "Miss Farquhar told us to drop in."

"Did she? Did she now?" said the proprietor looking up at Fergus with a thoughtful expression. For some reason Fergus couldn't identify, that look made him shiver.

"In that case you'd better come this way." The owner walked to the back of the shop obviously expecting them to follow him. At the last table, tucked around the end of the counter, he stopped. The big, burly man sitting there with a tea cup gripped in a hand that looked too massive and clumsy for such a delicate cup looked up.

"I offer one pot for the use of this table," said the proprietor.

The big man shook his head and said, "Two."

"One, but I will give you a free choice of any tea you wish."

"Seglesh agree," said the big man, with a broad grin spreading across his face. "Get favourite. Oolong. Not often afford that. Get next time Seglesh here." He finished what was left of his cup of tea in one gulp, stood up and stepped away from the table.

The shop owner indicated that Fergus and Duncan should sit. They did so while he remained standing next to the big man.

"I remember you," he said, looking at Fergus. "I must

say I didn't expect to see you again. Miss Farquhar wasn't too pleased with you so you'd better have a good reason for coming back here."

Fergus looked at the big man who was hovering nearby.

"It's all right," said the proprietor. "He knows Miss Farquhar too. You can talk in front of him. Anyway, we're private."

"Private?" said Fergus in surprise. Then he noticed he couldn't hear anything of the other conversations going on around them. *He's cast a Quiet Place spell on this table! I wonder if it's a glamour we're seeing. What does he really look like?*

"People can't just come in here throwing Miss Farquhar's name around like a password. You'll need to convince me you've got a good reason for it."

Fergus heard the implied threat in the proprietor's voice and said, "She told me to come here and call you Armach."

"Great stars above! What sort of trouble has she got herself into?"

"I can't tell you that. It's something we've got to tell Cridhe Igrainid about and it's best if she's the first to hear it. Neither of us can get to Eideann by ourselves. Will you take us through the lacuna, Mr Armach?"

The proprietor scowled as he looked round the busy room. He said, "Armach isn't my name. That's an emergency code. It tells me Miss Farquhar is seriously in need of help and asks me to do what I can to assist whoever gives me the message. If what she needs is for you to get to the Cridhe, then wait a bit. As soon as I can close up I'll see you through the lacuna and get you in to see her."

"Can't we go now?"

"Seglesh do it," said the big man before the proprietor had a chance to answer. "We go now, not wait for you close shop. Easier. Faster."

"But the appeal was to me."

"Yes, but Seglesh can do. No obligation."

"If you're sure … "

"Might get Seglesh back in favour with Cridhe," said the big man.

The proprietor's brow furrowed. He nodded slowly and said, "It might at that." He turned to Fergus and said, "We'll try it. This is Seglesh. He's as dedicated to Lady Trinafar as I am. He'll get you through the lacuna and take you to the Towers."

#

The elf on guard on the Eideann side of the lacuna was reluctant to let them pass until the big man removed a glamour and revealed himself to be a troll, well over eight feet tall with craggy blue skin, small horns spiralling backwards from his forehead and thick, cracked and fissured fingernails that looked like claws. He was really cramped in the limited space of the cave.

"Seglesh! It's good to see you again," said the elf as they slapped hands. "Are you back permanently?"

"Not know," said Seglesh. "Hope."

The elf looked disappointed. "Look me up if you are, Seglesh, you're a good drinking buddy. We'll spend a night out together again."

"Sound good," said Seglesh in a high-pitched voice that sounded incongruous coming from a massive troll, "but need be careful. Got drunk, cause trouble. Cridhe banish Seglesh. Don't want give Cridhe reason to banish again."

They left the elf at the lacuna and moved on up the path. Fergus enjoyed the awed expression on Duncan's face when he first saw Luchairt Eideann. It reminded him of his own reaction. Then he remembered why they were there and told Duncan to hurry up. "You'll have plenty time to enjoy the sights of Eideann."

When the goblin guard at the entrance to the Robhas Tower saw them coming he reached inside, rang a bell and shouted, "Alert! Turn out the watch! Alert!"

Half a dozen more guards, a mixture of goblins and elves, quickly appeared from inside the tower. Other people moving through the entrance rapidly got out of the way and the guard levelled pikes at them as they approached. Two of them nocked arrows and half-drew their bows.

"What are you doing here, Seglesh?" asked one of the goblins. "You were banished until next Beltane for brawling."

"Was," agreed Seglesh, "but cross-breeds got important message for Cridhe. Need help get from Edinburgh."

"What's the message about?"

"He can't tell you that," said Fergus. "He doesn't know. I can't tell you either. It's for the Cridhe's ears only."

"Know it about Lady Trinafar," said Seglesh.

"Well you can't see the Cridhe right now," said the goblin who seemed to be in charge of the watch. "She's in a meeting of the full council. You'll just have to wait until it's done. I'm not going to disturb them for news of Trinafar. She's let us all down and her doings aren't important enough for me to bother the council with. Her name on its own isn't enough to persuade me to disturb the Cridhe."

"It *is* urgent," said Fergus, hoping that Duncan and Seglesh would keep quiet when they heard Trinafar being denigrated.

A hiss from Seglesh made the goblin step back and put a hand on his sword.

"No, Seglesh. Let's not get into trouble," said Fergus, worried by the potential for mayhem. "It won't do Lady Trinafar any good."

Seglesh stepped back, still glowering, but clearly backing off from the confrontation.

Fergus asked, "Can't you even get a message to the Cridhe to say Fergus Monteith and Duncan Kirkpatrick are waiting to see her. She'll recognise our names."

The goblin shook his head, but a couple of elves nodded. One of them pointed at Fergus and said, "I remember seeing him talking to Commander Misghel as they left a meeting with the Cridhe. He is known. I think sending in a message would be acceptable."

The goblin scowled and, with obvious reluctance, told one of the elves to arrange a message if he was willing to take responsibility for bothering the council. Then he told everyone to get out of the way and stop blocking traffic.

Fergus, Duncan and Seglesh were escorted up the stairs to one of the doors adjacent to the throne room. It was a waiting room with an assortment of chairs made to suit every race from goblin to ogre. One of the guardgoblins went into the throne room with a message.

The leader of the escort said, "Sit here and wait quietly. We don't want any trouble. You hear me, Seglesh?"

Seglesh grunted and sat down on the only chair big enough for him. He licked his fingers and started polishing his horns with them.

Fergus noticed how nervous this behaviour made the goblins. He said, "Seglesh, think about Lady Trinafar. She's in trouble. Don't get us thrown out before we can tell the Cridhe what we know."

"Half-a-dozen goblins not enough throw Seglesh out.

About an hour passed with Seglesh getting increasingly restless and needing to be reassured time and again that he had been right to bring Fergus and Duncan through the lacuna. Eventually the door opened and an elf beckoned them into the throne room.

Seglesh reacted first, jumping to his feet. His high-pitched voice became even higher as he said, "What if Cridhe angry? She banish Seglesh forever!"

"You should have thought of that before you brought a pair of cross-breeds into the Luchairt," said the goblin in charge of the escort. "Too late to change your mind now. In you go."

"Follow my lead, Duncan," said Fergus. He went into the throne room, stopped three paces from the throne and went to his knees. From the corner of his eye he saw Duncan do likewise. Seglesh thumped down on his knees, then prostrated himself in front of Igrainid.

"You may rise," she said after a short pause during which Fergus saw her attention was on him.

As he got to his feet Fergus saw there were nine other people in the room. He recognised three of them; Misghel, Yuseth and one of Trinafar's sisters. *Which one is she? She's wearing blue. That makes her Saefan, doesn't it? I suppose the others must be councillors. A goblin, two elves, another fay, a dwarf and an anthrop who would look completely human if she didn't have tusks. Quite a mixture.*

"Introduce your companion, Fergus."

"Yes, Cridhe. This is my friend Duncan Kirkpatrick. He is the son of Rulidh Trischan Farnist of Obharden."

Saefan gasped and made a grasping gesture in Duncan's direction. The blue and silver shimmer of a shield appeared wrapped closely around him and he froze where he was, halfway through rising from his knees. Misghel stepped forward putting himself between Duncan and Igrainid, and Igrainid herself looked shocked. Seglesh gave a high-pitched moan and prostrated himself again.

"You didn't tell me about Duncan's relationship to Rulidh before you went off to Aberdeen."

"No I didn't, Cridhe, because I didn't know it at the time. May I tell you what happened to us in Aberdeen?"

"I think you should. But before that, tell me what part this troll plays in your story. Was he with you in Obharden? Why is he here? He is well known to us as an occasional troublemaker. Do you need him to tell your story or can you do without him?"

Seglesh wailed when Igrainid said that and mumbled, "Told me message about Lady Trinafar. Said important. Didn't mean no harm. Seglesh swear it, Cridhe. If Seglesh done wrong bringing them is because they fool Seglesh."

Fergus explained their association with Seglesh. Igrainid nodded and said, "Seglesh, since this doesn't involve you directly you don't need to hear any more of this discussion. Leave us, with my thanks for what you have done."

Seglesh stood up, mouth open and eyes wide. "Thanks?

Cridhe not angry with Seglesh?"

"No, Seglesh, I'm not. Bringing them through the lacuna was the right thing to do. Well done. Your banishment is rescinded, but be very careful not to get in trouble again or you'll be banished for longer. You may stay in Eideann but in return you are obliged to stay silent about this business. Remember that and do not speak of it to anyone. Don't even hint of it in gossip. Do you understand?"

"Yes, Cridhe. Thank you, thank you. Seglesh say nothing. Promise. Thank you." Still muttering thanks, Seglesh backed across the throne room, pulled the door open and said, to the globin standing outside, "Seglesh stay! Cridhe say can stay!"

Igrainid nodded to the goblin, confirming what Seglesh said, and watched the door close behind him.

She bent to activate one of the Quiet Place spells and said, "Now Fergus. What has happened and where is my daughter?"

ın obharden

Trinafar followed Rulidh down the narrow but well-lit servants' stair into the basement wondering how she was going to get out of this mess. *If he thinks mother will submit quietly to his demands just because he's holding me captive he's wrong, she won't. She'll not submit to being coerced even if my safety is at stake. She'll grieve for me if she has to, but that won't stop her putting the Domain first. And she knows I'd feel and do the same in her place. I'll just have to stay alert for any opportunities and make the best use of the resources I've got, limited though they are.*

Two of the doors at the bottom of the stairs were standing ajar. She could see one led to a storeroom containing, among other things, strings of onions, wheels of cheese and sacks of flour. The other opened into a well-stocked wine cellar. As she passed an archway the appetising smells wafting from it made it clear that's where the kitchen was. She looked around as Rulidh stopped in front of another door and made a twisting gesture. The lock clicked and the door swung open. The life-candle, burning steadily in the lantern, illuminated a passage leading gently downwards for about sixty paces with another door at the end. Halfway down the passageway Trinafar got a feeling of unreality, as if she was standing inside a soap bubble ready to burst. She recognised the sensation as indicating she was near a lacuna and guessed it lay beyond the far door.

"Go on," said Rulidh, indicating the door at the far end of the passage.

She opened it and stepped through into a forest. It was mostly pines, with an occasional holly, birch or rowan. Despite her predicament she relaxed slightly when she took a deep breath of the intense, fresh, slightly astringent smell of the pines. She turned to watch Maedron then Rulidh shimmer into view under a shallow overhang, the only feature giving any hint of the position of the lacuna on this side.

"You've never been here before, have you?" said Rulidh, adding, "I didn't think so," when Trinafar shook her head. He pointed west and said, "Luchairt Obhardenan is about half a mile that way."

Cridhe Peruch's base wasn't as famous as her mother's, but then few were. She had never heard a description of it and had no idea what to expect when, about twenty minutes later, Rulidh pointed into a shallow valley and said, "There it is."

She looked ahead, uncertain of what he was indicating. It wasn't until she saw people moving in and out of some of the low, dark-green bumps in the landscape that she realised they were buildings covered in foliage.

Rulidh pointed to one of the larger bumps and said, "That one is Cridhe Peruch's base. It's a pity you've come at the wrong time of year. The rhododendrons covering it are glorious in April and May."

"We can always go back and come again later," growled Maedron.

Trinafar smiled. *He's not given up.*

"I'm afraid that won't work," said Rulidh, showing no evidence of appreciating Maedron's attempt at a jest. He guided them to a door in the middle of the western side of the mound he had identified as their destination.

Half a dozen gnomes wearing hauberks and carrying pikes stood at the door. They bowed to Rulidh and allowed him to lead Trinafar and Maedron inside. Two of them left their position at the door to follow them into the mound.

With foliage completely covering the building Trinafar expected the interior to be dark and gloomy. She was glad to be wrong. Light was supplied by hundreds of glass globes, each about the size of a hen's egg, hanging from the rafters. They gave off a gentle, yellowish glow. Individually they weren't very bright but collectively they provided plenty of illumination. Reflections from the mica inclusions in the granite pillars supporting the roof produced a shimmering, sparkling effect. She gazed around. *It's effective, and it's quite attractive, but perhaps it's just a little bit over-the-top.*

Another squad of gnomish guards, these wearing loricated armour, were standing at one of the six other doors leading from the hall. The door they were guarding caught her attention. It was polished to a high gloss and inset with green and yellow gems forming the image of a snarling wildcat, the badge of the Realm of Obharden. *It's the most impressive door and the only one with a guard. It must lead to the Cridhe's throne room.* As she expected, Rulidh went straight to this door and demanded to be let in to see Peruch.

The gnome commanding the squad glowered at Rulidh. Trinafar thought he sounded pleased to be able to tell Rulidh that he would have to wait. "You can't just barge in on the Cridhe," he said, "you know that. Nobody gets in until he tells me to admit them. You'll need to wait until he's ready to see you. You can sit over there." He waved his hand towards a table and chairs in one corner of the hall. Then he turned his back on Rulidh.

Trinafar saw Rulidh's jaw clench and thought she heard his teeth grinding. He swung round, stalked across to the indicated corner and flung himself into one of the chairs.

She sat down too, noticing as she did so that almost all of the chairs in the hall, not just the ones in that corner, were sized for gnomes. It didn't matter to her because she was quite small, but it was a problem for Maedron. She saw him look around, probably for a larger chair and shrug when he didn't see one. Then he leant back against the wall, managing to look reasonably comfortable. *He's probably more at risk than I am. I do hope he can be patient. He looks a lot calmer than I feel.*

As Trinafar waited she watched the activity in the hall. She noticed a few elves and a couple of goblins passing through one or other of the doors, but most of the people she saw were gnomes. The scarcity of goblins wasn't a surprise given the traditional antagonism between goblins and gnomes but it struck her as odd that she saw no fay, anthrops or dwarves at all. *I suppose it makes sense for gnomes to be the majority here because that's what Peruch is, but there don't seem to be many of any other race, at least not among those with business in the palace. I'd be seeing many more different shapes in Eideann.*

Three times over the next hour the door opened to let people leave the Cridhe's chambers. Each time the gnome in charge of the guard went into the throne room and returned to admit another group. Each time Rulidh was left waiting.

Trinafar was certain Rulidh had to be furious at being ignored for so long. Eventually the door stayed open after half-a-dozen gnomes, all wearing elaborate brocaded jackets like Rulidh's, had exited through it talking animatedly among themselves and looking very satisfied. The officer commanding the door guard stepped into the throne room, said something to someone inside, then turned to beckon Rulidh forward.

Rulidh stood up slowly, brushed at his jacket to make sure it was hanging properly, gestured for her to get up, and started walking, in no hurry, towards the throne room. His behaviour suggested to Trinafar that he didn't want to appear to be responding to the summons of the guardgoblin, someone he must consider an inferior.

Maedron offered his arm to assist Trinafar to rise, not that she needed it. He bowed over her hand and in that position, when nobody except her could see his face, she saw his eyebrow feathers ripple slightly. Left eye, right eye, pause, then right and left. It was a signal in the private language of the Eideannach Domain Guard meaning 'stay alert'. She knew the language well enough but, like all the guard who were not elves, she had to improvise and use other facial movements to make herself understood. As Maedron had once teased her, she spoke Guardish with an accent. She smiled to herself. *He's trying to encourage me by reminding me I'm not alone. He's much more sensitive than people give him credit for.* The guard officer was frantically gesturing at Rulidh to hurry up, but without success. He was taking his time. She was sure that they were so wrapped up in their private battle for dominance that they were ignoring her, so she risked responding to Maedron. Flaring her nostrils and briefly opening both eyes wide she sent him the message 'be careful, don't take risks'.

When she took a step into the throne room she stopped, impressed, despite herself, by what she saw. It wasn't Cridhe Peruch who took her breath away but the furnishings of the room. The throne itself was a massive slab of red granite shaped into a chair big enough to seat a troll. Its arms were carved in the likeness of wildcats. Plentiful velvet cushions prevented Peruch being overwhelmed by the sheer size of the throne. Rich tapestries and delicate paintings of flowers, fish and waterfowl lined the walls.

The floor in front of the throne was covered by a yellow and green carpet with a maze pattern. It grabbed her attention. *It's a trap, isn't it. Start tracing the curves and the magic will ensnare the watcher.* She knew she should ignore it, but it was difficult. *It must give Peruch an advantage over any visitors.* It took a lot of concentration, but she did manage to drag her eyes away from the maze and look somewhere else.

Even with the effort she had put into breaking the mesmeric effect it wasn't until Cridhe Peruch spoke that she was completely free of the influence of the carpet and really had a chance to look at him. He was short, even for a gnome, and stout. His dark-blue doublet, heavily embroidered with silver, was stretched over a substantial paunch.

"Well, Rulidh. What has brought you back from the second world so quickly?"

"A piece of good fortune, Cridhe," replied Rulidh, straightening up after a deep bow. "Allow me to introduce my guests."

Peruch waved a hand, "Go ahead," and leaned back into the velvet cushions. He sat up again suddenly when Rulidh named Trinafar and Maedron. "How, under the gaze of the Starmaker, did you get hold of them?"

"They more or less fell into my lap, Cridhe. I found them at my home in Aberdeen and – ah, *persuaded* them to come here with me."

Trinafar smiled to herself at the slight quaver in Peruch's voice when he pointed at Maedron and said, "You have him under control, I hope."

"Of course, Cridhe. I made sure of that. I don't think he's going to do anything stupid or take any risks while I hold this." He lifted the lantern and said, "It's Trinafar's life-candle."

"Her life-candle! That should do it." Peruch looked thoughtful, then said, "The obvious thing to do is use her to put pressure on Igrainid."

"That was my thought too, Cridhe. I have already dispatched a cross-breed who was with them to Eideann to tell Igrainid we have her daughter."

"Why did you take it on yourself to do that?" snarled Peruch. "That sort of decision is mine. You're getting above yourself. As strong as you are, don't forget that you are limited to using the latency I generate. If I withdraw my favour you'll have nothing. I thought you would understand that by now."

"Forgive me, Cridhe," said Rulidh, going to one knee. "It seemed the best way to make use of our good fortune."

"You may be right. I am sure having them captive here will be to our advantage, particularly if our agent in Eideann can use that information. But I think it might have been better to keep Igrainid in ignorance of that fact, at least for the present. Remember it's me who makes the decisions here, not you."

Trinafar saw Rulidh's face show flickers of anger, fear and resignation before settling into impassivity. *Nice to know they're not in harmony. I wonder if we can take advantage of that.*

"Lady Trinafar," said Peruch, switching his attention from Rulidh to her, "you and your companion are welcome to Luchairt Obhardenan. We will make you as comfortable as we can here. I'm sure you will understand that your movements will have to be restricted to some extent. However, I can assure you that you will not be mistreated or harmed in any way. Unless, that is, you do something foolish like attempting to leave without my permission. I look forward to talking with you later. For the moment the business of the Realm must take precedence. Go with Rulidh. He will find suitable accommodation for you."

Despite him giving her the courtesy of a welcome Trinafar had a sour taste in her mouth at the idea of being in his power. She knew she was likely to be safe until her mother refused to accede to Peruch's demands, whatever they might be. *After that, who knows?* She acknowledged her dismissal with a bare minimum bow to Peruch, and followed Rulidh from the throne room.

He took them to a smaller building about a quarter mile from Peruch's base and told them it was where they housed Peruch's special guests. It was guarded by a squad of five goblins armed with short swords. The one who seemed to be in charge also had a crossbow. The only entrance was through the guardroom.

"You will be quite comfortable here," said Rulidh, indicating a corridor with five rooms opening off it. "There is no one else in residence at the moment so you can choose whichever of these rooms you want. Food will be brought here for you and you will eat here unless the Cridhe wants you to dine with him. He probably will at some stage but it won't be tonight, he has another engagement. I'm sure you realise we can't allow you to wander freely but there is no reason to confine you to this building. As long as you don't go too far, and have an escort, you can look round and see the Luchairt. If you need anything you have only to ask and it will be provided if I decide it is a reasonable request. If you want to talk to me one of the guard will bring you to my rooms. They are in the next building to the east. I wouldn't advise you to try to escape. Remember I still have the life-candle and I'm going to leave Maedron cut off from any latent power."

"I'm not likely to forget," said Trinafar and turned away from him to examine their new rooms leaving him looking at her back.

Rulidh grunted and stomped out.

"That's got rid of him," said Trinafar with a sigh of relief. "I hope we don't have to spend too much time in his company."

"Or in Peruch's," said Maedron.

Trinafar shuddered. "I want to avoid Peruch as much as possible. There's something about him that makes me feel unclean."

"My lady, did you notice that Peruch made a mistake? I don't suppose he meant to let us know that he has an agent in Eideann. I wonder who it could be?"

"So do I. But I don't think we need to concern ourselves about it until we get back to Eideann, if then. Actually, I'm not sure he did make a mistake. It's possible he's trying to worry us with disinformation."

"True. I wish you hadn't thought of that."

ʒɑCheRinʒ

Sumethla was the first to arrive in the place-that-doesn't-exist for the next scheduled meeting of the Group of Eleven.

She welcomed her colleagues and opened the meeting by describing the new anomaly she had previously discussed with Dhugalt.

The reactions of the others made it obvious to Dhugalt that she had had one-to-one meetings with at least three of the others on the same topic. He took careful note of the way she had used multiple one-on-ones to generate support from the rest of the Group before allowing a general discussion of a possibly contentious issue. It was a technique frequently used.

"I haven't told you before, but I have previous experience of this type of anomaly," said Sumethla. "You all know that I have been a member of the Group for longer than anyone else."

There was a murmur of agreement.

"Eight years after I became one of the Group there was an anomaly just like this one. It was as much of a surprise then as it is now. A couple of years later it was followed by three Failed Sources.

She paused waiting for a reaction. When there wasn't one she said, "A year after that a worldline shift occurred."

The rest of the Group reacted to the mention of a worldline shift in various ways. There were expressions of incredulity, some laughter, and arguments about the existence, or non-existence, of worldline shifts. They all knew about the tales of the Lost Worlds, but almost all of them dismissed them as myths.

The magi observing from around the margins of the place-that-doesn't-exist crowded closer. The number of minivortices, and other perceptible disturbances in the ambient space, increased. The Eleven could feel the pressure building up.

"Some of you are laughing at the idea of worldline

shifts," said Sumethla. "I don't really blame you but, believe me, they are real. And they're nothing to laugh about. I have experienced one, as has one other member of the present Eleven. When I became a member of the Group the lacunae didn't lead to the second world we know as the Empire but to a different world known as the Principalities. Isn't that right, Brangret?"

"It is," said one of the two goblins among the Eleven. "I wish it wasn't, but I have to admit Sumethla is telling the truth. I joined the Group three years after she did. As most of us do, I then spent some time in the second world."

"But, Brangret, you never go to the second world," said Tredun, the other goblin.

"No, I don't. I'm afraid to. You see, I barely made it back to Tirog from the Principalities. A worldline shift happened something like ten or fifteen minutes after I came back. Two of the people I was travelling with delayed in the second world for one reason or another and they never made it back. Nobody ever saw them again. Since then, I've never been able to convince myself to step through a lacuna."

"The Principalities *were* real," said Sumethla. "Brangret and I are probably the only people still living who can attest to that. The Principalities were just as the Lost World stories say. Eorp was fragmented into more than a hundred small countries, some of them so small a man could ride across them in a day. Each of them was very jealous of its territory, and wars, or at least skirmishes, among them were common. The history of that world was all about a series of would-be conquerors who tried to expand their kingdoms. Some of them succeeded for their own lifetimes but the combined territories they ruled usually broke up into their constituent parts within days of the conquerors' deaths. Few of these mini-empires survived more than one generation of rulers."

There was a profound silence. Even the pressure from the halo of hopeful faded somewhat.

"Sumethla, are you suggesting there is some association between a worldline shift and anomalous inheritance?"

"I am. I don't know for sure but, as I told you, there was a cluster of anomalies a few years before the worldline shift I experienced. I can't help wondering if the two anomalies we know about now are an indication of trouble to come?"

A rather subdued Eleven dispersed, agreeing to search all available records for more information about anomalies.

in eιϑeαnn

Fergus took a deep breath, then went to his knees in front of Igrainid again before saying anything. Barely able to speak around the lump in his throat, he told her what had happened to Trinafar in Obharden.

" … Rulidh sent me to tell you he has Trinafar and will keep her safe. He said he will send a message before the next full moon telling you what he wants you to do."

Igrainid sat unmoving, her forehead gradually creasing into a frown. Some of the councillors started fidgeting and turning to look at each other.

Fergus saw Saefan lift her head as if she was going to say something, then she shook her head as if changing her mind and stayed silent.

"That is not acceptable," said Igrainid in a very quiet voice. Then she said it again, much louder, with emphasis on the 'not' which was accompanied by her thumping a fist on the arm of the throne.

"I agree," said one of the elvish councillors Fergus didn't know. "Cridhe, I have in the past expressed my disapproval of the way you treat Lady Trinafar – as if she had the skills and abilities expected of one of her heritage when she clearly does not. However, that opinion is irrelevant in view of this blatant attempt at coercion by Peruch. I will support you in whatever decision you make."

Fergus listened to the other councillors expressing their endorsement of that position. He looked up at Igrainid and was shocked to see tears in her eyes. *Surely she can't be surprised by the strength of their support? Or is she crying for Trinafar?*

"Have you any more news for me, Fergus?

He bowed his head and said, "I do, Cridhe."

"More bad news?" she asked.

"I don't know if it's good or bad, but it's to do with why we went to Aberdeen in the first place. I think you need to hear what Duncan has to say."

"Do I?"

"Yes, mother," said Saefan before he could respond, "I agree with Fergus. We sent an expedition to Aberdeen hoping to get some information. We might as well hear what it has produced … "

Misghel interrupted, saying, "We should also remember that the message Fergus brought is from Rulidh and not from Peruch. Since we have Duncan we have as much of a hold over him as he has over us."

"I'm afraid not," said Fergus. "From the way Rulidh treated Duncan it's obvious he doesn't care much about his son."

Saefan and several of the councillors looked shocked and made sounds of surprise when he said that.

Fergus looked across the room to where Duncan was still encased in the shimmer of a shield, then back to Igrainid. "Can he hear us?"

"Saefan, it is you holding the shield, isn't it? Are you allowing him to hear us?

Saefan confirmed that the shield was hers and that it was isolating Duncan as well as immobilising him. "He can't hear anything."

"Good," said Igrainid.

Fergus felt a shiver running down his spine when Igrainid switched her attention back to him and said, "Stand up and tell me why you brought him here."

Fergus climbed to his feet, glanced again at Duncan and said, "Before Lady Trinafar was taken Duncan answered some of the questions we had about the blurring and he came with me from Obharden to put his knowledge at your disposal." Fergus paused and looked at the councillors seeing blank looks on most of their faces. *Does she want them to know about the NEbox and her premonition?* Then he turned back to Igrainid and waited for her reaction.

Igrainid frowned. She looked around the half-circle of the councillors, nodded and said, "Of those present, only Saefan, Misghel, Yuseth and Fergus know why I sent Trinafar to Aberdeen. It's quite a complex tale and I don't want to take the time to explain it at the moment.

Please forgive me for asking the rest of you to leave me now and to remain silent about what you have heard."

Fergus watched the councillors muttering among themselves as they stood, bowed to Igrainid, and left. The elf who spoke earlier to support Igrainid paused on the threshold. His violet crest fluttered as he said, "Cridhe, I have confidence in the ability of Misghel and Lady Saefan to keep you safe should this cross-breed wish you harm. However, I would be happier if you had even more protection. I offer my skills, such as they are."

"Thank you for your concern, Councillor Hurilt," said Igrainid. "While I'm sure you would make a significant addition to the security I already have I don't want to spend time explaining why Trinafar went to Aberdeen. Do not worry about my safety, I have adequate protection. Leave us."

Fergus noticed Igrainid's glance towards him when she said she had 'adequate protection'. He felt a warm glow of pleasure and contentment at the idea of being included in that description. *That's a surprise. It seems a geas can reward as well as punish!*

The last of the councillors had left the room when Saefan snorted and commented that Hurilt was being his usual irritating self, trying, as always, to push himself forward.

"Just ignore Hurilt," said Igrainid, then she switched her attention from Saefan to Fergus, asking him, "are you sure Duncan isn't a threat?"

He took a deep breath. "Yes, Cridhe, I think he truly wants to assist."

Igrainid nodded and said, "I know you believe that, Fergus. The geas would have killed you by now if you didn't. I hope you aren't mistaken."

She turned to Saefan, told her to release the shield and asked Misghel to step aside so she didn't have to peer around him to see Duncan.

Audible cracks from Duncan's spine accompanied his straightening up from the half-crouch the shield had held him in and Fergus winced imagining how stiff he must be after spending so long in that position.

"You are the son of Rulidh Trischan Farnist," said Igrainid, leaning forward to question Duncan. "Do you understand that is not a relationship that will win you friends here in Eideann?"

"Aye, Cridhe, I ken that. But I hae some knowledge and information that I believe will help ye."

"Why would you want to do that?"

"I dinnae like what my father has done, kidnapping Lady Trinafar. I want tae make amends."

"And how do you propose to do that?"

"I'll share some discoveries I've made with ye. Lady Trinafar said they're revolutionary – as important as Neuven's Principles, she said."

"What!" The exclamation burst from Saefan and she quickly apologised to her mother for the interruption.

"Your pardon, Cridhe," said Fergus, "So far you've only heard what happened to us after Rulidh turned up because that seemed most important. However, we do have other news. I think it might be better if we began at the beginning with our arrival in Aberdeen and take it step by step."

"Yes, that does sound like a good idea."

#

For the next hour or so Fergus and Duncan demonstrated the NEbox and the changes Duncan had made to it. The final image, of the caged candle flame, made Misghel grimace and say, "I recognise that. It *is* the life-candle spell."

Saefan frowned at the image and, after a short pause said, "Not quite, I think. I've never had occasion to use it myself but I did study its structure when I was researching restraint spells eight or nine years ago. I'm sure there's something different about the link where the cage around the flame becomes a chain. Shouldn't it be a single twist rather than than the double one that image shows?"

"You may be right, Lady Saefan," said Misghel after a moment's consideration. "I have used this spell, but only once, and that was more than thirty years ago. I could be misremembering it."

"Rulidh did say he had modified the spell, so that might be why it looks different," said Fergus. "Do you think being able to see the magic will be as useful as Trinafar suggested?"

"Let's find out," said Saefan. "Mother, I will lift something – that cup by your left hand. Use the NEbox to watch my magic and try to unravel it."

Saefan made a lifting movement and the porcelain cup she had indicated, with its decoration of enamelled red and yellow roses, floated up into the air. It stopped at head height. Igrainid watched it rise, then looked at the image on the box, touched the screen with the thumb and index finger of her right hand and made a delicate pinching movement.

The cup fell.

Saefan exclaimed, "No!" and grabbed at the cup with both hands. The cup stopped bare inches above the floor, her hands nowhere near it.

"I made a bad choice there," she said with a quaver in her voice. "I should have picked something less precious to experiment with. Who caught it?"

"I did," said Igrainid, "by the grace of the Starmaker I was just fast enough. I was shocked to find it was so easy to change your spell."

Fergus said, "Duncan has something else to add to the NEbox. He hasn't told me what it is or what he expects it to do, probably because he's not sure if it will work. He hasn't been able to try it before now because a moving train isn't the best place to do delicate work."

"What you've shown us so far is impressive enough, Duncan. And I think I might well agree with Trinafar's opinion about its significance," said Igrainid. "What is this something else?"

"When we went tae the lab last night I picked up some bits and pieces. One o' them was a sheet o' tactomer."

"What's that?" asked Fergus. "I've never heard of it."

"I'd be worried if you had. It's a company secret and none o' it is supposed to be taken out of the lab – in a way I suppose ye could say I've stolen it from myself. We're planning on using it in the second generation o' the boxes. It's a smart material that I think will combine showing images with being an input device."

"I fear that means nothing to me," said Igrainid. "Go ahead and make whatever changes you think are necessary."

"Thank you, Cridhe," said Duncan, clearing a space on the table in front of him. He opened the NEbox and started to move some of the components around. About twenty minutes later he made a sound of annoyance and undid what he had just done.

"I'm sorry, Cridhe. That configuration's no going tae work. I'll need for tae start again. This is going to take a while longer than I thought."

"No matter," said Igrainid. "Take as long as you need." She looked at the others and said, "There is no need for all of you to stay if there is something else you should be doing."

"I will stay for your protection," said Misghel, "there is nothing more important than that."

"With your permission, Cridhe, I will leave," said Yuseth. "Interesting though this is, I have other duties." When Igrainid nodded, he stood, bowed and left the room.

"I would prefer to stay, mother," said Saefan. "Seeing the beginning of what might be a revolution in combining magic and technology is something I don't want to miss." She helped herself to tea and sat back ready to watch every move Duncan made.

"Gie me a hand, Fergus," said Duncan.

"I can't help, Duncan. I don't know what you're doing."

"Ye can haud things in position for me when my twa hands arenae enough."

It took Duncan, with some help from Fergus when he

needed an extra hand, more than an hour to make the changes he wanted. Most of that time was spent spreading the tactomer, a delicate sheet of thin opalescent material, carefully over the existing display and trimming it to size. Most importantly, according to Duncan, they made sure there were no air bubbles under it. After that making the protonic connections was simple enough and Duncan did that without assistance before closing the box again.

"Done?" asked Fergus when Duncan sat back.

"Aye. At least I think so. The only way tae be sure is tae try it."

Igrainid asked, "What does it do?"

"The first thing is pretty simple. You can use the screen like a piece of paper and your finger like a pen to write on it. Then store the image of the writing tae be brought back later." Duncan demonstrated this, then said, "It'll dae something else as well and I think that'll be mair useful."

"What's that?" asked Igrainid.

"Best if I find out if it works rather than telling ye what it's supposed tae do and find it disnae."

Fergus saw Igrainid looking at him with one eyebrow raised. He said, "I believe you can trust him, Cridhe."

"Very well, Duncan, you may go ahead with your demonstration."

"Thank you, Cridhe. I want somebody tae lift something again. It had better be something less fragile than that cup this time in case it disnae work – or maybe in case it does."

The ambiguity in Duncan's remark raised a few eyebrows.

Igrainid asked Saefan to do the lifting and Duncan said, "Whenever ye're ready."

Saefan chose a silver spoon from the tea caddy and lifted it to head height.

"Fergus, look at the box. Can ye see the magic holding the spoon up?"

"Yes."

"Touch the image on the screen and try tae rub out one of the lines o' magic."

The clatter of the spoon hitting the floor was drowned out by curses from Misghel, gasps of amazement from Igrainid and Saefan, and the thud of Saefan's chair being overturned as she jumped up from it.

Fergus found himself wrapped in a fine network of sparkling blue and silver threads applying a firm, unyielding, even pressure to every part of his body. He could breathe and blink, but, otherwise, he was unable to move. From the corner of his eye he could see a similar shield surrounding Duncan.

"How is that possible?" asked Igrainid, echoing Fergus's own thoughts.

"The Starmaker might know, but I don't," said Saefan, fumbling behind her legs for her fallen chair while keeping her eyes firmly fixed on Fergus.

"Who is shielding them?"

"I am, Cridhe," said Misghel.

"Both at once! That was well done, Misghel. A very fast reaction."

Misghel bowed, acknowledging the compliment, but he kept his attention on Duncan.

"Can they hear us?"

"Yes, Cridhe. I didn't have time to do more than a basic shield for each of them."

"Release their tongues, please," said Igrainid. "I have questions for them."

"They can talk now, Cridhe," said Misghel, moving to stand between Igrainid and Duncan.

Igrainid frowned, took a few moments to adjust the cushions on her throne, leaned back into them and took a deep breath. She looked straight at Fergus and said, "Explain this."

"I can't, Cridhe," he replied. "I just did what Duncan told me to. There was a faint prickling sensation when I rubbed the screen, like touching a nettle. Then the line I touched blurred and vanished and the spoon fell. I was as surprised as any of you."

"I doubt it," said Saefan, "I'm not just surprised, I'm astonished and shocked."

"I think we all are," said Igrainid.

"Well, Duncan, can you explain?"

"Aye, Cridhe. The tactomer screen converted Fergus's touch intae a signal that changed the image and feedback from the changed image altered reality the same way magic does."

"Why didn't you warn us what would happen?"

"Because I wisnae sure it would work and I didnae want tae look foolish in front of all of ye if it didnae."

Fergus snorted. "Did you not think what the reaction would be if I suddenly started doing magic?"

"No, I've got tae admit it never occurred tae me. I suppose I should have given ye some warning."

"That would have been a good idea," said Igrainid. "As it is, you leave me in a quandary. I know Fergus believes you're not a danger to me because he's still alive. However, he could be honestly mistaken and now I don't know whether to trust you or not." She hesitated, then told Misghel to stop their ears and still their tongues.

Fergus waited as calmly as he could. It wasn't easy. His heart rate increased, he found himself breathing faster and he could feel sweat trickling down between his shoulder blades.

He saw Saefan apparently arguing with Misghel while Igrainid sat quietly. Her gaze moved from one to the other as she followed the arguments, looking at whoever was speaking.

Some twenty minutes later she clapped her hands and the others stopped talking.

Fergus found he could hear and move again when Igrainid asked him, "Will you return to Obharden tomorrow and take a message to Cridhe Peruch for me?"

"Of course, Cridhe."

"We will discuss it later. For the moment I want to find out more about the capabilities of this – this box of tricks."

For the next couple of hours Duncan, Fergus and

Saefan experimented with the NEbox trying to find out its limitations for modifying or abolishing spells. Igrainid and Misghel also contributed to the ideas they tested. They were so engrossed in this that cups of tea were allowed to grow cold and had to be reheated several times.

Eventually Igrainid said, "We could carry on with this all night, and probably all tomorrow too. Fascinating though it is, there are other things I need to do. Saefan and Duncan, you seem to work together well. Will the two of you carry on experimenting?"

"Yes, mother, I'd love to. It's fascinating."

"Cridhe, I would be very happy tae work with Lady Saefan."

"Good, that's settled. Now, Fergus, you said you would carry a message to Peruch for me."

"Certainly, Cridhe."

"Don't be so quick to agree when you don't know the risks involved."

"Cridhe, the geas binds me to serve you, so the risks are irrelevant."

"Your enforced service to me does not give me the right to place you in danger without your agreement. Rulidh said Cridhe Peruch is plotting to rule in the second world as well as in Tirog. If that is true it suggests he won't have any regard for a cross-breed and he might well blame the messenger for the content of the message. Imprisonment is the least of what he might do to you."

Fergus felt he could breathe more easily when Igrainid told him she wouldn't force him to carry the message. *She's given me permission to choose – but do I really have a choice with Trinafar in danger? Maybe Igrainid's just good at manipulating people and getting them to do what she wants. Doesn't make any difference, I've got to do it.*

"Yes, Cridhe. I understand. What is the message?"

"Deliver it to Peruch himself and nobody else. In particular, I don't want you to tell Rulidh before Peruch. He can hear it at the same time but not before. Say that I will ensure the Synod hears about this plot and I will encourage it to take action against any attempt to dominate and rule the second world."

"Mother, he must realise the Synod will act against him," said Saefan.

"I'm sure he must, and he must have plans to deal with that. However, I suspect his plans aren't complete yet. He can't have expected to capture Trinafar and that may force him to move earlier than he intended."

Fergus saw Misghel nodding vigorously, then he switched his attention back to Igrainid when she said, "One more thing, Fergus, before you go. You might be able to call on the services of my ambassador to Obharden. Unfortunately, I cannot promise that because it depends on Peruch allowing you access to her. She is an elf called Volissen vul Birres. If you do get the chance to meet her then you can identify yourself as my messenger by talking about the village of Saltpans. It's quite near here."

"Saltpans? Is that the place that's called Prestonpans in the second world? If it is, I've been there, Cridhe."

"Have you? That's convenient. How far away from Edinburgh is it?"

"Hmm, about eight miles, I'd say."

"Yes, and no. It *is* eight miles, but tell Volissen it's sixteen miles and she will know I've sent you."

Fergus nodded. "I understand."

"It's important you tell Peruch about your geas as soon as you can so that he knows you're unable to tell him anything other than the message. He will understand he can't extract any more information from you."

"Yes, Cridhe. I will do that."

"Come here, Fergus, and give me your hand."

Fergus was shocked and elated when Igrainid took his hand, turned it over and and kissed the back of it. He felt his face get warm and was sure he was blushing.

"Will you no send me back with Fergus?" asked Duncan. "You cannae send him on his ain."

"No, I don't think you should go back. You are

involved somehow in the premonition I had. I'd like you to stay here while we try to work out what it means."

"Might I suggest," said Saefan, "that Fergus takes the modified NEbox with him. He can use the geas to avoid telling Peruch, Rulidh or any of their people anything about it. It might be a useful thing to have. Duncan and I can experiment with the other one. I'd really like to be involved in inventing new uses for it."

"Good idea. We'll do it that way."

Theory

The Eleven came together again in the place-that-doesn't-exist at the request of Fuormil, a fay member. She wanted to recap on whatever was known about the relationship between the worlds. She admitted to having been skeptical about the existence of worldline shifts, but had been convinced by Sumethla and Brangret at the previous meeting. She had spent every moment she could spare in examining all the records she could find, correlating stories of the Lost Worlds with changes in the membership of the Group of Eleven and anomalies in the lineage of Sources.

The declared topic attracted a lot of attention from the halo. According to Sumethla and Brangret the previous worldline shift had been accompanied by major changes in the composition of the Eleven, so the hopeful were there in unusually large numbers. They all hoped they might benefit from this discussion, and get some clues as to how changes came about.

Dhugalt felt this was probably a pointless, redundant, exercise but repeated what he had previously told the Eleven about Trinafar and her failure to produce any latent power despite the appropriate lineage.

Then Sumethla reported she had confirmed the anomaly discussed at the last meeting where a too-short lineage had resulted in a Source.

Fuormil then revealed that she had recently discovered yet another anomaly in one of the territories she visited; another Failed Source.

Everyone wanted to know what was causing the anomalies, but nobody had a clear answer.

Various suggestions were made, bringing together ideas that had been raised in the past. These included one speculation that all the worlds, including the Lost Worlds, were always linked together. In this scenario, only two of them, Tirog and whichever the second world was, were 'real' at any one time.

The dwarf who argued for this interpretation also suggested a possible cause for worldline shifts. "Perhaps," he said, "the linkage between the worlds is put under stress by people moving from world to world through the lacunae. Eventually the stresses become too much and a worldline shift occurs to stabilize the network of worlds."

Nobody liked that idea, because it put the blame for worldline shifts on the inhabitants of Tirog and their unrestricted use of the lacunae.

This theory made Sumethla recall an incident from early in her career as a member of the Eleven. One of the Group at that time had been dissatisfied with where a lacuna opened in the second world and had, as he described it, 'forced' it to open somewhere more to his liking.

Sumethla couldn't describe how this was done and nobody else, as far as she knew, had ever managed to do it, but it did show that magi could interact with the lacunae.

The halo reacted badly to the suggestion that people going through lacunae were responsible for causing worldline shifts by increasing the stress on the network of lacunae. They put more pressure on the Eleven for permitting this to happen. One or more of them might well have ousted a member of the Eleven if the counter argument hadn't been so strong. That suggested they too had been equally responsible for using and allowing the unlimited use of lacunae.

With mixed feelings of disgust and resignation, the meeting ended and everyone left the place-that-doesn't-exist to return to the real world.

back to obharden

As Fergus followed Misghel down the path to the lacuna he kept remembering the feel of Igrainid's lips on the back of his hand. The memory of that gentle touch, and the trust in him it showed, distracted him from the risk he was taking. He was amazed by how calm he felt.

"I can get you through the lacuna here," said Misghel when they were getting close to it. "But how are you going to manage the crossing in Aberdeen?"

"I'm not sure. I know where the lacuna is so I think I'll need to hang around there hoping to find a way to let Rulidh know I'm there. Then wait for his reaction."

"I think it's very brave of you to do this. It's a pity you're a cross-breed or I'd have you in the Domain Guard."

"You wouldn't accept a cross-breed in the Guard?"

"No. No offense, Fergus. You've proved you're different but, on the whole, I don't trust cross-breeds any more than I trust shapechangers."

Fergus was startled by Misghel's comment. The only evidence of discrimination or racial prejudice he had come across in Tirog had been on his arrival when Maedron had questioned him about his mother. Even that was just him doing his job as a sentry. Ever since Igrainid had accepted him Maedron had treated him as a colleague. It worried him to find someone as close to the Cridhe as Misghel with that attitude in what seemed to be a functioning multi-racial society. *How widespread is that sort of belief?*

He stopped on the path and said, "But you're trusting me with this mission and I'm half shapechanger."

"It's the Cridhe who is trusting you. She showed you that with her kiss. It's a rare accolade, and I don't think it's ever been given to a cross-breed before. She trusts you, so I do too. Anyway, like I said, you're different. You've shown yourself to be worthy of trust despite being a cross-breed."

"Why don't you trust cross-breeds?"

"I just don't understand how anyone can form a liaison with somebody from another race – it's disloyal to your own."

"So you blame me for my parents' choice."

"No, not at all," said Misghel, sounding flustered. "That's not what I mean. It's just that, well … "

"Cridhe Igrainid has seven mixed race children."

"But she's the Cridhe!"

"Yes, and I'm happy to serve her and have her trust. But her children are still mixed race, whether you like it or not. I think you need to do some serious thinking about your attitudes." He paused and, before Misghel could answer, added, "I don't want to get into an argument right now so let's just leave it there for the moment. If you want to we can talk about it again after I get back. Open the lacuna for me and I'll be on my way."

Misghel started to say something but stopped and opened the lacuna.

Much to his surprise, as Fergus stepped through the lacuna he heard Misghel mutter, "May the Starmaker shine on you."

Then Fergus was through, coughing and spluttering in the dirty air of Edinburgh.

#

It was mid-afternoon when Fergus arrived at Union Station in Aberdeen. He set out immediately for Rubislaw Hill, thankful that the weather was better than it had been on his last visit.

He rang the bell and waited for someone to answer, rehearsing in his mind how he was going to introduce himself.

He recognised the servant who answered the bell. *Thank goodness. He should remember me.*

"How may I assist you?" asked the servant.

"My name is Fergus Montieth. I was here a few days ago visiting Duncan." He waited for the servant to nod and admit to recognising him. "I know Duncan's not here at the moment, but I was hoping to see his father instead."

"I am afraid Mr Kirkpatrick is not at home, sir. I do not expect to see him until Wednesday. May I take a message for him?"

"I have something important to tell him. I don't mean to offend you, but I think he should hear it directly from me."

"I do have a way of getting urgent messages to him," said the servant. "Write a note for him and I will ensure he receives it. Come with me. I will provide you with writing materials."

I suppose that means he, or somebody else here, can pass through to Tirog. I hope I can persuade him to take me, thought Fergus as he followed the servant. He took advantage of being behind his guide while walking along the corridor to slip the NEbox from his pocket without it being seen, switch it on and glance at the screen. As he expected it showed the reality behind a glamour – the servant was a gnome.

Their destination was a library where the guide indicated an old-fashioned, roll-top mahogany writing desk standing in front of a window.

Fergus decided to take a chance, took a deep breath and, instead of sitting at the desk, said, "I presume Duncan's father is in Obharden. Wouldn't it be better to let me through the lacuna so that I can deliver the message in person?"

The servant hesitated. Then, after Fergus again emphasised the urgency of the message, said, "That does make sense if it's that important. Very well, follow me."

Fergus followed him down the servant's stair and along the tunnel to the lacuna. The servant indicated the door and said, "That will take you to Obharden."

"I've never been to Obharden and don't know my way around. Will you guide me to wherever I can find Rulidh Trischan Farnist? In return I promise to tell him how helpful you have been."

The servant lifted his head to look up at Fergus when he mentioned a promise. After a short delay during which Fergus assumed he was considering the possible benefits, he said, "I accept your bargain."

Trinafar did say to be careful about promises. I hope I got this one right. If Rulidh isn't pleased with me turning up and with him helping me then there's a chance he'll get blamed for it more than I will.

Fergus enjoyed the walk through the forest from the lacuna to Luchairt Obhardenan. The strong scent of the pines and the springy feel of the carpet of fallen needles under the trees reminded him of the countryside where he had been brought up.

His guide seemed to be in a hurry and set a fast pace which Fergus, with his longer legs, matched easily. Less than a quarter of an hour later the guide stopped, pointed ahead and said "Luchairt Obhardenan."

"Where?" said Fergus, then he realised that the green mounds he was seeing were buildings smothered in vegetation. He said, "It's very different from what I was expecting. I'm glad you agreed to show me the way, I'd be completely lost without you."

His guide grunted and took him to a low mound covered in ivy. "This is the master's residence. If he isn't here it's likely he will be with the Cridhe." He tapped a rectangular piece of metal hanging by the door. It was a gong and produced a sweet, high-pitched note that lingered in the air for a couple of minutes.

The goblin servant who answered the gong confirmed that Rulidh was at home and told his guide to take Fergus into his presence.

The gnome he was following ushered Fergus into a cosy room with dark wood panelling where Rulidh was sitting in an overstuffed leather armchair with two glowing globes hovering in mid-air over his head.

Fergus heard surprise in Rulidh's voice when he recognised him and said, "You're that cross-breed my son brought to the house in Aberdeen. What are you doing here? And how did you manage to get through the lacuna?"

"My name is Fergus Monteith. I come with a message from Cridhe Igrainid." He indicated his guide and said, "This gnome has been very helpful in getting me here."

Fergus saw a scowl on Rulidh's face as he looked at the gnome. *I don't think that's the sort of reception the gnome was hoping for. He was expecting praise. Too bad!*

"You don't have the authority to make decisions like that," said Rulidh with a snarl. "Leave us. I'll deal with you later."

The gnome hurriedly left the room.

"Well! What's the message from Igrainid? I don't suppose you're going to tell me she'll agree to do whatever Peruch wants to save Trinafar, are you?"

"No, I'm not."

"Pity, because that's the only message Peruch will listen to. Tell me exactly what Igrainid said.

"I can't. I'm under a geas and my message is for Cridhe Peruch's ears."

Rulidh put the book he was reading down on a small table, rose from his chair, stepped up close to Fergus and gazed into his eyes. He sighed and said, "Yes, I can see the shadow of the geas. I don't understand why Igrainid did that. Cridhe Peruch will tell me her message anyway so why not let you tell me? It's very inconvenient." He sighed again, "I'd better take you to him. Follow me."

Fergus followed Rulidh to the largest of the foliage covered mounds and into the Cridhe's study, a comfortable room lined with books and maps. He would have liked to explore it. One of the maps displayed on an easel showed the familiar outline of Alba. *I suppose those overlapping lines on it must be the boundaries of the Domains and Realms.*

"What is it this time?" asked Peruch, looking up from the only chair in the room, a well padded rocking chair.

Rulidh told Peruch that Fergus was a messenger from Igrainid.

"You have him under control, of course," said Peruch.

"I do, Cridhe. He isn't shielded, but I have my hand

around his heart and can crush it in a moment if needed. Anyway, he's a cross-breed with no magic and he's not even carrying a knife. He's not a threat."

Peruch looked at Fergus curiously and asked. "Does Igrainid really trust a cross-breed with a diplomatic message? It's the sort of thing I might expect from her, but still I am surprised. I think I will send for her ambassador and have her confirm you are the messenger you say you are."

After a short wait a very tall elf arrived. She had bright lemon-yellow eyes, her crest was pale-blue and her eyebrow and ear feathers a slightly darker shade of blue. She bowed to Peruch and said, "You sent for me, Cridhe."

"Ah, yes! Ambassador Volissen. Good of you to come. This cross-breed claims to have a message for me from Igrainid. Can you vouch for him?"

Volissen studied Fergus and said, "I have not met him previously, Cridhe. If he comes from Igrainid she will have provided him with some means of identification. Allow me to establish a Quiet Place and I will find out."

Peruch frowned, then gave her the permission she asked for.

Volissen walked over to one corner of the room and asked Fergus to join her. She raised an arm overhead and made a spiralling motion.

Fergus recognised the dull, enclosed feeling of a Quiet Place with its lack of echoes as it formed around him.

Volissen put her hand in front of her face and said, "Conceal your mouth. I suspect Peruch may have learned the art of lip-reading."

She waited until Fergus raised his hand and then said. "Give me proof that you come from Cridhe Igrainid."

"She told me Saltpans is sixteen miles from Eideann."

"I think you'll find it is only eight."

"No, she definitely told me sixteen."

"Good. Give me a hint of what your message is so I can decide how I will respond to it."

"I can't give you the message. I'm under a geas to

deliver it to Cridhe Peruch and nobody else.

"That's awkward."

"I think I might be able to tell you that Peruch is holding Lady Tr … "

Fergus felt as if his head was being squeezed, saw flickering multicoloured lights closing in from the periphery of his vision. He put his hand to his throat, started coughing and, gasping for breath, said, "Can't – say – more."

The feathers of Volissen's crest laid flat against her skull. "Curse it," she said. "I couldn't stop myself reacting to what I think you tried to say. Stop there. Don't kill yourself trying to circumvent the geas."

She dismissed the Quiet Place spell and said to Peruch, "I have verified that he is indeed a messenger sent by Cridhe Igrainid. You may be certain the message he brings is from her."

"Well, cross-breed. What have you got to say?"

"First of all, Cridhe, I must tell you I am under a geas."

"Is he, Rulidh?" asked Peruch before Fergus could say any more.

"Yes, Cridhe. I confirmed that before bringing him here."

"Well, what message does Igrainid have for me.

"Cridhe Igrainid sends word that the Synod will hear of your plot to dominate the second world and she will encourage it to take action to prevent this happening."

With the message delivered Fergus waited, slightly apprehensively, for Peruch's reaction. After a short silence, Peruch jumped to his feet and demanded, "Is that all you have to say?"

"That is what Cridhe Igrainid told me to say."

"Did she say nothing about me holding Trinafar?"

"I have told you everything she wanted me to say. The geas prohibits me from saying any more."

Peruch glared at Fergus and growled, "Get out of my sight. You too, Rulidh, your meddling hasn't done us any good. I don't want to see you again today unless you have something positive to offer. I'll send for you when I want you. Meanwhile put the cross-breed wherever you've put Trinafar."

"Cridhe, I want to see Lady Trinafar," said Volissen as Peruch settled himself back into his chair. "As an ambassador from her mother I have a duty to her. You can't force me to ignore that."

Peruch glowered at her but, having accepted Volissen as an ambassador, he had also acknowledged her obligation to do her duty and had to allow her request. "Very well, you can see her. It probably won't do any good, but you never know. You might be able to persuade her to plead with her mother for support."

Rulidh led Fergus and Volissen to the building where Trinafar and Maedron were held. He told the guards that Fergus was to stay there too. Then he left them there in a small room furnished with dark oak settles around a low table standing on a red and blue rug.

Fergus was relieved to see Trinafar uninjured and able to smile at him. He asked, "Are they treating you well?" as soon as the last of the guardgnomes left the room.

Volissen bowed to Trinafar, echoed the question Fergus had asked and added, "My lady. I must apologise for not coming to see you before this. I didn't know you were here until about half-an-hour ago when I was summoned to vouch for Fergus."

"I suspected you hadn't been told I was here," said Trinafar. "I know you think I've let Eideann down by not being a Source but I didn't think that would prevent you doing your duty as ambassador. Mother has faith in you."

"I haven't changed my mind about you," said Volissen, "but I am loyal to your mother and will do what I can for you."

"Thank you."

"The question is, what *can* I do for you? I assume Peruch has some sort of hold on you."

"Yes. Rulidh has a life-candle linked to me and, somehow or other, has severed Maedron's access to latent power."

Volissen's crest flattened against her skull again. "That

limits our options rather severely."

Fergus hesitated. *She thinks Trinafar is responsible for not being a Source.* He wondered if the ambassador was trustworthy. *I think I'll wait until she's gone before telling Trinafar about the NEbox. Then she can decide whether or not to tell Volissen.* He shook his head, let it drop and tried to look disconsolate.

"Your pardon, Ambassador Volissen," said Maedron. "When we arrived here and Rulidh took us to see Cridhe Peruch it was obvious that the two of them were not entirely in accord. Is there any way we can take advantage of that? Can you tell us anything about their relationship?"

Volissen shook her head and denied any knowledge of a discord between Peruch and Rulidh. However, as she did so she laid a finger across her lips and indicated by gesture that the others should seat themselves. She raised one hand overhead and made a spiral movement.

Fergus immediately felt the, now familiar, sensation of being in a Quiet Place, a slightly confined feeling with a complete absence of echoes.

SURPRISE

The next meeting of the Eleven produced a surprise. Almost before the place-that-doesn't-exist had established itself one of the Eleven made an announcement.

Sumethla was the longest serving of the Eleven but the one who spoke could claim to be the oldest in terms of years. He had spent forty-two years in the cloud of the hopeful before succeeding in finding a place in the Eleven. Add to that the more than fifty years as one of the Eleven and the time before he had grown strong enough to join the halo and his claim to be the oldest was believable.

It had been, he said, good to be one of the Eleven. However, he admitted he was getting weary of the continual stress that went with membership and, with the prospect of a worldline shift in the offing, he felt it was time for him to step down.

Surprise, disbelief and shock rocked the place-that-was-not. Abdication was a recognised way of leaving the Eleven, but hadn't happened for a long time. Most members chose to hang on to their position as long as they could and, when necessary, fight for survival. Even Sumethla could remember only two previous abdications.

Inevitably the announcement attracted those in the halo. Here was a possible route to power and influence. The ambient space became full of almost visible presences as all the hopeful prepared themselves for the struggle ahead.

Then the abdicator surprised them again by naming someone he thought would be a suitable replacement and donating some power to the one he named. This caught everyone else off balance; the unexpected nominee slid into place as part of the Eleven without difficulty; and the retiree quietly disappeared from view.

For a short time it was still possible to get a hint of his existence out in the margins of the halo. However, the donation of power to the new member meant the abdicator had weakened himself and become vulnerable to attack. Those who had hoped to fight for membership resented not being given the opportunity and took their revenge on the abdicator.

He had effectively committed suicide.

planning

Volissen took the seat opposite Trinafar and said, "I can speak now without fear of being overheard by Rulidh. He doesn't like the rift between himself and Peruch being discussed."

"What is their relationship?" asked Trinafar. "Apart from the obvious fact that Peruch generates the latency Rulidh uses."

"I've been here as ambassador for only a little over two years," said Volissen, "so I don't know the full story. Nierell, who was ambassador here before me, told me what his predecessors had passed on to him, and I've learned a little more from odd bits of conversations I've overheard."

"I understand," said Trinafar. "You're saying what you can tell us is, at best, second-hand information and might not be accurate."

"Exactly so, my lady."

"I'll bear that in mind."

"Good," said Volissen. "There's quite a lot to tell you so I suggest we make ourselves as comfortable as possible. There should be a tea service in one of the cupboards."

"Good idea," said Trinafar. "I could do with a cup."

Fergus made a face. Coffee seemed to be unknown in Tirog and, although he had got used to drinking tea, he still didn't like it. However, he helped Maedron find the tea service and distribute the cups of fragrant liquid Volissen made.

"The first thing you need to know," said Volissen once they all settled down with their tea, "is that Peruch and Rulidh are half-brothers with the same father. They were born on the same day only minutes apart. What's more, their mothers are both seventh children."

Not being used to thinking in terms of Cridhe inheritance it took Fergus a moment or two to realise what this meant. Trinafar and Maedron caught on much faster. Trinafar gasped, "So Rulidh could have been

Cridhe instead of Peruch. Thank the Starmaker he isn't. Peruch is bad enough, I think Rulidh would be worse."

"Yes, if their birth order was reversed Rulidh would be Cridhe. As it is, Rulidh, being born first, is the sixth child of his father and Peruch is his father's seventh child – and both of them are unhappy about it."

"I can understand why Rulidh is unhappy about not being Cridhe," said Trinafar, "but I don't see why Peruch shouldn't be satisfied with the situation."

"Because his magic is very weak. He's barely able to lift as much as a single acorn, and he resents Rulidh's strength."

"I see," said Maedron, nodding. "Peruch thinks he would prefer being a stronger magic user to being Cridhe, despite having the political power."

"Exactly," said Volissen, "and there is no doubt in my mind that Rulidh envies Peruch and would rather be Cridhe."

"I'd have thought Rulidh would move away from Obharden to get away from Peruch's domination if they don't get along," said Fergus.

"He's tried that," said Volissen. "He went to live in Gresche for a while."

"That's where I first met him," said Trinafar.

"He spent five or six years there and seemed to be well settled," said Volissen, "then he fell foul of a very powerful magic user called Fliorign."

"I know her," said Maedron. "What did he do to upset her?"

"I don't know the details," replied Volissen. "It took me a long time to find out even that much. What I do know is that, somehow or other, he insulted her. She demanded satisfaction and they fought a duel."

"Oh! You mean he didn't apologise for whatever the insult was?"

"No, he didn't."

"That doesn't speak well for his good sense," said Maedron. "I wouldn't want to risk a serious duel with Fliorign. She's very, very good both with magic and with a sword. I've come up against her twice at the Alban Games and she's beaten me both times."

"Well," said Volissen, "she defeated Rulidh and had Cridhe Hulben banish him from Glesche. He had to return to Obharden because, if I've got this right, Hulben destroyed his ability to use latent power everywhere except in the Domain of his birth. Peruch is now the only Source who can supply him with it. Rulidh is very strong here in Obharden, but he's completely powerless anywhere else."

"So that's why Peruch dominates Rulidh," said Trinafar. "That's a very severe punishment. When did this happen?"

"A little more than three years ago."

"That makes sense," said Trinafar. "It fits with when I first met him in Glesche."

"It's no wonder they don't get along. What could the insult have been?"

"I don't know. What I've told you has come from my counterpart in Glesche and I haven't followed it up because I don't want to put him at risk by being too nosy."

"I can appreciate that," said Trinafar. "Thank you for telling us what you do know."

Volissen stood up, inclined her head towards Trinafar and said, "There doesn't seem to be anything we can do except wait. Send for me if you think of any way I can help make you more comfortable. I will leave the Quiet Place spell active so that you can have privacy." With another nod towards Trinafar she left the room.

Maedron stood, stretched until his shoulders cracked, and started pacing around the room. "All that is very interesting, but I'm not sure how we can make use of it."

"There's something I've got to tell you," said Fergus, rising to his feet and reaching into his jacket pocket to get the NEbox.

Trinafar raised an eyebrow. "Oh?"

Fergus switched the box on, wrote on the screen and held it out for Trinafar and Maedron to read. Maedron's eyebrow feathers flattened against his skull for a moment and then perked up again as he read what Fergus had written.

< *Can the person casting a Quiet Place spell hear what is said inside it after she has left it?* >

Trinafar shook her head and said, "No … " Then she paused as Maedron held up a hand in a warning gesture.

He took the NEbox from Fergus, examined it, drew a finger across the screen and nodded when he saw how the message function worked. He used it to write something he then showed to both Trinafar and Fergus.

< *Yes, it is possible. It requires only a slight modification of the spell. Why do you ask?* >

Fergus took the box back and wrote on it again.

< *I don't have any reason to distrust Volissen, I'm just being cautious. As well as this writing function Duncan has added another new feature to the box that should be helpful. I want to tell you about it but it's important to keep it to ourselves and not discuss it where there is any risk we might be overheard.* >

Trinafar looked thoughtful as she took the box and continued the written conversation.

< *As far as I know she is trustworthy. I admit I don't particularly like her but that's more because of her dislike of me and my 'problem' rather than any reason to suspect her loyalty.* >

Maedron lifted his head, his crest flaring and his eyebrow and ear feathers going flat against his skull. He grabbed the box from Trinafar, switched it into image mode and, looking intently at the screen, scanned around the room while the others watched.

When he finished looking at every part of the room he smiled and said. "I just remembered this gadget can see magic. The Starmaker be praised, Volissen used a standard Quiet Place spell. There's no trace of an eavesdropper modification. We can talk freely."

"Are you sure?"

"Yes, my lady. I can see the spell she used quite clearly. There's nothing unusual about it."

"Can you see any other spells?" asked Fergus.

"Yes," said Maedron. "I was concentrating on the Quiet Place spell but I can also see the life-candle spell."

"That's what I was hoping," said Fergus. "You see, Duncan has modified the box so that the screen doesn't just show magic but lets you change it by touching the screen."

"Impossible!" exclaimed Maedron at the same moment as Trinafar said, "Incredible!"

"It's true," said Fergus. "I've seen it happen. We were experimenting with the changes Duncan made and the Cridhe broke a spell Lady Saefan had cast by simply manipulating the image of her magic on the screen. You could use that ability to cancel the life-candle spell."

"But I don't have access to latency," said Maedron.

"Doesn't matter," replied Fergus. "Even I can change the magic by using the box."

Maedron's crest stood upright again. "You're not serious!"

"Yes, I am. I've done it when we were finding out what this latest version of the NEbox can do. I'm sure I could change the life-candle spell but I'm afraid to touch it because I don't know anything about how spells are constructed. I don't know what changes it would be safe to make and I don't want to risk harming Lady Trinafar. But, Maedron, you're used to magic and I'm sure you'll be able do it."

Maedron looked at Trinafar and said "My lady?"

"Yes, do it, please do it, Maedron. You know how that spell is put together, don't you? I trust you to dismantle it safely."

Fergus found it difficult to read Maedron's expression but he saw him swallow several times.

"What do I do with it?" asked Maedron, looking at Fergus.

"When Lady Saefan experimented with it she said she could treat the image of the magic the box shows as if it's her own magic she's seeing."

Trinafar closed her eyes, unable to watch as Maedron took a deep breath and touched the NEbox tentatively with one fingertip. Then he added a second and moved the two as if untwisting something. He hesitated for a moment, frowned, then taking a deep breath he dragged one finger down the screen and back up again with a rubbing motion. While doing this the erratic, disorganised movements of his eyebrow and ear feathers made Fergus think that Maedron was nervous. Then he exhaled and said, "It's done, my lady."

"Are you sure?" she said. "I don't feel any difference – but then the life-candle spell didn't produce any sensation either."

Fergus took the box from Maedron, looked at the screen then pointed it at Trinafar and captured an image. He showed it to her, saying, "Here, my lady, you can see you're free of that spell."

"Thank the Starmaker, and both of you." said Trinafar, gazing at the screen with tears in her eyes. Then she turned to Fergus and asked, "Will you be able to do anything for Maedron? Do you think the NEbox can be used to restore his ability to draw on latent power?"

"I doubt it," said Fergus after a moment's thought. "The box lets us change, or at least delete, existing magic but I think giving Maedron his magic back would mean adding something and I don't have the faintest idea how to do that."

"Too bad," said Maedron, "but at least you're free from that threat, my lady."

"Will Rulidh be aware of the change to his spell?" asked Fergus.

"I don't know. What do you think, Maedron?"

"I think not, at least not immediately. I get the impression he relies a lot on the status his powerful magic gives him so it's not likely to be the only spell he has active. Unless he's paying particular attention to it I don't think he's going to notice one, relatively small change among his active spells. I'd be more concerned about Peruch noticing a reduction in the usage of the latency he generates. Anyway, it's done and we have to accept that risk."

"Perhaps we should have thought of what we're going to do before cancelling the life-candle spell. We need to get out of here before he does realise the spell is broken," said Fergus. "He's not going to be happy to discover you're not under his control anymore."

"Maybe so, but I can't bring myself to regret getting free of the life-candle. It feels so good to know it's not hanging over me. Now we need to do some planning. How can we get out of here? We have no magic, and no weapons except a shadow-knife …"

Fergus didn't know what Trinafar meant by that. He realised, from the movements of Maedron's eyebrows and crest that he was surprised by it. However Maedron said nothing and Trinafar carried on speaking, "… The only way out is through the guard room and I'm not strong enough to cope with even one of the guards on my own, never mind five."

"If we can take the guard by surprise and I can get hold of a weapon then I should be able to deal with at least two of them, possibly more," said Maedron. "Unfortunately, that still leaves three if what we've seen so far is the normal complement."

"I'm big enough that I might be able to handle one goblin," said Fergus, "I'm not a trained fighter but I can provide a distraction."

"Volissen."

"What about her, my lady?"

"She's offered her support and I know her magic is quite strong. Her involvement in an escape would take the guard by surprise, and wouldn't violate whatever ambassadorial oaths Peruch has asked of her. "Tell one of the guard we need to see her. We need to move quickly and hope she gets here before Rulidh becomes aware that the spell is broken."

181

question

Klinmerd, the goblin who was now the newest member of the Group of Eleven made his presence known at the next meeting saying that he was worried. "I have been observing the meetings of the Eleven for more than nineteen years," he said. "At one of the earliest meetings I attended the subject was the Failed Source in Eideann. Now there is another Failed Source and I am becoming somewhat worried."

"We all are," said Sumethla. "These anomalies might be indicating a possible worldline shift."

"I know that but it's not what worries me. It's that there is no possibility of either of the involved lineages producing a new Source and neither of them has an alternate line."

"True," said Sumethla.

"Should we not be more proactive?" asked Klinmerd.

"What do you mean?"

"As well as the two Failed Sources there are at least fifteen of the Domains and Realms of Alba and Anglaya, not to mention a dozen or so in Eorp and Affrik, in which there is no successor to the existing Cridhe," said Klinmerd. "And in some Domains the line of succession is two or even three generations short of producing a new Cridhe. Tawe is a good example."

"Tawe has time. Cridhe Jiltin is young and is well aware of her duty to her Realm."

"True, but Tawe is just one example, and by no means the worst. The records indicate there are more such potential problems at present than at any time in the past."

"You must have some solution in mind or you wouldn't raise this. What do you suggest we do?"

"There is a vast untapped reservoir of talent just outside this non-place where we're meeting," said Klinmerd. "We have all been there and we know the desire that drives the magi to congregate there seeking power –

primacy among our peers – glory – whatever you want to call it – whatever it was that drove you to join the hopeful."

"What of it?" asked one of the Eleven.

The question was echoed by two more and a feeling of tension developed as the onlookers became aware of some disharmony among the Eleven.

"The rumours we encourage about the magi say, amongst other things, that we don't generate latency. This is usually interpreted as 'can't' but all of us know that to be inaccurate. We can but, unlike Sources, for us generating latency is a conscious act."

"So?"

"If a Cridhe with no successor could be replaced with one of us they could provide latent power and avoid the sort of catastrophe that befell Belfeir and Gertseay."

"Why would we want to become mere generators of latency? That would make us no better than the Cridhe."

"Don't sneer at the Cridhe," said Sumethla. "Their function is vital to the Domains and Realms."

Unusually, the hopeful, gathering around the edges of the non-space, made their opinions clear to the Eleven. Normally, if any meeting of the Eleven could be said to be normal, the onlookers simply observed, waiting and hoping for opportunities.

This time many of them went farther and intruded into the deliberations of the Eleven. The majority agreed with Klinmerd; others agreed in principle but argued it wasn't required until an heirless Cridhe was dying.

"Not so," said one of them, pointing out that Belfeir and Gertseay had both been abandoned well before their last Cridhe had died and that had caused severe disruptions in those and the adjacent Domains.

"It may well become necessary in Eideann, but not for a long time," said Dhugalt. "Igrainid is relatively young as Sources go and I don't think she's likely to die soon. Should it become necessary, I will undertake to supply latent power to Eideann. I am related to Igrainid and I wouldn't want to see her Domain or her children suffer.

The rest of you should think of possible effects on your families too before dismissing the idea."

The appeal to family was enough for the rest of the Eleven, and the vast majority of the onlookers, to agree to the suggestion – albeit some of them showed considerable reluctance. Some of them accepted the proposal in principle knowing that their relatives were secure from any risk and the chance of them actually having to replace a Cridhe was small.

By any objective assessment this meeting of the Eleven had taken longer than most but, as always, time in the quasi-space was variable. When the Eleven returned to wherever they had been before joining the meeting the time that had elapsed was anywhere from a few minutes to several hours.

escape

A little over two hours after Trinafar had asked the guard to send for the ambassador, Volissen arrived to find her restless and nervous with a glass of tea cold and abandoned on the table in front of her.

"I'm sorry to have taken so long …"

"Don't worry about that now. We've got to get out of here as soon as we can," said Trinafar. "There's no time to explain why. We need to go before Rulidh comes to investigate and we need your help."

"But he'll snuff your life-candle."

"Probably, but it won't do him any good. That spell is broken."

Volissen looked startled. "How?"

"We'll explain later. We need to leave right now before anybody comes to investigate. Can you stupefy the guard and let us get away from here?"

"I suppose I could, but …"

"You'll have to come with us of course. I don't like to think what Rulidh or Peruch would do to you if they find out you've helped us escape."

It took another ten minutes of questioning with Trinafar getting more and more nervous as time passed before Volissen accepted that she was free of the life-candle.

Once she was convinced, Volissen said, "I'm required by my position to give assistance to anyone from Eideann so, yes, I will help you. But helping prisoners escape is well outside the remit of an ambassador and you will be in debt to me."

"I know. I accept that we will incur an obligation to you. I will personally repay it on behalf of all three of us. The debt *will* be balanced." Trinafar took the silver ritual knife from her belt, stabbed her thumb and said, "I swear it."

Volissen nodded and signalled for them to follow her as she turned to the door.

She stepped into the guard room making wide

sweeping gestures with both hands. Four of the five guards collapsed where they were standing. The fifth, who was busy sharpening his sword, was unaffected by Volissen's spell.

"Look out," she shouted as the others followed her into the room, "One hasn't gone down."

Maedron ran across the room, grabbed the weapon one of the stupefied guardgoblins had dropped and threw himself at the remaining guard, knocking him over.

The goblin twisted round, pulled Maedron's feet from under him and brought him crashing to the floor.

Although Maedron was bigger, his opponent was strong. They were well matched. Each of them managed to get a grip of the other's wrist and keep their opponents' blades from their throats. The room echoed with grunts as they struggled. They rolled over and over, wrestling for dominance.

Trinafar reached into her skirt pocket to touch the tattoo on her thigh. She felt the hilt of the shadow-knife acquire substance.

Maedron managed to flip his adversary on to his back.

He couldn't hold him down.

The goblin kept rolling, taking Maedron with him on an erratic course through the furniture.

They ended up with Maedron pinned underneath the goblin, with the hand holding his blade pushed far to the side and trapped under a chair that had been overturned during the struggle.

"Go!" shouted Maedron. "Get away."

Trinafar took a deep breath, gripped the hilt of the shadow-knife firmly and pulled. She knew she would sacrifice some of her flesh to give substance to the black blade, and that it would hurt.

Even knowing it was going to happen she screamed when the blade came fully free. The pain was so much worse than she expected.

Lunging forward, she rammed the knife into the goblin's neck. His blood poured across her hand. He made a gurgling noise, let go of Maedron's wrist and brought his hand to his throat in a vain attempt to staunch the bleeding.

The sensation as the goblin's body spasmed and went limp made Trinafar shudder. It was the first time she had killed anybody and she didn't like the feeling of knowing someone, even an enemy, was dead as a result of her actions. She was nauseated by his dead stare. It looked as if it was accusing her. She almost dropped the shadow-knife as she pulled it free of his body. *No! I've got to keep hold of it. I can't afford to lose it. I might need it again.*

Maedron twisted and threw the goblin's body aside. He stood up and assisted Trinafar to her feet. "I didn't know you had a shadow-knife before today, my lady. Tell me about it, please. I need to know what assets we have. Whose working is it? How long will it last? Can you resheath it?"

"It was made by a salmad called Bernu, directing a gang of five."

"I know of him. He has a reputation for doing good work."

She told him "Now that I've drawn it I have to keep hold of it or the spell will dissipate. It can't be resheathed. Like all shadow-knives only the flesh donor can use it so I've got to hold it or lose it."

"Good," said Maedron, "It could be better but I'm happy you've got it."

"Where did you get that knife from?" asked Fergus, looking puzzled. "I don't understand. If you had it why didn't you give it to Maedron to use before we attacked the guards?"

"I couldn't. It didn't exist then except as a tattoo on my thigh. It's built from my flesh so I'm the only one who can wield it."

Maedron examined the short sword his opponent had been wielding. "That's why he didn't succumb to your spell, Volissen. This blade is iron. It must have negated your spell. Thank the Starmaker, the iron probably prevented him casting any spells of his own."

"Never mind that," said Volissen. "We've got to go! Hurry, before anybody else turns up."

"Calm down," said Maedron. "We will go, but we can't rush. We have to behave as if we have a perfect right to be walking around."

He paused long enough to take and sheath the goblin's iron weapon and told Volissen and Fergus that each of them should take one of the other blades dropped by the goblins. "Best if we all have weapons. Lady Trinafar, have you anything to wear to replace that blood-stained blouse?"

"Yes. I'll go and change.

"And see if you can find a way of concealing the shadow-knife. I don't want you to abandon it. It may come in useful again.

"I'll take the crossbow," said Fergus. "I'll do better with that than a sword."

"No," said Maedron, "I don't think you should. The crossbow is too obvious. There's no good reason why we should have one and somebody might get suspicious. We've got to be as inconspicuous as possible." Then he turned to Volissen and asked her, "Which way should we go?"

Volissen said, "We'll go to my office first. Nobody will be surprised to see us going there. It's on the edge of the Luchairt and we should be able to slip away unobtrusively."

Sure enough nobody paid particular attention to them, at least until they reached the building that housed Volissen's office. It was small but, with two towering pines built into and supporting the endwalls, it was quite imposing.

"Your pardon, my lady," said Volissen when they reached her office. She spoke loudly enough to be sure the two goblins waiting in an anteroom could hear her. "I must deal with these enquiries before we can go sightseeing." She indicated a door and said, "There is a tea service in that room. Please help yourselves and I will join you as soon as I can."

"More tea," grumbled Fergus when the door was closed behind them. "Isn't there any coffee?"

"So few Sidhe like it that it's not worth the trouble or expense of importing it." said Trinafar, "Getting tea is difficult enough."

"What do you mean?"

Trinafar initially shrugged off the question. She was more concerned with the delay in their escape than with anything else but she understood the need for Volissen to behave as normally as possible to avoid raising suspicions, and she supposed that meant the diplomat had to deal with those who wanted to talk to the Eideannach ambassador. *Don't know how long she's going to need, so I might as well answer Fergus's question. It's as good a way as any of passing the time.*

She sat down and patted the chair beside her. Fergus sat too.

"Tea has to be shipped halfway round the second world from its origin, be that Qin, Sarandib, Assand or wherever. Shipping in the second world is a lot easier and faster than it would be in Tirog but it still has to be brought through a lacuna and distributed to the Domains and Realms. There are several companies who specialise in that and make a good living from it. If it wasn't for them we'd be drinking chamil, or rosehip or some other tisane."

Half an hour later all of them were getting increasingly anxious, wondering if they still had time to get away before anybody started chasing them.

Maedron stood behind the door looking at a map of the area. With sword in hand he was ready to attack anyone coming through it.

The door opened and Volissen entered. Everyone stood up and crowded round her.

"Good," she said, "I've got rid of the people who wanted me. It took a while but I think it was worth it. Taking the time to deal with them will suggest we aren't in a hurry. Also, I've used them to lay a false trail. I mentioned that I was going to take you on a sight-seeing trip to Hazlehead. It's well enough known as a local beauty spot to be a believable destination. If we take some food with us anyone who sees us will think we're going for a picnic and that won't raise any suspicions."

"I suppose we're not actually going there," said Trinafar.

"Certainly not."

"You do have a destination in mind, I hope."

"Yes. We're going to Girdle Ness. It's only about five miles away." She pointed it out on the map Maedron was studying. "There's a lacuna there. It doesn't get a lot of traffic because it's one of the intermittent ones, only accessible under certain conditions and it's out in a fairly desolate area. The one you came through from Rulidh's mansion is so much more convenient and gets much more use. I think Girdle Ness is likely to be our best bet."

"Good. Let's go."

A few people saw them walking out into the forest surrounding the Luchairt. Volissen was well enough known that nobody, apart from a few who acknowledged her with a nod or wave, paid particular attention to them.

They set off west towards Hazlehead, walking into the thickest part of the forest, along the course of a small stream. When they were out of sight of any of the buildings of the Luchairt Volissen swung their route southwards away from the stream saying following the stream would take them to the river Dee but by a roundabout route. "This way is faster," she assured them.

When they reached the Dee about twenty minutes later she led them downstream along a riverside path to a small cluster of buildings where a solidly built bridge with granite footings and wooden superstructure carried a narrow road across the river.

"Brig o' Dee," she said. "We need to cross here."

"Can we?" asked Trinafar. "It's busier than I expected from what you said. Quite a few people are using that bridge. Somebody's bound to see us."

"I really do think we need to cross here," said Volissen, explaining that the course of the river would force them north again and farther away from their destination if they didn't. "We want to go more to the east, towards Neig Bay. There are several downstream crossings we could use but they'll likely be busier than this one."

"In that case, would we be better going upstream to cross?" asked Maedron.

"There aren't any other crossings for at least a mile, maybe a mile and a half, upstream. Going that way would take us back towards the Luchairt and would waste time. I think it's got to be here."

"If we just walk across somebody will see us and possibly tell any pursuit where we've gone," said Maedron. "Can you generate a cloak?"

Volissen shook her head. "Not one that's good enough. There are too many of us. The best cloaking spell I can cast needs me to be holding hands with anybody I want to conceal."

They stood looking at the bridge for a few minutes, watching a fairly steady stream of people on foot or driving carts crossing it. "What do we do?" asked Trinafar.

"I have an idea," said Fergus. "Rulidh is going to start looking for us soon, if he hasn't already. He's dismissive of cross-breeds, so I think he's likely to pay less attention to finding me and concentrate on the three of you. Why don't you take advantage of Volissen's cloaking spell while I go across by myself. Hopefully, any search party isn't going to be looking for me."

"You can't go on your own, Fergus. It's too dangerous," said Trinafar. "What if something goes wrong and we can't meet up again?"

"Just hope it doesn't," said Fergus with a shrug.

"Your pardon, my lady," said Maedron. "I think he is right. It *is* our best bet." He turned towards Fergus and bowed. "Fergus Monteith, I am in your debt for accepting a risk that should properly fall to me. Give me your hand."

Fergus did as Maedron asked.

Maedron said, "I acknowledge the debt I have to you

for sharing my duty as a bodyguard to the Lady Trinafar Chiolet Fion Eideannach." He held up the blade he had taken from the goblin, looked into Fergus's eyes and said, "Will you permit the sharing of blood between us?"

Fergus blinked in surprise. He nodded, then gritted his teeth as Maedron drew the edge of the short sword across their thumbs and let their blood mix.

"Fergus," said Trinafar, "I don't think you have any idea of what an honour it is to be joined by blood to an elf like Maedron. You are now a member of his family, the House of Mochri."

"I'm surprised you're willing to adopt me. I got the impression you didn't like, or trust, cross-breeds," said Fergus. "I know your father doesn't. He told me so to my face."

"There are maybe a dozen cross-breeds in Eideann that I know of," said Maedron, "but only a few of them live near the Towers and I don't know any of them very well. I'm ashamed to say I haven't questioned the commonly held opinion of them. You have made me do so. I am sure my father will change his mind when I tell him what you have done. He will be obliged to accept my adoption of you into the family."

Trinafar said, "It would be nice if everyone was accepted for what they do and say instead of being prejudged by what they are. Unfortunately that seems to be too much to ask."

Fergus pinched his thumb and finger together to stop the bleeding and asked Maedron if he should go before the rest of them or after.

"You should go first, I think. Go a quarter mile or so beyond the bridge and wait for us somewhere prominent, like a branch in the road or a cluster of trees. We'll follow about ten minutes behind you. We'll see you waiting and let you know when we've caught up with you. If we went first you wouldn't have any way of knowing where we were."

Fergus nodded to them, took a deep breath and stepped out on to the road a couple of hundred yards before the bridge. He strode along the road and on to the bridge trying to look as if he belonged there.

He was about halfway across when his hand started aching. He shook it, trying to relieve the discomfort but the sensation spread from the cut and increased in severity. Soon it was a burning feeling running up his arm. He couldn't see anything untoward when he examined it. Within minutes the feeling reached his chest and was painful enough to make him gasp for breath.

He staggered and almost fell.

Has Maedron poisoned me? No! Why would he do that?

The pain constricted his breathing. Gasping, he stumbled onwards, made it across the bridge and staggered on for about another hundred yards. He tripped over his own feet and fell in a heap by the roadside.

What am I doing? What's happening? Why am I here?

The darkness flooding over him was almost welcome.

manipulations

At the next meeting of the Eleven Wardlik asked his usual question and, once again, Kragum criticised him for wasting time.

"Why can't you accept what we have established about the Failed Source," he demanded. "I don't understand why it has happened any more than you do, but I don't see any point in going on and on about it. If anybody *does* discover anything new then I'm sure we will hear all about it."

Wardlik grunted. *I'd better not push this much more.*

"I just don't think we should ignore it," he said. "I believe it may be more important than we know."

I don't want to provoke a confrontation.

He thought back to his very first visit to the place-that-was-not as one of the Eleven. He had been surprised to find a message waiting for him. It wasn't addressed to him by name, but to 'My successor'.

He was still uncertain, even after many years, if the message was a trap. He could imagine himself wanting to be revenged on whoever replaced him when he eventually lost his position as one of the Group.

On the other hand, he could imagine a 'goody-goody' member, like Sumethla, Brangret or Dhugalt wanting to warn their successor of what the message had implied. The possible link between anomalous inheritance and a worldline shift was potentially valuable – or dangerous – information.

The recent example of a sixth child becoming a Source left Wardlik wondering how that could happen; he couldn't think of any way to bring that about. When the meeting ended Wardlik returned to the place-that-was-not as soon as he could, thinking it might be worth experiencing the message again. *In case I missed something that would explain this new anomaly.*

The first part of it confirmed that it wasn't from his immediate predecessor only, but from a series of three who had all passed it on to their successors. *Can I trust three of them any more than I can trust one? The message chain would surely have broken down if any of them were untrustworthy, so perhaps ...*

The second part was, as always, more difficult to believe. It said that a worldline shift could be forced by creating enough instances of anomalous inheritance and suggested a way of doing this. The person who controlled the shift would also control the second world that formed as a result.

Once again Wardlik felt the appeal of more power. It was that which had convinced him to join the halo and fight for a place in the Eleven. Ten years after finding the message from the past he eventually convinced himself it was worth trying to force the formation of an anomaly in the way the communication had suggested.

He sighed as he thought of his attempts. He had tried to create a Failed Source on five occasions. Of all of them, only the fourth was a success. In each case he had encapsulated a newborn seventh child within a shield compounded of negation, denial and exclusion and then settled down to wait for the child to reach the age of seven. The first became a Source, albeit a very weak one, and Wardlik wondered if he had let the child get too old for the technique to work before shielding it. Then the next two had died of the spotted fever before they were old enough to produce latency. His only success had followed, and confirmed the efficacy of the technique. To his surprise the fourth actually fed latency to him directly and he had gained in strength as a result.

Pity I waited so long before my most recent attempt, he's still too young to know if he's a Source or not. Waiting until he is old enough will be a waste of time.

I think I will try again soon.

lacuna

Trinafar watched Fergus walk away. She soon lost sight of him as he merged into a group of people approaching the bridge. *I hope we can find each other on the other side.*

Volissen grasped their hands. She warned them not to speak, then cast her cloaking spell. Trinafar had evidence of how effective the cloak was when the others disappeared from her view. She assumed she was also invisible to them as they kept bumping into each other while walking along the narrow riverside path. Once on the road, with a bit more space, they gradually got used to walking in step. Their progress along the road and on to the bridge was slow but steady.

People they might have collided with made room for them without apparently being aware of their presence. Trinafar realised it was a subtle effect of the cloaking spell. *I haven't seen that effect before. It's really good.* She made a mental note to congratulate the ambassador when she dropped the cloak and they could speak again.

After they had gone a good bit more than a quarter of a mile beyond the bridge Volissen tugged them to one side where a cart track led through a copse to a farm. "There's nobody in sight on this track," she said, "and the trees will hide us from anybody on the road. This is a good place to shed the cloak, nobody will see us suddenly appear."

"Yes," agreed Trinafar, and let go of Volissen's hand. "Where's Fergus? I haven't seen him."

"Nor have I," said Maedron, "and we should have passed him if he did what we agreed."

"What do we do? Go back towards the bridge and wait for him?"

"We can't go back," said Volissen, and Maedron agreed with her.

"But …"

"No, my lady. We need to keep going. Getting you safely away has to be our priority. Fergus knew there was a chance the plan might go wrong and chose to accept the risk."

Trinafar shook her head but said nothing.

"Back to the road then," said Maedron. "Keep looking for Fergus."

They didn't see him anywhere along the next mile of the road and had to admit they'd lost him.

A standing stone, with a runic inscription, stood where a track branched off the road. Volissen was happy to see it; it perfectly fitted the description she had been given of the route to Girdle Ness.

She led them eastwards along the track for about quarter of a mile before they reached a pile of stones that had once been a building.

"I don't feel the lacuna. Is this where it's supposed to be?" asked Maedron.

"No," replied Volissen. "This is just an old shepherd's hut. We need to go a bit farther; the lacuna is on the shore. The person who told me about it said to follow the stream by the ruin."

Trinafar looked with dismay at the shore when they got that far. A shallow slope, decorated with tussocks of grass and a scattering of sea pinks, samphire and broom ran down to an irregular, crumbling edge. Rocks peeking through the grass were covered in lichen and moss. Five or six feet below the edge a narrow strip of sand dotted with exposed rocks, seaweed and tidal pools waited for them. Clambering down to the beach wouldn't be easy.

"Where do we go?"

"I'm not sure," said Volissen. "I've never been here myself. I've only heard descriptions."

"Well, tell us what you've been told. What should we be looking for? What do you know about this lacuna?" said Trinafar. "You did say it's intermittent."

"Yes. Haven't I mentioned the opening conditions? It's only available at low tide during the three days of the full moon. You can't get through if it's wet underfoot. I wouldn't even have considered it a possibility if the moon wasn't right."

"Thank the Starmaker it's nothing more complicated than that."

"I was told the lacuna is in an alcove on the south side of a small promontory, between two pillar-like rocks about eight feet high. Oh, yes, the promontory is to the south of the stream from the ruin, and it's supposed to have a flat top with a crack about four inches wide running across it from north to south."

"What's the state of the tide now?" asked Trinafar.

"How should I know?" said Maedron, looking around with a frown. "I don't live by the sea. All I can say is it's not high tide but I don't know if it's ebbing or incoming."

"But you know which way north is, don't you?" she said.

"Of course I do. It's that way," said Maedron confidently, facing out to sea and pointing to his left. "I think we should take a good look around. Try not to lose sight of each other but see if you can recognise anything from the description. Be careful with where you put your feet, that seaweed will be slippery." He led the way down on to the beach assisting Trinafar who had only one free hand, the other still clutching the shadow-knife. Once down they separated to explore the area.

The better part of an hour later they met up again and agreed that the tide seemed to be coming in and that there were at least three places nearby that could conceivably fit Volissen's description.

"Which one do we try?"

"I'd go for the one nearest the stream," said Volissen. "The description specifically mentioned that."

"Yes. That would be my choice too." Maedron looked around and pointed in the direction of the possible site closest to the stream. "I don't think it can be that one. The sand within a couple of feet is already wet, and the other two are still dry."

Maedron looked landward, dropped to his knees and said, "Get down. Quickly. There are at least half-a-dozen people coming this way from the direction of Neig Bay. Maybe Rulidh has thought of this escape route. Worst case scenario is they've caught Fergus and forced him to tell them where we're going."

"Oh, I hope not."

"What do we do?"

"We're not going to be able to try both possibilities without being seen. If we pick the wrong one we'll have to run to get to the other before anybody else does and that could be a very close thing. Which one do you think we should we try, my lady?"

"The one by the stream."

"I agree. You and Volissen start working your way towards it. I'll let myself be seen and try to distract them. Shout as soon as you find the lacuna and I'll come as fast as I can."

"Be careful, Maedron."

"Pray to the Starmaker that we've made the right choice."

Trinafar and Volissen stayed crouched over, clambering over and between the rocks while trying to keep below the edge of the grassy slope and out of sight. Trinafar tried not to think of the spaces between rocks that were waiting to grab her ankle and twist it if she slipped. She stumbled and almost stabbed herself with the shadow-knife. *I need both hands for this! I'll have to let the knife go.* As it fell from her hand she saw it evaporate in a stream of black smoke before it hit the ground. Her thigh started aching where the flesh had been ripped away.

She started breathing hard – suppose Rulidh was with this search party, he'd do worse than a life-candle spell if he caught her. Even if he wasn't she could still be caught by someone else and turned over to him. That would be just as bad in the long term.

She realised Volissen was breathing just as hard and wondered what Peruch would do to her for what he would see as treachery?

Wriggling between two rocks she gasped in relief when she felt the typical sensation of being near a lacuna. She turned in place trying to localise the feeling. The surroundings didn't exactly match Volissen's description, but that had been rather vague. She was definitely close to a lacuna.

"I've got it," called Volissen from a gap between two stone pillars. "It's here."

"I know! I can feel it. You go first – Don't argue, just go."

Trinafar watched Volissen push into the tight space between the rocks and vanish.

She shouted Maedron's name as loudly as she could.

Where is he?

Falling rocks clattered behind her and she turned to see Maedron jump from one of the pillars. He didn't jump far enough to land securely on the sand. One of his feet came down on a loose rock. It rolled and she saw his foot twist into a position that made her wince. He grunted in pain as his ankle collapsed under him and he fell. When he tried to rise and put weight on that leg he staggered.

"Go, my lady. They're close."

"Not without you. Come on, lean on me."

"Never mind me. Go!"

Trinafar ignored Maedron's instructions and dragged him onwards. Together they lurched towards the lacuna. Maedron turned enough to force Trinafar through it first, then he fell through himself. It was only when he stifled a grunt of pain that she realised he had another injury as well as a twisted ankle. There was a crossbow bolt in his shoulder.

She snatched his sword from him and held it up, pointing at the lacuna. A goblin partly emerged. He screamed as he materialised around the iron blade. Then he fell backwards through the lacuna, the weight of his limp body dragging the sword from Trinafar's hand.

The sensation of proximity to a lacuna vanished.

"We're safe," she gasped. "That was close."

"The tide must have come in fast, my feet are wet," said Maedron. "We've got to climb."

"Can you manage?"

"I will have to, won't I."

RECOVERY

Fergus forced his eyes open and quickly closed them again because it was too bright and everything was blurred. He blinked several times and his vision cleared enough to let him see what the source of the light was. It was the moon, two days past full, riding high in the cloudless sky.

He tried to push himself up to a sitting position, but something prevented him rising and his arms wouldn't support his weight. He slumped back down on to something soft and, after a moment's confusion, realised he was wrapped in a blanket.

"You're in a real mess, aren't you?" said a deep voice to his left. He turned his head in that direction.

The blurred shape he saw standing there resolved into an elf when he blinked again. *Scarlet crest and brown feathers! I don't think I've met an elf with that colouring before, have I? Who is he?*

"Mess?" he said, or tried to. It came out as a croak from his dry throat.

"Congratulations," said the voice. "I had a bet with myself whether you'd say 'Who are you?', 'Where am I?', 'How did I get here?', or 'What happened?' You've spoiled my little wager by thinking of something different to ask, so I guess you win."

Fergus managed to croak, "Water."

"Oh, sorry. I should have thought of that." The mystery figure helped Fergus to sit up and drink from a thin-walled ceramic flask beaded with moisture. The water it contained was cold enough to make his teeth ache.

"What do you mean by saying I'm in a mess?"

"Well, just look at you – a shapechanging cross-breed with iron poisoning and under a geas staggering along a country lane not sure of where he's going. That's not something you see every day."

"Who are you? What happened?"

"Ah! I was sure you'd get to one of the standard

questions sooner or later! You can call me Dhugalt. I was ten, maybe fifteen, yards away from you when you started staggering all over the road, obviously in some sort of difficulty. You wandered off the road into a lane, tripped over your own feet and collapsed into the ditch alongside the path. Nobody else seemed to pay any attention. I expect they thought you were drunk, but I saw the stain of iron poisoning spreading up your arm and I thought I should do something about it."

"I'm grateful for your help." said Fergus, "I'm indebted to you. How can I repay you?"

Dhugalt smiled. "What about your geas?"

"Well, it has to take priority. However, as long as you don't ask me to do something against the interest of Cridhe Igrainid of Eideann I will do whatever necessary to meet my obligation to you."

"For someone only recently arrived in Tirog you show a good understanding of obligations and indebtedness."

"How do you know I've not been here long?"

"Because you told me. You've been delirious for three days and said all sorts of things about yourself and your companions during your ravings."

"Three days!"

"Yes. Your friends left you behind when they couldn't find you."

"They'd have been looking for me. How did they not see me?"

"I had no idea why three people who'd been hiding under a cloak were trying to find someone who was injured. They could have been your enemies. I thought it better to hide you."

"You saw through their cloak!"

"Well enough to know they were there but not to recognise them. It's not too difficult if you know what you're doing. I'm sorry if I spoiled your plan to meet up again, but you were obviously in no condition to go with them. I decided it would be better to heal you. So I kept you hidden and let them go on their way.

"Did they get through to the second world safely?"

"Now how would I know that? I was here looking after you."

What else did I tell him? Did I say anything about the NEbox? Where do I go now? How do I get back to tell Igrainid what's happened?

"Don't worry," said Dhugalt. "Your secrets are safe with me. Travel with me for a bit and I'll get you back to Eideann. I'm going there anyway. Igrainid will be expecting me to turn up sometime in the next couple of weeks. You'll be wanting to tell her your story, and it's also where you're most likely to meet your friends again."

"Why are you being so kind to a total stranger?"

"Two reasons. One is that I hate iron poisoning; the other is curiosity. I want to learn more about this gadget you think is so significant. Don't worry. You haven't said much about it, at least not much that makes sense to me. I could force you to tell me but I don't like to compel people to do things they don't want to."

Fergus felt his head spinning and slumped back with a mutter of apology to Dhugalt.

#

The next time he woke it was dark except for the streamers and curtains of green and orange twisting and waving in the sky. They provided enough light to see by. Fergus looked around and saw Dhugalt sitting on the trunk of a fallen tree watching the aurora.

He freed himself from the blankets piled over him and sat up. The effort involved produced a grunt and attracted Dhugalt's attention.

"Beautiful, isn't it?"

Fergus nodded in agreement. He shuffled across to sit next to Dhugalt, dragging the blankets with him because it was cold, and made himself as comfortable as he could on the tree trunk.

Dhugalt passed him a flask, saying "That'll warm you up."

Fergus sniffed it, felt his eyebrows rise and took a small sip. It was a thick, sweet liquid that tasted of whisky, heather and honey. It slid easily down his throat and, as Dhugalt suggested, it did warm him.

"What's that?"

"It's a concoction they make up north, around Shettan. They call it The Spirit of Heather. I'm rather fond of it."

"I'm not surprised. It's delicious."

They sat in silence for a bit, then Fergus remarked, "Aberdeen has a reputation for being a good place to see the aurora. It looks as if the same is true of Obharden."

"They're really the same place," said Dhugalt, "so it's not surprising."

The two of them sat entranced by the display for more than an hour, until it faded shortly before sunrise.

"A blessing from the Starmaker," sighed Dhugalt. He sat quietly for a while and Fergus thought he was meditating.

Twenty minutes or so later Dhugalt stood up and said, "Now, how about breakfast? Then we'll get going."

#

Fergus didn't recognise the lane that took them to the road, or the road itself, and said as much to Dhugalt.

"That's not surprising. You were in a bad way and almost unconscious. I really don't know how you managed to keep on your feet for as long as you did. I know many people who would have succumbed to the poison much faster."

"I don't understand," said Fergus, "You say I was suffering from iron poisoning and I've got to accept you know what you're talking about. The thing is, I've worked with raw iron and iron tools for years without any problems. How could I suddenly become susceptible?"

"Ah! I'm afraid that was probably Maedron's fault ..."

"You know Maedron!"

"Oh, yes, I know him quite well. In fact we are related. It's a complicated relationship over a couple of generations but we do have several ancestors in common. I'm sure he didn't intend to poison you. I can understand why he would want to acknowledge his debt to you, but the way he did it was a bit more extravagant than necessary. He's always been prone to grand gestures and sharing blood with you is just that."

"That doesn't explain about the iron poisoning."

"Well, somebody suddenly developing a sensitivity to iron isn't something I've come across previously, or heard about, so I'm not sure exactly what happened. I think it must have been a combination of the potential susceptibility inherited from your mother plus exposure to an elf's blood and Maedron's use of an iron knife to create the blood bond."

"So I've got to avoid iron from now on, have I."

"I'm not sure. As I said, I haven't come across this situation before. You might be able to handle iron safely but, equally, you might not. The only way to find out is to try it. I'm sure you will at some stage, but you must be very, very careful when you do and have somebody with you to treat you if necessary."

Nobody paid attention to them as they turned right out of the lane and joined the sparse stream of people on the road.

Fergus stopped when they got in sight of the bridge. He recognised it and realised they were heading back the way he had come, towards Obharden.

"Don't worry," said Dhugalt when Fergus said they shouldn't be going there. "It's quite safe. If you want I can keep you cloaked while we're in Obharden but it's not really necessary. Neither Peruch or Rulidh will dare to attack any companion of mine."

"Are you that powerful or that important?"

"Yes, to both," replied Dhugalt in a matter-of-fact tone. "I expect you've heard of magi."

"But ..."

"Yes, I know – they're a myth. That's a belief we encourage but, in fact, we *are* real."

"But, if you keep yourselves secret, why are you telling me?"

"We do like to keep our existence secret, and you will forget about me being a magus when we eventually part company. In the meantime, while we are together, it's easier if you do know. It avoids me continually having to make you forget. At the moment, and for as long as you're travelling with me, you can know what I am. However, you'll find you're unable to mention it to anybody."

"Why the secrecy?"

"Simply because if everyone knew about us we would continually be asked to produce miracles and cast spells others can't. We have a more important function than that – and I'm not going to tell you what that is."

"But …"

"Yes?"

Fergus, rather hesitatingly, said, "I don't want to insult you, but you've just contradicted yourself. Earlier you said you don't like to compel people, and now you said you make them forget you."

Dhugalt frowned. "I didn't say I liked making people forget. It's just something that goes with being a magus. Now, let's keep moving. I want to visit Obharden, and Dundhe before we get to Eideann."

"Do we have to go to Dundhe? I've heard Cridhe Ghara is intolerant of cross-breeds."

"He is. But the same applies to him as to Peruch. He won't risk my displeasure by mistreating you. Come on," said Dhugalt, starting towards the bridge. "I'd like to get to Luchairt Obhardenan tonight."

#

Fergus was still apprehensive about meeting Peruch and Rulidh again, despite Dhugalt's reassurances. He stopped when, about an hour before sunset, he recognised the building that held Volissen's office and realised they were already within the borders of Luchairt Obhardenan.

"What's wrong?" asked Dhugalt. "You're not still worried about their reaction to seeing you again, are you?"

"Yes, I am rather. Particularly Peruch's reaction. He was really put out by the message I brought from Igrainid."

"Well, if you feel that strongly about it, I'll cast a glamour over you. Stay in the background, act like a servant and they won't pay any attention to you."

"I …"

"Trust me."

I suppose I must.

Fergus followed Dhugalt through the Luchairt to Peruch's base. He felt a bit more comfortable when he saw everyone making way for them without hesitation. Even the guards at the door of the throne room deferred to Dhugalt and stepped aside to allow them immediate access. There was a gnome speaking to Peruch when they entered. He stopped talking and, with no fuss, left the room.

Peruch stood and said, "Dhugalt, I've been expecting you. As always, you are welcome to Obharden. How may we assist you?"

Fergus was, briefly, surprised by the deference Peruch showed. Then he stopped thinking about that, or about anything else, when his attention was caught by the maze woven into the carpet in front of the throne. He was vaguely conscious of time passing as his eyes followed the recursive loops over and over and over again. However, time wasn't relevant and he just kept on mentally tracing and retracing the curves.

He was only marginally aware of the arrival of Rulidh about half an hour later and, with his mind still entranced, the three-way conversation that resulted meant nothing to him. It wasn't until Dhugalt broke it by snapping his fingers that he was free of the carpet's spell and became aware of where he was. The audience was over. He followed Dhugalt from the throne room and was startled to see the sun had set and something like three hours had passed.

"We'll stay here tonight," said Dhugalt, "and head for Dundhe tomorrow." He led Fergus through the buildings of the Luchairt to a guest room and settled into a sofa with a sigh of relief. He poured a few drops of Spirit of Heather into a cup of tea, took a sip and sighed contentedly. "I'm glad that chore is over. Of the nine Domains and Realms I visit regularly this is the one I like least. Peruch isn't one of my favourite people, and I always try to move on as quickly as possible.

"Was he angry about Trinafar and the others escaping?" asked Fergus.

"He barely mentioned them except as welcome guests who stayed for a few days and have now gone home."

"But that's not true. They were forced to come here and were kept prisoner."

Dhugalt turned to Fergus and said, "I know you believe they were captives but, when you told me that, you were delirious. I didn't pay too much attention to what you were saying because you were rather incoherent. The way Peruch and Rulidh behaved and spoke gave me no reason to doubt them."

Fergus started to argue that Peruch was going to use Trinafar as a hostage. He didn't have time to do more than start talking when Dhugalt stopped with his tea cup halfway to his lips. It looked as if his attention was somewhere far beyond Fergus.

ARGUMENT

There was a dispute in the place-that-doesn't-exist. Two of the Eleven had arrived more or less simultaneously to take advantage of the place as an observation point. Unfortunately, they couldn't agree on what to observe.

One of them was an advocate of trying to do something about the incipient worldline shift. Although she admitted to being uncertain what they could do she did feel strongly that they should try to do something.

The other claimed that the resurgence of the sidhe supremacy movement was a more important issue as, unlike a worldline shift, it was something they *could* deal with. He insisted that there was nothing the Eleven could do about inheritance anomalies or whatever was going to happen to Tirog and the second world; though he agreed it was an important problem, he also insisted they should ignore that particular issue unless somebody came up with new insight.

More of the Eleven joined their colleagues in that place as soon as it became evident there was a problem. The intensity of the debate was such that they were drawn in whether they wanted to join in or not.

Sumethla favoured dealing with the sidhe supremacy movement first. She said it was the most important thing they could do. She named six Cridhe in southern Alba and north-east Anglaya who were involved. Two of those she identified were Peruch of Obharden and Ghara of Dundhe. Because both of them were in the territory covered by Dhugalt he was the subject of a powerful attack by those on that side of the ongoing argument.

The pressure applied to him increased, until he started feeling very insecure. He only managed to save himself by letting the Eleven know he was in Obharden, and already in place to deliver an ultimatum to Peruch.

The meeting ended with three of the Eleven still thinking Dhugalt should be ejected from the Group and

Dhugalt feeling the pressure from the halo of magi around the non-place.

Sumethla pointed out it would take time to get anybody else in position to squash Peruch's plot and they might as well take advantage of Dhugalt being where he was.

Her last words before the place-that-doesn't-exist vanished again were addressed to Dhugalt, and were to the effect that he was lucky to be in the right place to take action immediately.

on to dunðhe

Dhugalt's attention returned to the room in Luchairt Obhardenan and he completed the movement he had started, lifting the cup to his lips and drinking from it.

"You went – away – for a moment," said Fergus. "What happened? Are you alright?"

"Yes, yes I am, but that was uncomfortably close."

"What was?"

"I was pulled into a meeting of the Group of Eleven – I suppose you could call it the ruling body of the magi, but that's not really an accurate description. It was a pretty contentious meeting and I barely survived the experience. What was said there makes me think you had better tell me more about how Maedron and Trinafar ended up here."

Fergus described in detail how Trinafar and Maedron had been captured, how they had been forced to accompany Rulidh to Obharden and what Rulidh had said about applying pressure on Igrainid.

"Rulidh wanted to use his capture of Trinafar to force Igrainid to support him and Peruch because they want to conquer and rule Aberdeen as well as Obharden."

"Hmm. You didn't say anything about that when I was looking after you."

"I didn't? I'd have thought that would be on my mind and come out when I was delirious."

"What you've just told me fits with what I heard during the meeting of the Eleven. I need to look into this some more," said Dhugalt. "Come with me."

They returned to the throne room through the torrential rain that had started falling in the last few minutes. Peruch and Rulidh were still discussing some of the things Dhugalt had told them during their meeting.

"I have heard something disturbing," said Dhugalt. "Fergus tells me you are planning an attack on the second world. Is that true?"

Peruch glared at Fergus then addressed Dhugalt.

"I saw he was with you earlier but I don't pay attention

to cross-breeds, particularly when they're entranced by something as simple as that carpet. Look at him, caught in the maze again. Where did you find him? He was with Lady Trinafar's party and I thought he went with them when they left."

Dhugalt snapped his fingers to release Fergus from the effects of the carpet and asked him to explain again how Trinafar and Maedron had come to visit Obharden.

"His story doesn't match yours," said Dhugalt to Peruch when Fergus stopped speaking.

"He's a cross-breed. You can't believe anything he says."

"I have no reason to disbelieve him. Everything else he has told me has been true."

"How do I know you're not putting words in his mouth?"

"Stop trying to evade the issue. All that does is give me more reason to think there is something to what Fergus says. Tell me the truth."

"You've already decided against me, haven't you?"

"Cridhe Peruch, I strongly suspect, from your behaviour and from what Fergus tells me, that you are indeed planning an attack on the second world. I must warn you against this. The two of you are allowed at present to know I am a magus, but I am more than that. I can permit you to know of the Group of Eleven and tell you I am a member of it. I have evidence from other members of your intentions. On behalf of the Eleven, I tell you what you are planning is forbidden. You *must* not do this. Do you understand?"

Rulidh started to say something but Dhugalt cut him off, saying, "You already know what it's like to be denied access to latent power. Imagine what it would be like if your Cridhe was deprived of the ability to generate it."

"You can't do that! It would affect the entire population of Obharden," said Peruch. "The Realm would be devastated."

"I'm glad you have enough sense to realise what effect it would have. The Eleven will make a bargain with you to leave you able to generate latency if, in return, you give up your idea of conquering the second world. Do you understand?"

Fergus hadn't seen anything of Dhugalt being other than helpful. He was astonished at the power and presence he exhibited when delivering the ultimatum to Peruch. *I'm glad he's not angry at me.*

"Why are the magi so solicitous of the second world?" asked Peruch. "It doesn't make sense."

"You don't need to know why. Just accept that you may not, under any circumstances, try to conquer any part of it. Your co-conspirators will be warned as well. Do you understand?"

There was a reluctant grunt of agreement from Peruch.

Dhugalt knew that the threat had always been enough to squash conspiracies in the past. Although the threat had never been carried out he deliberately gave the impression that it had been on at least one occasion. Because it was important to his own survival he was quite prepared to lie to Peruch so that he was in no doubt about what could happen to him.

Dhugalt said. "Be assured that you will be carefully watched and the Eleven will not tolerate any actions taken against the second world. I can't permit you to remember the details of this conversation. However, any time you think about it you will be aware that trying to conquer the second world is a bad idea. I urge you to pay attention to that feeling."

Dhugalt stalked out of the throne room, closely followed by Fergus.

"Will he change his plans?" asked Fergus.

"I hope so. We *will* remove his ability to generate latent power if he doesn't. We might be able to find an alternative way to supply Obharden with latency for a couple of years, until his daughter is old enough to be a Source but that will rely on the Group of Eleven doing something we have never done before. It could happen, but I'm not optimistic about it. I just have to hope he has enough interest in the safety of his Realm to take my warning."

#

The kitchens of Luchairt Obhardenan provided a more than adequate supply of food for Dhugalt and Fergus when they set off the next morning on their way to Dundhe.

Four days later they arrived at Cridhe Ghara's court. The warning about Ghara's attitude to cross-breeds was confirmed with the disdainful way he behaved towards Fergus. However, that was as far as it went. Dhugalt's influence was enough to ensure that Fergus wasn't mistreated.

Ghara was quite young and inexperienced. He had become the sole Cridhe in Dundhe only three years previously on the death of his mother. When questioned he confirmed that he was part of Peruch's scheme. He was quite matter-of-fact about it and didn't try to evade the issue. When questioned he trotted out the usual arguments that accompanied belief in the fallacy; all about how the fay, and other races among the sidhe, were superior to humans and deserved to rule the second world. The prohibition from the Group of Eleven came as a complete shock to him and his opinion of Peruch plummeted.

"If it wasn't that Obharden is so much richer and stronger than Dundhe," said Ghara, "I think this might be enough to spark a feud. It might yet because my council will not be pleased with this attempt to manipulate me, and them. We will discuss this issue in council but I can assure you Peruch will not receive any support from me or my Domain. Hurilt will regret coming the next time he shows up in Dundhe to try to influence me."

"Good," said Dhugalt, "Now that that's sorted out I will be on my way. I'm hoping to get to Eideann in three days."

hunt

With some difficulty, and some help from Volissen, Trinafar helped Maedron pull himself on to the top of the rocks. The bolt was still stuck in his left shoulder and he grunted in pain as it jiggled with every movement. Even getting into a position where he could touch it was painful and it was impossible for him to get enough of a grip on it to remove it.

"Leave it to me," said Volissen, taking hold of his right hand to keep it away from the bolt.

Very carefully she used magic to break the shaft as close to his skin as she could, then pulled his clothing aside to examine the wound. "I'm going to work it free," she said. "It's going to hurt."

"Do it," replied Maedron, gritting his teeth.

Using magic as delicately as she could, she teased apart the fibres of the muscle the bolt was embedded in and gradually eased it back along the entry track.

"Thank the Starmaker. It's a pile tip not a broadhead or a bodkin. It doesn't seem to have done as much damage as it might – it hasn't gone as deep as I feared. I think it must have struck without much force and at a pretty shallow angle to end up in that position, perhaps it was a ricochet. It was stopped by your shoulder blade. I don't think it has cracked the bone. If it has it's not a major fracture and, fortunately, it hasn't penetrated deep enough to damage your lung."

"Thank you," Maedron said, when she tossed the fragments away. "It feels a lot better without that there. I am indebted to you."

Volissen rummaged in her pouch and found the food she had put there. She used the cloth it was wrapped in to bind the wound.

Maedron tried rotating his shoulder and said, "It hurts but I can move it."

"What about your ankle?" asked Trinafar. Can you stand on it?"

He tried to get up but putting any weight on his ankle was painful. A couple of limping steps later he reported he didn't think anything was broken, "but I don't think I can walk on it for long."

"I'm sorry I can't do anything for your ankle except bind it. Unlike the shoulder I can't actually see whatever damage you've done.

"We're still in trouble," said Trinafar. "We're in the second world and two of us obviously don't belong here. We can't use either of the lacunae we know to get back to Tirog. I don't suppose you know of another one we could use, Volissen."

"Not close enough to be useful with Maedron having difficulty walking. The nearest I can think of is about twenty miles away."

"That's not good," said Maedron with a grimace. "I doubt if I can walk that far in any reasonable time."

"Volissen, we are going to have to rely on your magic to hide what you and Maedron are. Are you happy to cloak us again or would you rather use a glamour?"

"A cloak would be simpler."

"But it will be easier for us to lose track of each other," said Maedron. "Look what happened last time we used a cloak; we lost Fergus."

"This time we've got enough hands to go round. I can make sure nobody will see us."

"Can we rest for a bit?" asked Maedron. "Perhaps at that ruin we passed. It would give us a little shelter and give me a chance to heal somewhat before what's going to be a difficult journey."

"Don't know what the ruin will be like in this world, if it exists at all," said Trinafar, "but it's worth a try."

It was difficult for Maedron to struggle up the slope with his ankle hurting. He needed support. Because of their height difference this was usually from Volissen and they often had their arms around each other during their clumsy progress up the hill.

Relieved to find a ruin in more or less the same place they settled down, making Maedron as comfortable as possible. This ruin was bigger and rather more intact than the one they had seen in Tirog during their escape. It even had one wall standing to waist height to provide some shelter from the gradually strengthening sea breeze.

"Water, shelter, what more could we want?" asked Trinafar in an attempt to raise their spirits as she helped Maedron find a comfortable, or at least a not too uncomfortable, position.

"I'd be happier if we had more than one knife between us," said Maedron, "and I'd heal faster with some food in me."

"We've got this," said Volissen, producing several packets from a pouch at her belt. "I said we could bring food without arousing suspicion. It's not a lot, but it's all I could find quickly before we left the Luchairt."

Each packet contained a piece of trailbread with a cheese and pickle filling, a rather wizened looking apple and a double handful of nuts. Volissen gave most of the contents of her packet to Maedron, telling him he needed it more than she did.

"Once more I am indebted to you," said Maedron. "I acknowledge this and I promise to find a way to repay you."

Volissen nodded to him then looked around to see Trinafar near the stream, peering intently into it.

"I had hoped there might be fish in the stream," said Trinafar on her return to the ruin, "but there aren't."

She agreed with Volissen that Maedron was most in need of the food they had and ate only the nuts from her packet.

#

They rested at the ruin for two days, surviving on some gull eggs they found and a couple of rabbits Volissen caught with her magic. The water from the stream was drinkable but all they had to carry it in was one small flask and they had to make frequent journeys to supply Maedron with the water he needed. They tried carrying water by soaking a cloth in the stream and wringing it dry back at the ruin. It worked after a fashion. The water they squeezed from the cloth wasn't foul, but it wasn't really palatable. They soon gave up on that idea and used the cloth to bind Maedron's ankle instead.

His ankle improved, but after two days' rest he still couldn't put much weight on it for very long.

What they were going to do next occupied their thoughts and most of their conversation for those two days.

Trinafar suggested going to a village called Curath. She was an avid follower of the doings of the Imperial Family and knew Crown Prince Karl, Princess Consort Marianne and their two younger children spent some time every year at Curath, where they had a quiet estate in the foothills of the Cairga mountains. Although she didn't know for sure there was a station there she thought there must be, as trains were the Crown Prince's favoured method of travel.

Volissen complained that Curath was something like forty miles away, far too far for Maedron to hobble. Instead, she argued in favour of going south to get a train at Stonehaven. That was only about a dozen miles. She knew the East Coast Line from Stonehaven would take them to Dundee and from there they could get a fast service to Edinburgh.

Maedron suggested heading for the other lacuna Volissen knew about. The one she had described as being twenty miles away from Brig o'Dee. He admitted it was farther away than Stonehaven but thought it might be a faster way to get them back to Tirog.

It was Maedron's ankle that eventually decided for them. They dropped the idea of going to Curath. The notion of hiking twice as far as necessary into the foothills to an uncertain destination didn't appeal when the alternative was walking along a well made, albeit fairly busy road. Also, as he said, going south still gave them the choice of a train from Stonehaven or a lacuna to take them back to Tirog. They wouldn't have to make that decision for several days.

When they set out that evening under a darkening sky with the temperature dropping, their progress was slow. Maedron had to stop frequently to rest his ankle. He kept apologising for slowing them down and Trinafar had to tell him to stop blaming himself.

They had managed only about a mile and a half when they were forced to stop for the third time. The road skirted a small wood that provided a place to rest. They moved deeper into the trees until they were out of sight of the road and felt secure enough for Volissen to let her cloak lapse.

Maedron examined the swelling around his ankle as best he could in the gathering gloom. He said, "Normally I could do thirty miles in a day quite easily but at the rate we're going we'll be lucky if I can manage two. I'm really holding us back."

"We are making progress. It might not be as fast as you'd like, but we're getting there."

"Yes, my lady, but we've got to get you back to Eideann as soon as we can. It might be better if I found somewhere to rest while you go on without me."

"No!"

"I could build a hide in this wood and you could send somebody back to collect me when you get to Eideann."

"Forget it," said Volissen. "You are in debt to me …"

"I know it."

"I've had time to think about it and I've decided what you can do to meet your obligation. Until you do I'm not letting you out of my sight. Not because I think you won't pay your debt – I won't insult you by suggesting that, you're too honourable – but now I know what I want I'm staying close to you."

Maedron's crest and ear feathers stood up. He asked, "What is it you want of me?"

"Give me a child."

Trinafar stifled a laugh at Maedron's nonplussed expression.

"A child! Of mine! Are you sure?"

"Yes! I wouldn't joke about something as serious as

that. I have three children so far, but I want more. Eventually seven of course. I think you would make an excellent father for my fourth."

Trinafar had been surprised by Volissen's request and amused by Maedron's reaction. "It would be a good match," she said.

"Are you sure?" asked Maedron again.

Volissen snorted. "That's a silly question! Of course I'm sure. Your family is one of the most prestigious in Eideann. Don't you have any idea how desirable a child of your line is? I'd wager that every eligible woman in Eideann would jump at the chance to carry a child of yours if you made it clear you were interested. My lineage is quite good, but it isn't even close to being as prominent, as important, as yours. In fact the gap is so big that I wouldn't dare ask if it wasn't for your obligation to me." She paused then and, in a slightly quavering voice, said, "Am I asking too much?"

Maedron heaved himself to his feet with assistance from Trinafar, bowed to Volissen and said, "No, lady, it's not too much. I'm deeply honoured by your request. Since meeting you I have come to admire and respect you for your actions. The answer is yes, of course. I will grant your request, but I must ask you for enough time to get us back to Eideann so that we can observe the proprieties."

"That's acceptable."

"May I be one of your witnesses?" asked Trinafar.

"That would be a boon I wouldn't dare ask, given the disparity in our ranks – but it would be wonderful if you witnessed our pledge."

"After our recent experiences, I should think we could become friends. I would be happy to stand with you."

There was a catch in Volissen's voice when she said, "Shall we move on?"

"It will be dark soon."

"That means fewer people on the road. We might as well take advantage of that."

#

Another couple of miles later they were resting again when the stars started being obscured by a mist that gradually thickened. Dense, low, grey clouds moved in from the west and the temperature dropped rapidly. Lightning flashed on the horizon and thunder boomed in the distance. They shivered, not just from the cold but from a developing feeling of menace.

"I don't like this," said Maedron. "Those clouds are moving against the wind and it shouldn't be as cold as this, not at this time of year. I think we are about to witness a riding of the Hunt."

"But we're in the second world," said Volissen. "The Hunt doesn't ride here too, does it?"

"It does. In fact the Wild Hunt happens simultaneously in both worlds," said Maedron. He paused, looking thoughtful, then said slowly, "Because it's in both worlds the Hunt has even been known to provide a way between the worlds – like a temporary lacuna – I wonder … "

"Don't even think about it," said Trinafar.

"About what?" asked Volissen.

"He's thinking about trying to bargain with the Master of the Hunt for passage to Tirog."

Volissen gasped.

"You can't," she said. "It's much too dangerous. You can't challenge the Hunt. Especially not in your present condition."

"I know. I was just speculating."

"Well, don't. Remember you still have a debt to fulfil. You can't do that if you're dead, or assimilated into the Hunt."

It started to rain. At first it was just a light drizzle, but it soon got heavier, and looked as if it would get heavier still.

"Help me build some sort of shelter," said Maedron.

He bent a few flexible saplings over, wincing at the strain that simple activity put on his shoulder but working through it.

While Volissen held them in position with magic, he used his belt to tie the saplings together into a rough dome, then he started weaving branches and twigs into the structure. The others joined in and helped him fill in the gaps with a canopy of leaves. It wasn't perfect, but it shed most of the rain and they snuggled together under it for warmth.

Lightning flared again and again, getting closer. For a few minutes it was almost continuously bright and the accompanying thunder was deafening. About twenty minutes later the storm gradually moved away. The intervals between lightning and thunder became progressively longer. The rain slowed and stopped. The temperature rose a little.

"Thank the Starmaker," said Trinafar when minutes had passed since the last peal. "If that was the Hunt, it didn't find us."

Maedron shook his head. "That *was* the Hunt. Didn't you hear the horns and the hooves among the thunder, or feel the terror that accompanies the Hunt? We are very fortunate that it didn't come any closer."

"No, I didn't hear anything, but I had my hands over my ears most of the time trying to muffle the noise."

"Shall we go on?" asked Volissen.

"Yes," replied Maedron, "we'll warm up faster if we're moving. I'll try for at least another mile before we have to stop again."

He didn't manage any more than three-quarters of a mile and that was slow.

Subsequent attempts were even less successful. By sunrise, after stopping three more times, they had travelled a total of only five or six miles from the ruin and they were looking again for a good resting place.

"Look, over there," said Trinafar, pointing at a stony outcrop on the uphill side of the road. "Isn't that a cave up there? We could rest there all day. Let you recover as much as possible and move on at night."

"But at this rate it's going to take another four or five days to get to Stonehaven," said Maedron.

"Never mind how long it takes. The important thing is to get there. A day's rest won't hurt us. We've been putting too much stress on your ankle."

It was a cave that Trinafar had seen, although a shallow one barely worthy of the name.

"Now let's have a closer look at that ankle," said Trinafar when Maedron had struggled up the slope to the cave. "I think you've been making light of how bad it is."

She asked Volissen to provide some light and, with the aid of the gentle glow between Volissen's hands, examined his ankle. Poking, prodding and manipulating it provoked grunts of pain from Maedron.

"You're right," she said, "I don't think it's broken but the ligaments are badly stretched, the swelling is getting worse and the joint's unstable. I can move the bones in ways they're not supposed to go. Pity we don't have anything else to bind it with. That cloth isn't doing much good. Anyway, you're not walking on that for at least another day. Now, what about your shoulder? We've been ignoring that."

"It's a lot better. Still a bit stiff, but I can move it." Maedron swung his arm around showing a good range of movement.

"Good. At least something's going right."

A full day's rest without putting any weight on his ankle let Maedron recover enough to move on the following day. Volissen tried a magic binding to support his ankle, but she wasn't able to be precise enough with its application and it wasn't very successful. They had to keep encouraging him and every time he complained about how slowly they were travelling they reassured him they were happy to be making progress of any sort.

The sky clouded over that evening. It started raining. There was nowhere to shelter. The surface deteriorated. Their feet started sliding in the mud and that didn't do Maedron's ankle any good.

The rain got heavier and they struggled on.

Trinafar started worrying about being so exposed when they began to hear thunder in the distance. Lightning flashed ahead of them. "Now what do we do?" she asked.

"If the storm gets any closer we'll have to lie down otherwise we're potential targets," replied Maedron.

The thunder got louder as the storm got nearer and nearer. Trinafar started imagining she heard the pounding of hooves in the sound. Then she realised she wasn't imagining it, there really were hoofbeats – and blasts of sound from hunting horns.

"It's the Hunt," she shouted over the noise.

Maedron replied, "I know."

Her heart sank.

A particularly brilliant flash showed her a mass of mounted people charging towards them. She couldn't count them, but it was obvious they were outnumbered many times over.

Another flash and she saw they were surrounded. Wherever direction she looked in she saw a continuous stream of riders going widdershins around them.

A loud blast on a horn and the storm fell silent although lightning continued to flash. The rain stopped. The riders came to a standstill. There were about forty of them, most being elves or goblins although there were also two anthrops, two humans and a couple of fay.

The obvious leader, wearing a helmet adorned with a splendid rack of antlers, rode his enormous horse forward to meet them.

"What do we have here?" he asked in a guttural voice. "Name yourselves that we may know your quality and your destiny in our meeting."

None of them spoke until the Huntsman repeated his demand for them to name themselves and added, "I ride for the glory of Cerne the Hunter that his name be exalted on both sides of the divide in these lands of Alba. I ask for the third time, who are you?"

Maedron reached out and prevented Trinafar from stepping forward. "Allow me to reply, my lady," he said quietly. "All the tales say that the Master of the Hunt respects power and authority so I will show him I'm your servant and that you have the right to command me."

He stepped forward, bowed his head slightly, then straightened up and addressed the Master of the Hunt. "I have the honour to be bodyguard and protector to the Lady Trinafar Chiolet Fion Eideannach. The other lady, Volissen vul Birres, is also under my protection."

"And who are you that you claim to protect these honoured ladies when you can scarcely stand?"

"I am Maedron hur Misghel hur Marind of the House of Mochri and I am escorting these ladies to their home in Eideann."

One of the riders moved her horse forward to stand beside the Master's. "Maedron? Is that really you?"

"It is," replied Maedron blinking in surprise at being addressed by someone who apparently knew him. The rider removed her helmet to reveal she was an elf with a green crest and violet eyebrow feathers. He recognised her immediately and groaned inwardly while saying, "I'm surprised to see you in the Hunt, Fliorign."

"I won my place with the Hunt almost two years ago." She turned to the Master and said, "We are indeed fortunate today. I have fought this elf twice in the past. Although I bested him on both occasions, it was a close contest both times. I would relish an opportunity to meet him again."

"How say you, Maedron hur Misghel hur Marind. Will you meet Fliorign vul Gentiss vul Tarov once again?"

Maedron bowed and said, "It would give me great pleasure, Master. However, I fear I could not provide much entertainment for you as I had the misfortune to damage my ankle a few days ago and, as you noticed, I can scarcely stand."

The Master snorted. "That can be remedied if you are willing to submit to my touch and accept the pain that comes with rapid healing. In return I ask that you demonstrate your skill in single combat against my champion Fliorign vul Gentiss vul Tarov."

Maedron looked at Trinafar and said, "With your permission, my lady."

"The Hunt relishes bravery, Lady Trinafar," said the

Master, "be it with sword in hand or with words and deeds of courage in a difficult situation."

"What are the stakes?" she asked the Master.

"As they always are. A victorious challenger is free to go his own way or to join us as an honoured member of the Hunt. The loser dies or becomes bound to the Hunt, most usually as a steed or a hound. Rarely, a vanquished opponent who has shown his mettle may be accepted into the hunt as a Rider. The status within the Hunt of the loser of such a challenge is dependent on their performance in the bout as judged by my Riders."

Trinafar looked at Maedron, saw his crest flare and his eyebrow feathers flutter in the pattern the Domain Guard used to signify acceptance.

Trinafar took a deep breath, accepting that she had no alternative. She was frightened for him but knew he would do his best, and knew his best was very good. She nodded to Maedron, giving him permission.

Volissen stepped forward. She lifted her head to gaze into the Master's eyes. What she saw there made her shiver, but she persisted and said, "I too have a stake in this affair. Maedron is significantly indebted to me."

The Master of the Hunt looked down at her and asked, "Will you risk your debt?"

Volissen swallowed and said, "I will."

"Excellent. This will indeed be an event to savour and remember. In return I will undertake to bear you swiftly to Eideann whatever the outcome of the bout. Come, Maedron, accept the healing touch."

The Master's horse was big enough to tower over Maedron when he limped forward to stand at the Master's stirrup. The Master had to lean a long way down before he could lay a hand on Maedron's head. When he did Maedron shuddered and gasped. He doubled over then straightened up and lifted his head to look the Master in the eye.

The antlered helmet lifted again and the Master said, "It is well done. There have been those who have not been able to tolerate my touch. Some have collapsed and been unable to fulfil their side of the bargain. I am pleased you are not one of them."

There was a burst of thunder as the riders beat their swords against their shields or armour.

"You see how my followers appreciate your courage."

"Master, there is a lack of equity here," said Fliorign. "Although you have restored his health he is weaponless and I can see he has also been severed from any latent power. Will you remedy this imbalance?"

The Master turned in his saddle to look at Fliorign and growled, "He did not bargain for correction of either of these lacks."

"True, he did not. But the glory of this encounter is diminished if we are so obviously unequal."

"On the other hand, the poignancy of an hopeless task has its own splendour."

"It has. However, that redounds to the honour of the hopeless, and its inevitability diminishes the victor. I would prefer it if I earned the triumph. Will you grant me the opportunity?"

"Very well," said the Master after a prolonged silence during which his gaze moved from Fliorign to Maedron and back again. "I will agree to your request if any of this company is willing to lend Maedron hur Misghel hur Marind a sword." He looked round at the mass of Riders and shouted, "A sword lease is needed. Will any here grant this elf the opportunity for an equal contest?"

Many of the riders shouted their agreement to this proposal and Maedron was offered a choice from a range of swords. Some he didn't bother examining as they were obviously too short or too heavy for him. He handled all the others trying out their length, weight and balance. Those he found wanting in some respect he returned to their owners with his thanks for the offer. The one he settled on resembled his own favourite sword, a two-edged hand-and-a-half blade with a cruciform hilt. He was even happier with it when he saw the weaponsmith's mark on the forte – it had been made by the same hand as his own.

After Maedron had made his choice he bowed low to thank to the owner who said, "I am Husret hur Bilnoc hur Lurul."

Maedron blinked, he recognised this Rider's name. He had had a long and successful career as the captain of the guard in one of the Domains to the west of Eideann, but that had been forty-odd years ago.

Husret said, "My sword is called Anmhor. I trust you will use her well and wield her with honour."

Maedron lifted Anmhor in salute to the Master and said, "I am satisfied with this weapon."

"Now you need your magic restored. I will permit you to draw on my power for the duration of the duel."

"You are gracious," said Maedron. He bowed to the Master, feeling a sensation of gentle warmth developing at the base of his throat. It accompanied the availability of latent power for the first time since he had been cut off by Rulidh.

anywhere

Dhugalt entered the place-that-was-not for the next scheduled meeting of the Eleven with some trepidation. His welcome was as he anticipated, more or less. His colleagues demanded that he give an accounting of what he had accomplished in Obharden and Dundhe.

His description of his interview with Peruch and Rulidh was mildly criticised for telling lies to them. However, Sumethla supported him saying that any of them might do the same.

The magi who had been most antagonistic towards him during the previous meeting were still critical of him. However, their attention was distracted by news of yet another inheritance anomaly. The new report brought the number of anomalies to four, two each of short lineages and Failed Sources.

Wardlik had been one of the most aggressive of the Eleven when Dhugalt was under threat but he was now almost conciliatory. He hadn't changed his opinion about the importance of suppressing the superiority movement, but he seemed to have become even more interested in anomalous inheritance than previously.

Now that Dhugalt had dealt with the ringleaders of the conspiracy those who had that as a priority calmed their demands and shifted their attention to what everyone agreed was an imminent worldline shift.

Wardlik was startled and frightened when one of the Eleven wondered if it might be possible to cause an anomaly. The one who said this speculated that knowing how an anomaly came about might lead to better understanding of them and their significance. This idea was met with approval by a significant majority of the Group.

It didn't meet with Wardlik's approval at all. There was too much danger of revealing his activities in causing potential Sources to fail; he was certain he wouldn't survive if his activities were exposed. He was startled when another of the Eleven described a message she had received from her predecessor. It duplicated the one Wardlik had received on joining the Eleven. He wondered if anyone else had been left one.

The only thing that gave him any feeling of security was that, having studied the subject for years, he ought to be able to misdirect any ideas the others developed.

Wardlik didn't want to get into a private discussion so he left the place-that-didn't-exist as quickly as possible after the end of the meeting.

ᚦuel

"Clear the field," said the Master of the Hunt. His riders pulled back, forming a circle about thirty paces across. "Come, stand beside me," he told Trinafar and Volissen. "No harm will befall you."

Fliorign dismounted and let one of the riders walk her horse away. She strode over to where Maedron was standing and touched her right hand to her chest. "It's an unexpected pleasure seeing you again."

"I wish I could say the same," he replied. "I would avoid fighting you if I could. My duty and allegiance lie with Lady Trinafar, and this is an interruption I could do without."

"Do you not rejoice in the glory of conflict?"

"Not when it interferes with my duty. At present that lies with Lady Trinafar. I mean no insult to you when I say this meeting is an unwelcome distraction."

The Master told them to get ready. "You may use any magic you wish to supplement your swords. However, in order that we may enjoy the contest, I will render you constantly visible to the witnesses whatever cloaks, shields or glamours you employ. Any such spells you choose to use will still be effective against each other. Do you understand?"

Nodding their understanding of the conditions they touched swords, backed away until they couldn't quite reach each other and waited to be told to start.

The Master kept them waiting for several minutes. Maedron felt the tension building and let it flow over and around him, refusing to be distracted by it.

"Fight!"

Maedron disappeared behind the red haze of a shield and stepped to his left.

Fliorign jumped forward with an exultant shout, her sword flashing through the space where Maedron had been standing.

He wasn't there. His shield, made visible to the

spectators by the Master's magic, showed him moving more to his left.

A moment later he appeared about three feet away from where he had been. His sword clanged off Fliorign's knocking it upwards and away from him.

She spun around with the force of the impact and vanished behind a cloak of her own.

Maedron also generated a cloak and, from Fliorign's viewpoint, vanished.

For several minutes they flickered in and out of each other's view. When they were visible their appearances were brief and seemed to be intended to draw the other into a rash move. Then both of them vanished again and stayed invisible for a longer period. The haze of their shields showed Maedron moving gradually towards the centre of the circle and Fliorign prowling round the periphery.

When Maedron appeared near the centre of the circle, facing away from the Master he didn't disappear again immediately. He gazed around, sword raised in a high guard position, turning slowly. He appeared to be trying to get some clue as to his opponent's whereabouts from seeing where the riders were looking.

Suddenly Fliorign was there, running at full speed from behind him with sword extended. Then he vanished and reappeared, not where he had appeared to be, but a couple of feet to the side. His sword was already swinging towards her. He missed her by not more than a couple of inches as she ran past the spot where he had seemed to be.

She laughed, lifted her sword in salute and shouted, "A most excellent glamour! Well done." Then she lunged at him.

Their swords clashed and clashed again. For the next few minutes there was no magic involved, just swordplay of the highest standard. Both of them deflected the other's strikes. Every parry was followed by a quick riposte, their swords ringing like bells. They shifted back and forth, each of them gaining a step or two then losing them again in the face of pressure.

The Hunters shouted encouragement and appreciation of the combatants' skills.

The attacks slowed slightly as the efforts each made started to take a toll.

By mutual and unspoken agreement they moved a little apart to give themselves some time to recover.

Fliorign let her point drop and said, "You're still as good as I remember."

Maedron lifted his sword in salute to acknowledge the compliment and went straight from the salute to an all-out attack trying to beat her back.

She diverted the attack saying, "You almost caught me with that when we fought before! I'm not about to fall for it now."

"You can't blame me for trying."

"Indeed I don't. I remember our previous encounters with pleasure. Nobody has ever made me work harder to win."

They separated once again.

Fliorign vanished from Maedron's sight.

He remembered she had one weakness, something he had realised during the second of their previous encounters but had been unable to take advantage of before she won the bout. He hoped she still had a tendency to be impatient, so he hid himself behind his cloak and stood still. Sooner or later she would give him a clue to where she was.

A few minutes later he saw a brief flicker away to his left, close to where Trinafar and Volissen were standing. He had seen that twisting, flickering effect, like looking through imperfect glass, on previous occasions. It was caused by somebody trying to see through his cloaking spell. It had never worked; his cloak was a very, very good one, better than most. He knew the finding spell that caused the flickering but didn't want to use it in case Fliorign knew it too.

He moved slowly in that direction mentally preparing another spell he hoped would let him see exactly where she was.

The flicker appeared again. *I knew it! She* is *getting impatient.*

He eased himself a bit farther forward, very carefully and cautiously.

When he thought he was close enough he cast a spell which produced a swirl of dirt and grass erupting from the ground where he thought she was. He saw what he was hoping for, an empty space near the centre of the resulting disturbance where the debris couldn't go because that's where she was.

Got her.

He extended his sword and lunged, sweeping his blade in a tight circle as he did so.

An impact, accompanied by a shout of pain, proved he had hit Fliorign. Her cloak vanished. She was lying on the ground bleeding from a gash in her right arm. Her arm was broken just above the elbow and bone showed through the wound.

Cheers erupted from the circle of riders. The Master dismounted and walked over to where Fliorign was lying.

"My champion has failed."

She struggled to her feet. "Forgive me, Master."

"What is life without a challenge?" said the Master. "Any contest may result in a defeat. That is a truth that has to be accepted. Now your status in the Hunt depends on the wishes of the other Riders."

He took the borrowed sword from Maedron and threw it across the circle to its owner who plucked it out of the air. Then he bent over Fliorign and said, "I will heal you in accordance with the judgement of the Riders," and put his hand on her head.

Fliorign screamed as the Master's healing took effect. She fell. Her body twisted and changed. It was a horse, not an elf, who stood up.

The Master said, "Maedron, the Hunt accepts only those who have proved their valour and skill. You have done so and may join us if you wish."

"I thank you for the invitation, Master. I am honoured but I must respectfully decline. I already have a commitment I must keep."

The antlered helmet nodded and the Master of the Hunt

said, "I thought that would be your answer, and I respect your dedication to your duty. You will be welcome to join us any time in the next year and a day should you change your mind. Meanwhile, I will take you to Eideann as promised. I will also restore your ability to draw on latent power from any Source."

He mounted, reared his horse and shouted, "I dedicate this encounter to the Glory of Cerne and the reputations of Maedron hur Misghel hur Marind of the House of Mochri, and his companions."

The Hunt roared their approval.

The Master gazed at Trinafar and Volissen. "I respect your steadfastness in standing by your champion. I regret I cannot offer you membership in the Hunt but I can provide you with transportation. Each of you, find a rider who is willing to carry you and mount behind them."

The rider who had given Maedron his sword offered to provide him with a mount too. "I enjoyed your bout. Your use of it has enhanced the worth of my sword and won me the wager I placed on the outcome."

"You bet against your champion?"

"Why not? I wasn't the only one and it seems I was right to do so."

"True," said Maedron, "but the bout could have gone the other way, as it has done on the two previous occasions I have fought Fliorign. I thank you for your support and for the use of Anmhor. May she serve you well."

"Is Fliorign permanently changed?" Trinafar asked the Rider who offered to carry her on his horse.

"Not at all. Many of us in the Hunt have spent time in other forms than our original ones. Membership of the Hunt confers long life. She can wait out her penance and, sooner or later, she'll be an elf again."

"Is she aware of being an elf in the form of a horse?"

"Of course she is. What would be the point of the transformation if she wasn't cognisant of the punishment for failure?"

Trinafar shivered.

The Master of the Hunt sounded his horn, the storm started again and the riders rode into the sky in a swirling mass.

When they descended again it was by the side of Duston Loch in Tirog in early morning, about a mile and a half from Luchairt Eideann.

They watched the Hunt disappear into the sky with relief.

"I know we're not actually there yet," said Trinafar when the Hunt had gone on its way, "but it already feels like we're home. Let's go and tell mother what's happened.

Reunited

"Has Fergus got back?" asked Trinafar wrapping herself around her mother as soon as the three of them were safely in Igrainid's study with the door shut, Misghel in attendance and a Quiet Place spell invoked.

Igrainid stepped back out of Trinafar's embrace and said, "Fergus? No, I haven't seen him. Isn't he with you?

Trinafar slumped into a chair with tears filling her eyes, hugged herself and sobbed, "What can have happened to him?"

Maedron and Volissen started to tell Igrainid and Misghel how they escaped from Obharden. Then Trinafar joined in. She had some trouble speaking around the lump in her throat, particularly when they were describing how they had lost Fergus.

"He was so brave," she said, "Just imagine how he must have felt out there on his own, in a different world, separated from the only people he knew there and with no idea where we were. I wish I knew what happened to him."

"He's quite resourceful," said Igrainid. "He managed to get into Luchairt Obhardenan to take my message to Peruch. Don't give up on him yet."

It took the better part of three hours, and more than a few cups of tea, for them to finish relating the events in Luchairt Obhardenan and on the road after their escape from Peruch's clutches.

Describing how she had stunned the guards Volissen told Igrainid she was worried that, by assisting with the escape, she had destroyed the relationship between Eidean and Obharden.

She was relieved and breathed more easily when Igrainid said, "Nonsense! You behaved entirely correctly. It's Peruch and Rulidh who are responsible for the breakdown in our relationship. I will not send any more ambassadors from here to Obharden while they are in power. You are not to blame in any way."

The part of their tale about the encounter with the Wild Hunt produced an amazed reaction when they described the feeling of terror that accompanied being surrounded by the Huntsmen. "The Master of the Hunt has a presence which is difficult to resist. It's oppressive, sinister, commanding and just about unbearable," said Maedron. "The way he treated us was more generous than I expected. It makes me think he was in a relatively benign mood. If so, we were fortunate. I would hate to meet him in a bad mood. He even accepted my refusal to join the Hunt with more toleration than I imagined he would show."

To satisfy his father's curiosity, Maedron gave a detailed, almost blow-by-blow, description of his duel with Fliorign. Trinafar and Volissen helped him with comments about the parts of the duel they had been able to see but he couldn't.

"Father," said Maedron, "we owe Fergus so much. He showed us how to break the life-candle spell and he acted as a decoy during our escape. I hope he manages to get back here to Eideann. Whether he does or not I must tell you I took it on myself to adopt him into the family. I hope you will endorse my action."

Misghel's crest flared briefly then settled back in place and he said, "I admit he did well and deserves some reward, but …"

There was an awkward silence for a few moments before Igrainid diverted the conversation by asking Trinafar about her use of the shadow-knife and how she felt about killing a goblin.

With her head down, and speaking in a whisper Trinafar said, "I think I killed two, not one. The first was when we escaped from the guards in Luchairt Obhardenan and the other at the lacuna when a goblin came partly through and impaled himself on the sword I was holding.

She shivered, and went on to describe as best she could the sickening sensation of holding a blade as it took someone's life.

Igrainid commiserated with her saying she had never killed anybody personally but she had been forced on four occasions to condemn people to death and witness their execution. "It is one of the most horrific things I've ever had to do."

"I have something else to tell you, Father," said Maedron, "I hope you will welcome Volissen vul Birres to the associate lineage of Mochri. I am deeply indebted to her and, at her request, I have agreed to discharge my debt by fathering her fourth child."

Once again Misghel's crest flared, but he quickly regained his composure, bowed to Volissen and welcomed her saying, "That is something I'm happy to hear and support. It's about time my son fathered another child and you are a worthy partner."

Volissen sighed with relief, her ear feathers fluttering gently. Misghel's possible disapproval was the last barrier she could think of to having Maedron's child and here he was accepting her without demur.

"The House of Mochri has a tradition of making breeding pledges at the solstices under the gaze of the Starmaker," said Misghel. "Does that meet your approval?"

Volissen's agreement was rather breathless. With the next solstice only a week away there was much to do before the ceremony. She had to meet the senior members of House Mochri, which meant she needed a suitably impressive wardrobe. Despite the limited time available she was excited. Not only would Trinafar stand as her witness but Cridhe Igrainid would be present, something she could never have imagined. Then after the ceremony she and Maedron would go into seclusion for at least a month, until she was pregnant.

#

Three days later Igrainid sent for Trinafar, as she had done every day. The two of them were gradually coming to terms with the emotions generated during Trinafar's captivity.

When Trinafar walked into the room at the top of the Robhas Tower, she was startled to find Fergus there. She stopped for a moment then ran across the room to greet him.

Maedron and Duncan arrived soon after Trinafar. They weren't quite as effusive in their welcome, Maedron being satisfied with exchanging a clasp of wrists and Duncan settling for a hug and a hearty slap on his back. They were joined by Saefan and Dhugalt before Igrainid decreed that the meeting was big enough and sealed the door.

"When did you get here? What happened to you?" and similar questions were asked of Fergus. They didn't really give him time to answer one before another was asked.

"Enough!" said Igrainid, trying to restore some order to proceedings. "Let Fergus speak."

"Before he does, Cridhe," said Misghel, "I would like to make an announcement, if I may."

Igrainid raised an eyebrow at the serious tone in Misghel's voice and gave him permission to speak.

Misghel crossed his arms on his chest, bowed low to Fergus and said, "I wish to apologise to you for what I said when you left to go to Obharden. I have thought about it a lot and I've realised I was in error. Your courage and dedication to the Cridhe's service goes well beyond what any geas demands. I think I wronged you when we spoke of my mistrust of cross-breeds. When Maedron told me of it, I must admit that the idea of accepting you into the House of Mochri took me by surprise and my initial reaction was to repudiate the adoption. However, I have had time to think and I would like to set matters right. Please tell me your father's name."

Fergus was startled but recovered enough to say, "My father was called Brendan Monteith."

Misghel nodded. "That is a good, solid name which will fit well into the Mochri lineage. I wish to make my acceptance of you quite clear by stating openly, in front of Cridhe Igrainid Luschet Sarel Eideannach and other witnesses, that I welcome you, Fergus hur Brendan, into the House of Mochri."

Igrainid smiled, told Misghel she was happy to witness Fergus's adoption, then she went on to ask Fergus to tell them his story.

Because Fergus also wanted to be brought up to date on how the others had fared, the session turned into a retelling of everything that had occurred since Fergus had left them at Brig o' Dee.

The way Fergus and Maedron had used the NEbox to free Trinafar attracted a lot of attention. "Cridhe, is it possible," asked Duncan, "that the use o' the box in that way accounts for the premonition? Ye did say ye thought it might be involved somehow."

"I don't know," said Igrainid. "Premonitions are rare and, apart from the sensory assault that accompanies them, each seems to be different. I have never heard of the cause of a premonition being recognised until after the event that provoked it. Then it usually becomes obvious what the stimulus was. That isn't the case here and I rather suspect that the event hasn't happened yet."

"Also," said Saefan, "from what I've read about them, a premonition is about something that threatens, or otherwise relates to, a Realm or Domain as a whole. They're not relevant to just one person, are they, Dhugalt?"

Dhugalt nodded, agreed with Saefan and said, "Premonitions are mysterious and I can't explain what causes them. I am intrigued by what I've heard about this box of yours. Despite being delirious when I found him Fergus didn't say much about it. I'd like to hear more."

Duncan was puzzled by the way people deferred to Dhugalt. He had to be told who he was, and have what that meant explained to him.

"I think I understand," said Duncan. "With your permission, Cridhe, I'm willing to tell Dhugalt more if he will agree to keep it secret."

Igrainid was taken aback at the idea of someone putting

conditions on a magus but accepted Duncan's request when she saw Dhugalt smile and nod.

"I think I can agree to that." He got up from his chair, moved over to sit next to Duncan and was joined by Saefan. Fascinated as she was with the NEbox and what it could achieve she had been virtually inseparable from Duncan since Fergus left for Obharden.

Although there was already a Quiet Place spell in operation in the room Dhugalt cast another one inside it to produce what he called a Place of Silence. Not only were the three of them isolated in what appeared to be to be a more intense version of a Quiet Place but everyone else seemed to forget they were there. The conversation of the others returned to Fergus's account of his journey through Obharden and Dundhe and the attitudes of Peruch and Ghara. Within the Place of Silence the sole topic was the NEbox and what it could do.

The gathering gradually broke up but Dhugalt, Duncan and Saefan stayed in Igrainid's study for a couple of hours longer, still discussing the NEbox.

"I would like to learn even more about the box myself, Duncan. Its potential is amazing," said Dhugalt. "Perhaps you can spare me some time later today ..." Then he lifted his head, looked out the window and saw it was getting dark. "Oh, I hadn't realised it was so late. Tomorrow would be better, if that suits you."

ꝼeꝺꞅꞇ

A feast celebrating Trinafar's homecoming was held the next day in the Great Hall on the third floor of Caedmon's Tower. The room was packed with people from all the races of Eideann.

The Great Table was normally occupied by members of the Domain Council as well as Igrainid and her children. However, on this occasion, three members of the Council were displaced to the High Tables so that Maedron, Volissen and Fergus could be rewarded with places befitting their roles in rescuing Trinafar.

Igrainid had carefully considered who to seat where. Two of the three councillors who ended up at one or other of the High Tables were people who she was confident meant the statements of pleasure or relief they had expressed at Trinafar's safe return. The third was Hurilt, who made no pretence of his disapproval of Trinafar and her failure to be a Source. However, he was open and honest about it. Igrainid was more confident of his attitude than of some of the others she kept at the Great Table. She suspected a couple of them of being insincere and wanted to observe their behaviour.

The cascade effect of people being displaced to a lower ranking table didn't seem to bother anyone except those who were moved from one of the High Tables, but even they were pleased to be at a Domain banquet.

Fergus remembered Trinafar telling him the clothes they had been wearing during his previous meal with Igrainid hadn't been formal. He had been surprised by that. However, now he could believe it. All the women at the feast were wearing elaborate gowns of layered, soft, delicate fabrics in pale colours with a richly embroidered overdress in an intense shade of a primary colour. The favoured jewellery was multiple strands of pearls woven into intricately braided hair. The effect was overwhelmingly opulent and he wondered how much was real and how much due to glamours.

His own garments, again supplied for his use by a pair of salmads, consisted of a knee length linen tunic vertically striped in purple and dark-green and worn over soft suede trousers. A badge at his left shoulder, in the form of a starburst made from seven diamonds, was a gift from Igrainid. Misghel had a similar badge and told him he should wear no other jewellery with it. The badge was known as the Cridhe's Kiss and was a sign of Igrainid's trust. There were only three others in existence.

Duncan was seated quite a long way from the High Table, at one of the smaller side-tables. He had been declared a guest of the Domain by Igrainid and this probably should have entitled him to a higher place. However, he was also known to be the son of Rulidh Trischan Farnist and that counted against him in the minds of the people who obsessed about the details of precedence.

Dhugalt sat down next to Duncan ignoring the efforts of the steward who tried to seat him elsewhere. He made a tiny gesture, like flicking a fly away, and the steward wandered off apparently satisfied.

"Now, Duncan. Last night you started to tell me about the way the NEbox responds to magic. I want to know more about that. How did you discover that, and what else do you think you can do with it."

"I dinnae ken what's possible. I want tae see all sorts o' magic in action and work out how to reproduce it using the box."

"An ambitious project."

"Ye're no going to stop me doing it, are ye?"

"No – No, I don't think so. Learning more about the way the world works is always a good idea. I will help you as much as I can before I have to move on. I'll need to get to Crioch sometime in the next fortnight but the journey won't take me more than three or four days."

"Ye'll help me, but ye'll make me forget what I learn if it suits ye."

"If it seems necessary, yes."

Duncan sighed. "That could make everything I've accomplished irrelevant."

"Sorry, but one of the functions of the Group of Eleven is to try to keep the two worlds stable and the NEbox is a potentially destabilising influence."

"I can see how ye can think that, but I dinnae have tae like it."

There was a steady stream of people walking up to the Great Table between courses to speak to Igrainid, Trinafar or one of the others seated there. During one of the breaks an elf with a violet crest caught Duncan's attention as he approached Igrainid. *Who's he? I'm sure I've seen him before, and in the Cridhe's company too.* He was puzzled for a minute or so then he remembered it had been in the throne room. *I was shielded at the time and I couldn't hear what he said but I saw an expression on his face that didn't look as if he agreed with Igrainid. Right now he doesn't look all that pleased to see Trinafar.*

He pointed the elf out to Dughalt saying, "D'ye ken whae he is?"

"Yes. His name is Hurilt ... May the Starmaker forgive me! I had forgotten all about it."

"About what?"

"Cridhe Ghara mentioned Hurilt while Fergus and I were in Dundhe. We were talking about Peruch's plan and Ghara said something about Hurilt being responsible for him joining the conspiracy. Ghara made it clear he thought Hurilt had deceived him and said he wouldn't be welcome in Dundhe in the future. He's got to be the same person. I've never met, or heard of, anybody else with that name, certainly not in Eideann or the other Domains and Realms I visit."

"D'ye mean he's a traitor?"

"I can't think of another explanation."

"Shouldn't we warn Igrainid that there's a traitor on her Council?" said Duncan.

"How? If we accuse him all he has to do is deny it and then he's been warned of our suspicions. Who knows what he might do."

"I hae an idea," said Duncan. "He might have picked

up some knowledge o' the NEbox and its capabilities during meetings of the Council, but he cannae ken everything it can do. Suppose we tell him it can separate truth and falsehood and convince him it can do that. Ye could ask some questions ye know the answers to and make the box change colour according to the truth or otherwise of the answers you get."

"And then I can ask him to deny being part of Peruch's plot – Yes!"

"He won't want tae admit it but he cannae risk the box saying he's lying. We've got him either way."

Duncan took advantage of a gap between courses to approach Saefan and whisper to her that it would be a good idea to convene the Domain Council after the feast. She looked at his expression and said, "This is something serious, isn't it?"

He nodded.

"Consider it done."

#

"Thank you all for coming," said Igrainid as the Council found their seats in the throne room. "Saefan, you asked for this meeting. What is it about?"

"I asked on behalf of Duncan. He doesn't have the status to do so himself but, I understand, he has discovered something important."

"Duncan? Explain."

"Aye, Cridhe. I have made a new discovery with the NEbox …"

"Not that damned box again," said Hurilt.

"Yes. That box again. I've been working on it some more. With the changes I've made the box is now capable of distinguishing truth from lies. This new ability, which I can demonstrate easily …"

"Nonsense," yelled Hurilt.

"… means we can use the box to confirm Dhugalt's discovery of a traitor in this council …"

Duncan was forced to stop talking as almost everyone

in the room objected vociferously to the idea that any one of them would be false to Igrainid.

"Silence!" Igrainid's command needed amplification with a spell before it was effective.

She went on to say, "What do you mean, Duncan? Explain yourself."

"Cridhe, we hae evidence that there's someone on this council whae's part o' Peruch of Obharden's plot tae subdue and rule the second world."

"That's a serious accusation."

"Aye, it is. Let me prove it tae ye."

Igrainid frowned then nodded. "You have my permission."

Duncan took a NEbox from his pocket and passed it to Igrainid saying, "Cridhe, please turn it on and write your full name on the screen."

She did so then twitched and almost dropped it when the box turned a bright sky blue.

"That means the statement written on the screen or said aloud is true. Now write something not true."

Igrainid didn't say what she had written but she twitched again when the box turned bright red.

Dhugalt's claim to be a magus made the box turn blue again, then Duncan provoked a bit of laughter when he turned the box red claiming to be a dwarf. When he insisted it was true, and added, "I was born in Aberdeen," the box started flashing alternately red and blue.

"I suppose that means your last statement was a mixture of truth and falsehood," said Igrainid."

"Yes, Cridhe. I *was* born in Aberdeen but, obviously, I'm not a dwarf."

"Is everyone satisfied that the box can recognise the truth?"

"With your permission, Cridhe," said Dhugalt and, when she nodded, he said, "Cridhe Igrainid, how many children do you have?"

"Seven."

The box stayed blue."

"Lady Saefan, how many younger sisters d'ye have?"

"Two."

The box turned red and stayed that way until Saefan corrected herself saying, "No, that's wrong, Trinafar is the only one of my sisters who is younger than me."

The blue returned.

Duncan bowed to Igrainid and asked, "Are ye satisfied that the box can tell the difference between truth and falsehood?"

Igrainid hesitated briefly then said, "Yes, you've convinced me. Tell me about this 'traitor'."

Duncan took a deep breath, bowed again and said, "With your permission Cridhe, I must ask Councillor Hurilt if he is associated with Cridhe Peruch's scheme to dominate the second world?"

Hurilt scowled and licked his lips, but said nothing.

"Councillor Hurilt. I ask again, are ye associated with Cridhe Peruch's scheme to dominate the second world?"

No response.

Every eye in the room was focussed on Hurilt. Maedron and Misghel stood and put themselves between Igrainid and Hurilt.

"Hurilt," said Igrainid. "This is the third time of asking. Are you or are you not involved in this plot? Will you respond, or is your silence a response in itself?"

When he still didn't answer layer upon layer of sparkling silver and blue threads surrounded him as at least five people shielded him.

Igrainid leaned forward to take a close look at Hurilt. She shook her head, looked at Misghel and told him, "Take him to the dungeon."

"With your approval, Cridhe," said Misghel. "I think that, before anyone leaves this room, we should all swear we are not involved in Peruch's plot. I am willing to go first."

Everyone else clamoured for a spot in the impromptu queue that formed.

Dhugalt spoke over the noise and said, "Igrainid, actually you don't need to interrogate anyone else."

"Why not? I don't suspect anyone of being a traitor, but

then I didn't suspect it of Hurilt. I need to know if there is another among us."

"I doubt if there is. I must confess that I had reason to suspect Hurilt, but no proof. This performance with the box was just that, a performance, intended to trap him into revealing himself. The box can't distinguish truth from fiction any more than any of us can. I provided the colours according to my knowledge of the correctness of the answers everyone provided. If you think about it you will realise I knew the correct answer to every question or statement the NEbox responded to."

"But – if he hadn't panicked …"

"He would have walked away apparently innocent. I hope you can forgive me for taking that risk."

Igrainid said nothing for a few minutes, then she sighed. "I suppose I can. But, please, don't do anything like that to me again."

"You should also thank Duncan since it was he who raised my suspicions and who devised that little charade."

"I will, although I wish I didn't have to. I would never have thought Hurilt a traitor. He's been a useful irritant on the Domain Council for years. Annoying, but I would have said harmless. I suppose Peruch must have offered him rulership of some part of the second world. What am I going to do with him?"

"Question him, then banish him to Obharden. Let him enjoy Peruch's company. If you don't think that's enough and want to punish him more I will remove his ability to use latent power from any Source."

"But …"

"I will also remove the memory of this meeting from everyone present so that nobody will believe that the NEbox can distinguish truth and falsehood. That means Hurilt can simply have made a mistake and given himself away."

"I suppose that's best," sighed Igrainid.

OpEN COURt

Twenty-odd people were waiting in the throne room for their opportunity to ask a favour of Cridhe Igrainid. Trinafar was the highest ranking and, as such, was first in line.

"What do you want of me?" asked Igrainid as Trinafar knelt in front of the throne.

"Mother, I want to go back to the second world to carry on with my research. May I have your permission to do so?"

Igrainid frowned. "I have already given you my permission. When you traded Fergus's service for a geas binding him to me I agreed you could spend another year and a day in the second world as recompense. Why do you think it necessary to ask again?"

Fergus, who was one of those waiting for his chance to speak to Igrainid, shivered a bit at the displeasure in Igrainid's voice. *She couldn't break that agreement with Trinafar, could she? Trinafar did tell me powerful fay could transfer promises and obligations to subordinates to avoid having to fulfil them, so I suppose someone as important as the Cridhe could. But surely she wouldn't treat her daughter like that, would she?*

"I do not think it necessary, mother. However, so many unexpected things have happened recently that I wanted confirmation so that those who still doubt my status would find no reason to grumble at my continued presence in the second world."

Igrainid nodded thoughtfully. "Well argued. I would prefer it if you stayed in Eideann but your request does make sense and I will hold to my agreement. You may go to the second world and stay there for up to a year and a day."

"Thank you, Cridhe."

Trinafar rose to her feet, kissed her mother and stepped back. As she did so, Yuseth announced, "Fergus Monteith, Recipient of the Cridhe's Kiss, requests a boon." Then he gestured for Fergus to step forward.

Mildly astonished at being ranked so high among the

supplicants at the open court Fergus knelt in front of Igrainid.

"What is it you want of me, Fergus?"

"Cridhe, when I left the second world to come to Eideann with Lady Trinafar I left several things undone in Edinburgh. Nothing of great significance but I would like your permission to go there to sort them out, settle my debts and collect some books and tools. Then I would like to return to Eideann and live here permanently, if that is acceptable." When Fergus implied that he might not have leave to stay in Eideann Trinafar almost spilled the tea she had poured for herself. She was about to ask Fergus why he wouldn't expect to stay but her mother spoke first.

"You have done me and the Domain a great service. What makes you think other than you are a welcome guest here?"

"Late last night as the feast was breaking up I was on my way to my room when I overheard a group of at least five elves, possibly as many as seven, muttering about 'Trinafar's problem'. I don't think any of them were aware I could hear them. At least three of them agreed that I should be sent back to the second world as I had made a serious mistake in rescuing Lady Trinafar from Obharden."

Igrainid sounded very angry when she asked, "What did you do?"

"There was nothing I could do, Cridhe. I would have liked to give them a good thumping but they outnumbered me and they would have magic on their side. Also I didn't want to cause trouble in the Luchairt."

"Would you recognise them?"

"Yes. At least I think I'd recognise the leader. There was just enough light to let me see that he was a young looking elf with yellow and orange feathers."

Igrainid twisted round to look at Misghel who was standing behind the throne.

"Hisellan?"

"Could be," said Misghel. "He is a bit of a hot-head."

"Question him," said Igrainid, "and if it was him make sure that he and his cronies are in no doubt about Fergus's status here."

"With pleasure, Cridhe."

"Show me your hand, Fergus."

He stretched his arm out towards Igrainid and felt a tingle at the place where she had bestowed her kiss.

"There, Fergus. The guards at the lacuna will see my mark. It will act as a token and permit you to pass in either direction."

"Thank you, Cridhe. I am relieved to have your permission to come and go. I don't want to let people like that drive me away."

He stood up, bowed again and backed away from the throne to make way for the next supplicant.

Igrainid acknowledged a new ambassador from the adjacent Domain of Bordiss and welcomed him to Eideann. She then refused Misghel's request to increase the size of the Domain Guard; gave Naod the gardener permission for a new planting of trees along the Luchairt Way and adjudicated a couple of property disputes before bringing the open court to an end.

Fergus and Trinafar found Duncan waiting for them in the Quiet Place in the garden and brought him up to date on the results of their appeals at the court.

"When are ye going tae take advantage of your permission tae travel between the worlds?" asked Duncan.

"I haven't decided yet, but it'll be sometime soon."

"I'm planning on going to the second world tomorrow," said Trinafar. "Why don't we go together?"

"I'd like that."

"And what about you, Duncan? You must be wanting to get back to Aberdeen and sort out NorEast, aren't you?"

"Aye, Lady, but I'm no in a hurry. I want tae learn as much aboot magic frae Dhugalt as I can while he's still around."

"Do you think what you learn from him will help you stand up to your father?"

"Och, aye. It'll dae that fine! I'll no be doin' what he wants just because he wants it. I'm done wi' being compliant. If he wants tae force me tae do something he'll need tae use magic on me – and he'll get a surprise if he does. I've had a few ideas about stopping that."

With Trinafar and Fergus listening with interest, Duncan described an enhancement Dhugalt had helped him make to the NEbox. He told them the latest version of the box had a new ability. As well as allowing the alteration or erasure of existing magic it allowed the holder to draw new magic on the screen.

He demonstrated this to the others by drawing a spell that lifted a piece of gravel from the ground and brought it to the table top without him touching it. The lifting spell looked like any other they had seen except that the magic appeared on the screen as dull red lines and not the usual violet. The movement was rather jerky and hesitant, but it did work. Duncan explained it was erratic because the interface with the tactomer sheet couldn't cope with fine detail. "I havnae learned the structure o' many spells yet and the ones I ken are relatively crude. But, thanks to Dhugalt, I'm getting there.

"He's helped me tae install twa new spells on my box. He approves o' them and says they should stop my faither, or anybody else, casting a compulsion spell on me. One of them makes the box into a mirror for magic and reflects any spell back on the caster."

"That'll make him sit up and take notice."

"Aye, it will. The other spell I've got acts like a sponge. It doesnae dae anything except soak up the caster's magic. It wid be nice if it made the absorbed magic available to the person holding the box but a' it can dae the noo is dissipate it. Using the absorbed magic will need finer control than I hae at present. Both o' thae spells are permanently active on my NEbox."

"The effect of those spells, particularly the mirror one, must be like cutting the caster off from latency," said Trinafar. "Are you going to make the same changes to the other box?"

"I cannae dae that yet. I dinnae hae ony mair tactomer. I'll need tae get tae the workshop in Aberdeen tae pick some up. There's nae urgency aboot me getting there but I'll happily gae wi' Fergus tae help him move if he wants my help wi' shifting things."

"Good," said Trinafar. "I'll arrange for a porter to help and I'll see you at the arch at mid-day tomorrow."

#

Fergus was delighted when he met the porter Trinafar had hired at the top of the path leading to the lacuna. "Seglesh! It's good to see you. Have you been behaving yourself?"

The troll nodded to Fergus, but bowed very low to Trinafar. His skin turned a duskier shade of blue and Fergus realised he was blushing.

"Behave yes. Seglesh good. No make trouble."

"How much can you carry?" asked Trinafar.

"Lots, Lady, lots. Much as three elves, maybe more."

"Will that be enough, Fergus, with you and Duncan carrying too?"

"I should think so."

"Good. Let's go."

They started off down the steep path to the lacuna. At the botton Seglesh cast a glamour that made him look like the big man Fergus and Duncan had met in the teashop and not the eight foot troll he really was.

Fergus paused near the lacuna looking around with a puzzled expression.

"What's wrong?" asked Trinafar. "You've been through this lacuna before. You know there's nothing to worry about."

"I'm not worried, just a bit confused. I can feel something – different. It's a sort of greasy feeling as if I had just washed and hadn't finished rinsing the soap off my skin."

"Are you feeling the proximity of the lacuna?"

"It could be that I suppose. But why should I be feeling it now when I never have before?"

"The only thing that's changed recently is your episode of iron poisoning. Might it be related to that?"

She called Duncan over and asked for his opinion.

"I dinnae ken why it should, but why ask me?" He replied. "Just because I've learnt a bit about magic frae Dhugald disnae make me an expert. Ye'd dae better asking him."

"That's exactly what we will do when we get back to the Three Towers. If you're all ready – let's go. You go first Seglesh and I'll go last."

The guard at the lacuna bowed to Trinafar and moved aside to allow them to pass. Fergus was surprised when he didn't start coughing in the Edinburgh air as soon as he stepped through. *Maybe I'm getting used to the change like Trinafar said I would. That's good.* He took a couple of steps forward and had to stop when he bumped into Duncan. Then Trinafar bumped into him. "Keep going," she said, pushing him onwards.

"I can't. Seglesh is in the way."

Seglesh turned round and looked back at her. Then he said, in an even higher pitched voice than usual, "Not right! Not right. Where we?"

"That's a good question," she said. "This," – she gestured at the exit from the lacuna – isn't Edinburgh."

Seglesh moaned, "Lost. We lost."

shift

The place-that-doesn't-exist was in turmoil as the need for an urgent meeting circulated among the Eleven and the pack of hopefuls. The feeling in the quasi-space approached panic as questions were asked and, mostly, left unanswered.

"What was that?"

"Did you feel that change?"

"It's happened!"

"What do you mean?"

"That was a worldline shift, wasn't it?"

"Are you sure?"

"What else could it be?"

One of the Eleven, the gnome Guloosh, didn't appear in response to the urgency of the summons. None of those present were certain why she wasn't there, but they all agreed that her failure to appear must be linked in some way to the to the convulsion they had all felt and which most of them agreed must have been a worldline shift. Sumethla suggested that Guloosh might have been in the second world when the shift took place and had been trapped there. "What else would keep her from this meeting?"

"What indeed? We must assume she is lost."

"Or dead."

"It amounts to the same thing."

The imbalance of having only ten at the core of the non-space let the onlookers apply more and more pressure as they tried to fill the gap. One of the strongest of those in the halo, a veteran who had almost succeeded on three previous attempts, switched his tactics. Instead of trying to force his way through and create a new gap, Barkeli offered to share his strength with the remnant ten and work with them.

This gambit worked and he slid easily into the vacancy. A new Eleven established itself and quickly reached a consensus. All agreed they needed to find out what the new second world was like.

"Be careful," said Sumethla. Don't be in too much of a hurry to try the lacunae. I remember they were unstable after the last worldline shift. Some vanished, others appeared and a few moved to nearby places. Who knows what effects this new shift has had. We don't want anybody else trapped in the wrong world. We know that happens occasionally anyway but the shift might well increase their frequency."

The tension in the place-that-doesn't-exist relaxed, slightly, and the Eleven dispersed to start their investigations.

options

When Fergus stepped into the lacuna he expected to see Seglesh holding a battered wooden door open for him and Duncan. Beyond the door should be a short straight tunnel, with a glimmer of daylight at its far end.

However, there was no door and the tunnel turned a corner ahead of Seglesh who was standing in a shaft of sunlight looking puzzled and alarmed. "Where we?" he asked again.

Trinafar whispered, "I don't know." She looked back at the others and added, "I don't think I want to know."

"What do you mean?" asked Fergus.

"It can't be … can it? … I suppose it must be … what else could it be?"

"You're no making sense," said Duncan.

"I think I might know where we are, but I don't know how we ended up here." Trinafar took another deep breath and said, "I think we might be in one of the Lost Worlds."

Fergus asked "What do you mean, Lost Worlds?"

"Didn't your mother tell you stories about places the lacunae used to connect to, but now don't? Places that used to be real but aren't any more?"

"Yes," replied Fergus. "I do remember her telling me that sort of story when I was three or four. She didn't call them Lost Worlds, just 'other places'. But she made it clear that these places weren't real."

"Were those stories of places like the Caliphate and Jorvikrike?" asked Duncan.

"Yes."

"My faither used tae tell me that sort o' story too when I was wee. He aye called them 'Lost Worlds'. When I got older he telt me they wisnae real and there was nae use trying to get tae them. I mind being so disappointed by that."

"Well," said Trinafar, "I think we might be in one of the Lost Worlds now."

Duncan scowled. "I hope no. Dhugalt said something

aboot other worlds tae me one night but I was awfy tired and I didnae really get what he said. I think he telt me the magi dinnae fully understand the relationship between Tirog and the second world. If I've got it right he said there can be sudden, unexplained shifts in whaur a lacuna leads. The magi ca' them worldline shifts. They're very rare and I got the impression the magi are a bit feared o' them."

"We'd better go back to Eideann," said Fergus.

"Good idea, but I'm not sure we can just turn around and go back. The other end of the lacuna might not be in Eideann any more. If what I think has happened is right then we're probably trapped here, wherever here is."

"I don't understand," said Fergus.

Trinafar told them that she and Yuseth had been researching stories of the Lost Worlds for more than four years. They matched up with what Dhugalt told Duncan. "We've come across references to people who have gone through a lacuna and never come back. And there's been three or four references to somebody arriving in Eideann, or one of the other Domains and Realms, from a second world they described as being different from the Empire. They've usually gone back through the lacuna they came through and never returned."

"Even if we are in one of these Lost Worlds we've got to try to go back to Eideann."

"Yes, Fergus, we need to try, but don't be surprised if we end up somewhere else."

"Let's have a look around here before we try to go back. If we can get there somebody is bound to ask us what we've seen here."

"Aye. I'll take a look."

Duncan cautiously poked his head round the corner. The shaft of sunlight illuminated a narrow street sloping up to his right between two massive stone buildings. From where he was standing he could see a dozen or more niches in the walls of the buildings, each one containing a statue.

He saw movement in the street and quickly pulled his head back into the shade. "Ah dinnae like the look o' what I'm seeing. Ah think we should leave."

Nobody argued.

They went back through the lacuna as quickly as they could, wondering if it would take them to Eideann.

It didn't.

The copse of ash and birch trees around the entrance of the lacuna they hoped to see wasn't there. Instead the irregular ground outside the cave was overgrown with clumps of nettles, thistles and fireweed.

Fergus turned round, stumbled and inadvertently dragged his right forearm through a mass of nettles. "Ow! Be careful, those things are vicious."

Seglesh sank on to his heels and muttered, "No magic."

"You're right," said Trinafar. "I should have noticed that myself. I can't feel any latency. Have you still got your own?"

"Yes, lady, but just Seglesh can use it."

"We started in Tirog and we've been through a lacuna twice so we should still be there. Obviously we're not – and there's not a trace of latency that I can use. I've got a nasty feeling about this world. We need to go up the path to see whatever the equivalent of the Towers is like here."

Seglesh took the lead as they climbed the path. His thick skin was impervious to the nettle stings and he broke the trail for them.

Fergus didn't want another encounter with the nettles and made sure he was following in Seglesh's footsteps. The stings he had suffered were bad enough to have already caused blisters and he couldn't help scratching his right forearm.

"What was it you saw in that other world, Fergus?" asked Trinafar. "You got us out of there in a hurry."

"There were a lot of statues in alcoves in the walls of both buildings I could see – dozens of them. I'd say they were life-size or even bigger. Some of them were really strange."

"Strange?"

"Yes. About half of them had animal heads. There was one with a bull's head, one with an eagle's, one with a ram's and so on. I didn't see any two the same. I got us out because there were two people walking down the street towards us and they were even odder than the statues. One of them had a horse's head and the other, well he seemed to have the head of a preying mantis but in proportion to his body. I'm not sure if either head was real, or if they were wearing helmets. They were both carrying spears. I don't think they saw me but I thought it better if we didn't stay around to find out."

Trinafar shivered. "I'm glad you did, but it still leaves us stranded here with no way to get home."

"People wi' animal heids!" said Duncan. "Like on Gyptic tomb paintings?"

"No. What I saw in the niches were definitely statues, and they looked pretty lifelike."

They saved their breath for the climb. Once they reached the top they gazed around in dismay. There were no buildings, at least none standing. Scrub grass and a few juniper and broom bushes covered rough, cracked and fissured rock. In a few places there were what could, with a little imagination, be called the remnants of walls.

"This place has been abandoned for a long time," said Duncan. "How long would it take for buildings tae decay tae this state?"

"I'd guess hundreds of years," said Fergus.

"And I can guess why it's like this," said Trinafar. "Seglesh says there isn't any latent power here and I believe him. I can't feel any either, not even as much as I usually can in the second world, far less what I can feel in Eideann. This must be what happens outside the range of a Cridhe's influence. People move away, the place is forsaken and falls into disrepair. I'm horribly afraid we're looking at the future of Eideann."

"Cannae be," said Duncan. "The lacunae aren't passages through time."

"I didn't mean literally the future. It's just that Eideann will become as deserted as this when my mother dies."

"What choices do we have?" asked Trinafar. She sat down on one of the rocky outcrops and ticked off the options on her fingers. "There doesn't seem to be much point in trying this lacuna again but we could do that. Or we could go to the next nearest lacuna, that's about ten miles away and try that. Or we could head for the nearest of the Domains and Realms adjacent to Eideann. That would be Bordiss."

"Bordiss good. Seglesh uncle live Bordiss."

"How far is that?"

"The overlap between Eideann and Bordiss would be about sixty miles away if we were in the Eideann I know, but I don't know if it would be the same in this world."

"You're sounding very composed about this, Trinafar," said Fergus.

"That's an illusion," she replied, "I'm terrified and just putting on a brave face. I've done a lot of research into the Lost Worlds. There's no doubt that people like me, who don't fit the usual pattern of Cridhe inheritance, are connected in some way with Lost Worlds and worldline shifts. I don't think we actually cause them, but there's certainly *some* association and I can't be sure this isn't my fault. It's as if I've always known something like this would happen and I'm sort of prepared for it."

It took them a good forty minutes of discussion and argument to make a decision. Finally they agreed to go back to the lacuna and use the NEbox to make some images of it, and of the other side, in case they got a chance to show people what they had encountered. Then they planned to go to the next nearest lacuna and see what happened when they went through that one.

"Ah think there's something we need to be careful aboot," said Duncan. "Something Dhugalt said makes me think the lacunae might be unstable after a change. If so, we might end up in different worlds if we lose contact wi' each other. Make sure you're a' touching somebody else when ye go through."

They set off back down the path to the lacuna with Seglesh once again leading the way, bashing his way through the nettles and muttering to himself, "Lost! Seglesh lost! Everybody lost! Trust Lady Trinafar. Get unlost."

lost worlds

"We need tae be careful," said Duncan, looking at the cave mouth. We need tae move fast and dae a quick turnaround on the ither side. The quicker we can go the less chance there is o'meeting somebody. Nae stopping for sightseeing."

"Do we really need to try this again?" asked Trinafar. "We already know that it won't take us back to Eideann."

"True, but let's not start the debate again. We did agree to give it another try."

Trinafar sighed, "Very well, Fergus. Let's do it. It's important that we all stay together. Seglesh will you go first and open the lacuna for Duncan and Fergus."

"Yes, Lady."

"I'll bring up the rear. Tell us when you're ready, Duncan."

"Just gie me a minute tae turn the NEbox on."

"May the Starmaker shine on us."

Duncan looked at the screen as soon as it lit up and immediately shouted, "Wait! Don't go, Seglesh. Nobody move!"

"What's wrong?"

"Ah dinnae ken. Come and take a look at this."

They all clustered round Duncan and gasped. The screen was showing a multicoloured blur instead of an image of the cave mouth.

"What does that mean? Is there something wrong with the box?"

"I've never pointed it at a lacuna before. This might be the normal way it sees one."

"Or it might be an indication of the instability of the lacunae after a worldline shift," said Trinafar.

"Aye, so it could. What do we dae noo?"

"Let's just wait a bit. If it's due to instability it might settle down."

"Seglesh got water. Want, Lady?"

"Yes, thank you, Seglesh. I would like some."

Duncan kept an eye on what the NEbox was showing while they waited. About half-an-hour later he attracted their attention with the news that the colours had stopped changing.

They saw a band of dark blue stretching across the image of the cave entrance.

"It looks like a threshold," said Trinafar, "and look, there's another band of the same colour going deeper into the cave and vanishing into the gloom. What do you think, Duncan? Is that a path? Should we try it?"

"It could be, but d'ye want tae take a chance on a guess?"

"Do you have a better idea?"

Duncan shook his head.

"Is everyone willing to try this possible path? – Yes? In that case let's stick to the same order. Seglesh, you first. Turn right around again and come back as soon as you've had a chance to see what's on the other side.

The band of colour indicating the path, if that's what it was, branched after a couple of steps.

Seglesh hesitated.

"Don't stop," said Trinafar, "Pick one to follow."

Seglesh groaned, muttered 'not want choose', but he started moving again and took the, slightly wider, left hand path. The others followed him to where the lacuna path ended in a patch of sunshine. "Know this place," he said. "Been here."

Voices ahead of them made them turn around in a hurry. The voices got louder and then they heard running feet behind them.

They followed the blue path in reverse. Fergus tripped just as he got clear of the entrance. He fell forward out of the cave and into a clump of nettles.

"Drown it," he shouted, followed by a tirade of curses directed at 'useless, bedamned, careless fishermen who can't look after their gear'. "May they get caught up in their own nets and drown!" He made a series of high pitched whistles and clicks. Then he gasped and apologised to Trinafar for his bad language.

"Don't worry," she said. "I'm not offended. In fact I

didn't recognise that you were swearing. Were those Lutran curses?"

"Yes, my lady, I'm afraid so," said Fergus, blushing. "I'm sorry. I just reacted without thinking when I bumped into more of those Starlost nettles."

"Then you are forgiven – as long as you teach me some. I'd like to be able to curse without anyone knowing what I'm saying. Meanwhile, let's try to get you out of the nettles."

"Barith!"

"Anesses!"

"I hope whoever those voices belong to aren't going to follow us."

"So do I. They sound angry."

"Anesses krafk!"

"Barith fen zellac nilen ...!"

"Konashk!"

"Aargh ..."

The voices ended when a scream from close behind them faded into silence.

"Consider yersel' lucky," Duncan pointed at a six foot spear quivering in the ground only a foot or so to the left of where Fergus was lying. "Yon spear just missed ye, and no by much. Stumbling might hae saved ye."

When Trinafar looked at the cave mouth she saw a body lying there with a spear embedded in its back and blood all around. Her hand went to her throat.

"Whoever they are they've killed one of their own."

"Spearman killed for throw. Punished," said Seglesh. "He told no to throw."

"How do you know that? And why did you say you've been there before?"

"Have been. Where Duncan saw animal heads."

"Was that the same place?"

Duncan looked up from where he was trying to help Fergus out of the nettles. "Aye, it could be the same place. And the blade on that spear looks like the ones I saw before. Seglesh, it sounds as if you understood what they were shouting."

"Understand some."

"How? Different world. Surely a different language. How could you understand? It's not possible."

"Actually it's not only possible, it's not even very surprising," said Trinafar. "If you read the histories of the growth of the Empire and correlate them with the lists of trolls who enrolled in the Empire army you'll find that the trolls could often translate languages they had never heard before. That was a huge benefit to the armies of the Empire. Nobody knows for sure how the translation ability works but one suggestion is that there's some sort of mental link through the lacunae. As far as I know the ability is unique to trolls."

"How d'ye feel, Fergus?"

"Like somebody's taken a scrubbing brush to my face and arms. They've got so sensitive. Even a bit of wind across my forehead is enough to make me cringe."

"I can't think of anything we can do to help I'm afraid. Can you?"

"Fraid not."

"How much did you understand of what they said, Seglesh?"

"Most. Leader say wanted catch we, not kill. Him angry."

"They haven't followed us," said Trinafar. "Perhaps the one they killed was the only one able to pass a lacuna."

"That's possible."

At Duncan's suggestion they went back up the hill to where they could sit on rocks without the risk of being stung. He also suggested they should try again but take the right hand path when it branched. The consensus was they had little to lose so, after resting for a couple of hours they set off down the hill again.

Their passage through the lacuna was promising because when they went right at the branch they saw tall trees ahead. At first they were disappointed when they realised the trees were pines and not the ash and birch they were hoping for, but were somewhat encouraged again when Seglesh said, "Magic here."

"A Second World with some latency!"

"Yes, Lady."

Trinafar looked up. "You're right,"she said. "It feels like about as much as in the Empire, but that's not enough to let me do much magic. Now what? It's not very promising that there's no sign of a path leading up towards where the Three Towers would be."

Without a defined path to follow, climbing the hill was a slow process. As they got nearer the top they went even slower trying to avoid being seen. Seglesh used his glamour to maintain his usual 'big man' look. It wasn't necessary; they saw nobody. Some smoke rising from roughly the position of the Tron was the only sign of life they saw and they decided not to investigate it.

"Just keeping going up and down the hill seems pointless," said Trinafar. "Anybody got any better ideas?"

"I'd like tae use the NEbox tae watch the cave entrance. That's the only thing that seems tae offer a way tae break this loop. It's shown a bit o' instability so we just have tae hope the lacunae are still changing."

"That's as good an idea as any," said Fergus. "Duncan, you should carry on making images of everywhere we end up. They might be useful."

Trinafar sighed. "Then down we go again."

When they reached the lacuna Duncan produced the box and they could see there was a band of colour across the cave entrance as before – but it was yellow, not blue."

"Hopefully it'll take us somewhere else. Shall we try it?"

Unusually Seglesh took the lead without being prompted saying, "Yes. Go different place. Find we."

"Not so fast, Seglesh. Wait for us."

Seglesh didn't wait but vanished through the entrance to the lacuna before Duncan could get hold of him.

Trinafar wanted to follow, but was restrained by Duncan. He pulled her back and said, "We've got to stay in contact wi' each other. It's no sure we'll arrive at the same place if we dinnae.

"I know that, but we can't just abandon him!"

They argued among themselves for several minutes until Seglesh suddenly reappeared. "Eideann. Seglesh been Eideann."

"Thank the Starmaker. Let's go."

Inside the lacuna the path branched.

"Which way Seglesh? No, you won't know, will you, you didn't have the box."

"Seglesh keep left until coming back."

"Fine. We'll keep left too."

They found themselves in a dark tunnel closed by a battered-looking door with squeaking hinges. Fergus started coughing as soon as he set foot beyond the door.

"This place looks familiar."

"And Fergus's reaction tae the dirty air makes it sound as if we're in the Empire. I think this is Edinburgh."

Once Fergus had stopped coughing he suggested going to his lodgings and getting something to eat.

Seglesh agreed, saying he was hungry, but Trinafar rejected the idea; she thought it urgent they go to the tea shop and warn the proprietor about the worldline shift. "We don't want anybody to get lost trying to get from here to Eideann."

Fergus was somewhat uneasy as they walked through the streets of Edinburgh. He wasn't sure why. He noticed Trinafar frowning slightly as she looked around. "Is there something wrong?" he asked.

"I'm not sure," she replied. "I keep seeing things I've never noticed before. The columns on that portico, for instance. If you'd asked me earlier what style they were I would have said Doric, but they're Corinthian. I guess I'm not as observant as I thought."

"I know what you mean. I've lived in Edinburgh for years and I would have said I know it pretty well but, as I look around, I keep seeing things I don't expect. It's the details that are catching me out. I guess I don't know Edinburgh as well as I thought I did."

They hurried up the hill and into the tangle of streets near Nicolson Square. Then both Trinafar and Fergus came to an abrupt halt. The shop they were standing outside was painted dark blue, not the reddish brown they expected to see, and the sign etched on the glass identified it as '*The Brewmester's Coffee Emporium*'.

Trinafar gasped and said, "This isn't Edinburgh after all! It looks enough like it to fool us, but it's not!"

"Not right!" said Seglesh, gazing at the door with a stunned expression. "Where we?"

Trinafar turned and hurried them away, back towards the lacuna. They were all confused, and walked disconsolately back through the streets of Edinbugh.

Once back among the nettles and thistles they asked each other, "What now?"

Trinafar wrapped her arms around herself and told the others this barren version of Eideann made her feel lost and she'd rather be in that world that wasn't quite Edinburgh.

Fergus wanted to know if she wouldn't feel just as bad wandering streets she almost knew?

She scowled but didn't answer his question.

"I'm no sure it would be a good idea tae bide in that version o' Edinburgh," said Duncan.

"Why not?"

"It's like enough tae the place ye ken tae fool ye. It might be there's a version of one of us there too, or one just a wee bit different. Fergus is maist likely tae hae a duplicate in that other city. He's spent years living in Edinburgh, so he sort of fits in there. Suppose he does have a double in the other version and the two o' them chance tae meet. There are tales about what happens when identical people encounter each other, and they never end well."

"You're talking about doppelgängers?" said Trinafar. "But they're just horror stories from the second world, aren't they? I've never heard any convincing stories about them in Tirog."

"Are ye sure? From what ah've heard you can hear about doppelgängers from almost anywhere in eastern Eorp. And it's said two identical people meeting results in their mutual annihilation. We dinnae want tae take the risk o' meeting different versions of ourselves from the wrong side of a lacuna."

"That's a frightening idea," said Trinafar. "What do you suggest we do, Fergus?"

"Even if Duncan thinks I'm most at risk I've got to say I think the possibility is low and I'm prepared to chance it."

"What does the box show now, Duncan?"

"Take a look yourself."

Trinafar saw the threshold of the lacuna was green. "Shall we follow the green path?"

"No," said Duncan. "I think we should try a different branch o' the yellow one because the yellow one we tried took us tae somewhere nearly right and I just wonder if similar colours might lead tae similar places."

After crossing the yellow threshold the band of colour split, as they had anticipated.

"Three shades of yellow. Which one do we try?"

"I cannae really see enough o' a difference tae remember which one we used before."

"I can," said Trinafar confidently. "My colour discrimination is very good. We followed the left hand one. Let's try the middle one this time."

"No," said Duncan. "Let's go right. It's just occurred tae me that the middle one is thicker than the others, and might be the default route for anybody going through the lacuna. We already ken the left path will take us tae the 'false' Edinburgh, so it might be we should take the right hand one this time."

"Makes sense."

Once again they found themselves in a short tunnel blocked by a battered wooden door.

"Looks good," said Fergus, "but then the last one looked good too."

They made their way cautiously through the streets noticing that this time the portico had Corinthian columns, and the other anomalies they had seen were back to what they considered normal.

Sighs of relief greeted their arrival at '*The T Shoppe*' which looked just as it should. The proprietor greeted Trinafar, ushered all of them to one of the tables at the back of the shop and offered tea.

Fergus laughed, "I never thought I'd see the day when I was glad to get tea."

paths

Trinafar sighed with contentment when a cup of green tea was placed in front of her and she inhaled the aroma.

"Dinnae get too comfortable. We've still got tae get tae Eideann and warn Cridhe Igrainid aboot what's happened tae the lacunae."

"We've got that sorted," said Trinafar. "We know how to get back to Eideann now."

"Do we?" Fergus asked in surprise. "The last time we went through the lacuna from here we ended up in that world where we had spears thrown at us. Do you want to go there again?"

"Starmakers blessings! No, certainly not."

"We need some ideas. What do we do next?"

"All I can think of is to try as many different paths through the lacunae as we can. One o' them is bound tae lead us tae Eideann."

Trinafar sighed. "And here was I thinking our travels were over."

"Not until we can tell your mother where each path leads."

"You can't mean that. There must be hundreds of possibilities."

"What do we know so far?'

"Yellow will take us to Edinburgh …"

"… and at least one similar place."

"Blue goes tae yon Gyptic-looking place and back again."

"Let's choose a different colour and try that."

"Red?"

"Why no? Unless we're awfy lucky we'll need tae try several paths. Red is as good a choice as any."

But red was no better than blue or yellow.

After several more attempts they tried a green path which delivered them to a cave in a small copse of ash and birch trees.

"This looks promising," said Fergus, "and it smells right too."

"And there's latency," Trinafar exclaimed, "Strong enough to be home."

A movement among the trees attracted her attention. She turned and saw an elf wearing a brown and green gambeson and carrying a sword approaching them. Then three more, one of whom she recognised as a frequent member of the Cridhe's escort, appeared from behind glamours.

"Sentries! Starmaker preserve us. There's always a sentry at the entrance to the Eideann lacuna. I should have thought of that. It might have simplified our search."

One of the sentries bowed, welcomed Trinafar by name and asked if she vouched for the other members of the party.

"I do," she replied. "We need to see my mother as soon as possible. I'm certain she will prohibit passage through the lacuna as soon as she hears what we have to say. Take my word for it and don't allow anyone else through."

"The Cridhe has already banned passage through the lacuna, my lady. That's why there are more of us here than usual," said one of the sentries. "However the ban applies only to those seeking to leave Eideann. You may pass freely."

#

"I need to speak with my mother," said Trinafar to the guards at the entrance to the Robhas Tower. "It's urgent."

She insisted that Fergus and Duncan were admitted too. She tried to include Seglesh as well, but the commander of the door guard was reluctant to allow him into the Tower saying he was unreliable and couldn't be trusted.

"Not worry. Seglesh understand. Not want disturb Cridhe. Wait here. Perhaps see Cridhe later."

"That's very considerate of you, Seglesh," said Trinafar.

His blue skin took on a darker tone and he turned away.

"Now you've embarrassed him," said Fergus as they started climbing the stairs to Igrainid's study.

They knelt in front of Igrainid who looked up from the pile of documents on the low table in front of her. Before she even had time to give them permission to speak Trinafar said, "Mother, we must close the lacuna. It's changed and now it's dangerous. People trying to use it will get lost."

Igrainid frowned. "How do you know about that? Explain yourself!"

"Please believe me, mother. I swear by the Starmaker that what I'm going to tell you is the truth. Give orders to close the lacuna and I will explain why it's necessary."

"Very well," said Igrainid. She made a flicking gesture with her right hand and a gong sounded on the other side of the room. Immediately the door burst open. Several guardsmen ran into the room arranging themselves in an arc between the door and Igrainid's chair. Igrainid pointed to one of them and said, "Passage through the lacuna is forbidden. See to it."

He bowed, turned and ran from the room.

Then she pointed to another of the guardsmen. "Find Commander Misghel and Lady Saefan as quick as you can."

"And Dhugalt," said Trinafar.

"Yes," said Fergus, "We'll need him too."

#

"I'm not sure I understand all your travels since you left for the second world," said Dhugalt after Trinafar, Duncan and Fergus had described what had happened to them and shown everyone the images they had captured of the worlds they had been in.

"You say you have been in a barren, desolate world before you managed to find your way back here."

"Yes."

"And you have also been in two versions of what we know as the Empire."

"That's right," replied Fergus. "They're so similar it's difficult to distinguish between them. We started calling them 'real' and 'false' so we knew which we were talking about."

"How did you avoid getting lost in all these other worlds?" asked Igrainid. "Since yesterday we've had reports of at least two people who haven't returned from a journey through the lacuna."

Dhugalt said thoughtfully, "It sounds to me as if you had the advantage of the NEbox acting as a sort of guide for you."

"Aye. Being able tae see coloured paths saved us. If it wisnae for them we'd still be wandering the maze o' the lacunae."

Igrainid suggested that their desire to get back to Eideann might have influenced where the lacunae delivered them to wherever they wanted or needed to be.

"No, Cridhe, ah dinnae think that's likely. After a' ending up in any o' the 'false' worlds we saw wisnae something we wanted."

"I agree with you, Duncan," said Dhugalt, "It doesn't seem likely to me."

He paused, then said, "However, I remember one discussion the Group of Eleven had about the lacunae. One of our number recounted an incident which implied that a powerful enough magus could divert a lacuna and have it open somewhere else."

"That doesn't help us," said Trinafar. "None of the four of us who went world-jumping have anything like the power of a magus. In fact two us us have no magic ability at all."

"I'd really like to see what the NEbox shows when you point it at a lacuna," said Dhugalt. "Can we go and take a look."

"I think that's a good idea," said Igrainid. "I'd like to see it too.

She turned to Misghel. "I expect you'll be wanting me to have an escort."

"Yes, Cridhe, definitely. I will organise one."

"Do we need anybody else?"

"What about Maedron? He'll be interested too."

"I'm sure he would be," said Misghel, "but he and Volissen are still in seclusion and will be for the rest of this moon at least."

The escort Misghel arranged consisted of twenty of the Domain Guard carrying swords and bows. The unexpected appearance of the Cridhe and her guard in the streets of Eideann produced an impromptu crowd who watched and cheered as the procession made its way from the Robhas Tower.

Igrainid was pleased to see half-a-dozen members of the Guard and Seglesh at the cave mouth ready to prevent passage through the lacuna.

"There isn't enough space around the lacuna to fit in more than six or seven people, Cridhe," said Misghel. "Obviously Fergus, Duncan and Lady Trinafar must be among them. Who else?"

"You'd better be there, Misghel, if only to keep you from worrying, and we need Dhugalt too. I think that should be enough. Clear as big a space in front of the lacuna as you can."

#

Once Misghel had the group organised to his satisfaction he invited Igrainid to step forward but he wouldn't let her get closer than three paces from the cave mouth.

She looked at the lacuna and sighed. "I haven't been here for years. Not since my father died."

"Has it changed," asked Dhugalt.

"No, it still looks much the same as I remember it."

"Do you miss being able to travel to the second world?"

"Yes, Fergus. I do – to some extent. However, I miss being able to wander around the Domain even more."

Fergus was baffled. *Why can't she move around freely?*

Igrainid noticed his confusion and explained, "If I go more than a mile or two from the Towers in any direction

I deprive people living that far away in the opposite direction from access to latency."

"Oh!" said Duncan. "I didnae realise access to latent power was so dependent on distance."

"It is," said Dhugalt, "but we can talk about that some other time. We came to see what the NEbox shows us about the lacuna."

The box happened to be pointing at Dhugalt when Duncan switched it on. The screen showed a brilliantly iridescent figure.

"D'ye suppose that's how the box sees a magus?"

"What are you talking about?" asked Dhugalt. "I can't see the screen when the box is pointing at me."

"Sorry," said Duncan, "Here, I've made an image of you. What d'ye think o' that?"

Dhugalt studied the image. "Interesting! I think you're right about what it means."

"Hae we no seen iridescence like that before?"

"You're right, Duncan! It was in Aberdeen, wasn't it? When you made the first modification to the box.

"Aye, there was that wee patch between her eyes when ye pointed the box at Trinafar."

"What! Trinafar showed iridescence like that? You've never mentioned that before."

"It never occurred to me to tell you about it because I had no idea what to make of it."

Dhugalt wanted to know if the patch was still there.

Duncan pointed the box at Trinafar and confirmed he could still see it. Studying it more closely he noticed the patch wasn't circular as he had originally thought. He magnified the image to occupy almost the whole screen and showed it to the others.

"That looks like a thin spot in a fabric partly repaired with something folded over it and sewn in place, like a patch. What can it be?"

"It reminds me of something else that was discussed at a meeting of the Eleven some time ago. We were talking about possible ways an inheritance anomaly could happen. One of us suggested that if a potential Source was shielded somehow before they were old enough to start generating latency, it might have the effect of producing a Failed Source."

"Like me, you mean? Why would anyone want to do that?"

Dhugalt shrugged. "I can only think it might be seen as a way to get power. Perhaps it would have the effect of draining latency from a Source as soon as it's generated so that they were never able to supply it properly."

"How much strength would it take to shield somebody in that way?"

"I don't know. I think it would take someone very strong to do it," said Dhugalt, "probably a magus."

"But," said Igrainid, "aren't magi powerful enough anyway?"

"Are we? Power of one sort or another is always an attraction. Just look at what Peruch and Rulidh were planning, and all for a little more power. I'm satisfied with what I've got but I can think of at least three members of the Group of Eleven who might be tempted."

"I want to know more about this," said Trinafar, tapping her forehead. "Can it be undone?"

Everybody looked at Dhugalt who shrugged. "I suppose I could try."

"What would the result be if you succeeded?"

Dhugalt shook his head and said he didn't want to speculate.

"Please! This is so important to me. Even if it makes no difference I'll know we have tried everything. What about asking the Group of Eleven? You did say they're interested in the Failed Sources."

"They are, very much so. One of them in particular has asked me for information about you at every meeting of the Eleven since we knew you were a Failed Source. I've never told them much, and I've been criticised for that."

"I don't mind you telling them more if it helps us understand this," said Trinafar, pointing at her forehead.

"There's one more thing to consider. The Group knows nothing about the NEbox. I've never mentioned it, or even hinted about its existence. They're not going to be happy about that, but I can't see any way of avoiding telling them all about it and what it's shown us."

Dhugalt didn't fancy a debate with the rest of the Eleven. The very idea made him shiver. He could see, all too clearly, the possibility of it becoming acrimonious. "I very much don't like the idea," he told the others "but, if you really want me to, I can ask for a meeting of the Group and do my best to bargain with them."

"Will it be dangerous for you?"

"Possibly, Trinafar, possibly. However, I am willing to take the risk."

"I assume you can call a meeting from anywhere," said Igrainid.

Dhugalt nodded.

"In that case let's go back to my study and get comfortable."

It took Misghel about twenty minutes to turn the guard escort around and pointed back towards the Three Towers.

ᴅesɪʀes

Back in Igrainid's study they settled into cosy armchairs and, at her invitation, helped themselves to tea.

"Are you certain you want me to call for a meeting of the Group of Eleven?"

"Yes please, Dhugalt," said Trinafar before anyone else had time to speak.

Igrainid sighed. *If we do this and something goes wrong then I could lose my daughter or uncle Dhugalt, or possibly both.* She was tempted to tell Trinafar 'no', but remained silent. *I've no right to prevent her taking the risk, if that's what she wants.*

"When I call for a meeting of the Eleven I will seem to be in a trance," said Dhugalt. "Don't worry about it. Fergus will tell you he's seen me in that state before. Time may seem to pass very slowly, or very quickly. It varies and I can't predict what it will be like for you. Just wait patiently and be ready to answer any questions I pass on from the Group.

Dhugalt closed his eyes. His head slumped. His breathing stopped, or perhaps it just became very slow and shallow.

The place-that-is-not came into being around him. He was well used to the pale silvery-grey radiance from some ill-defined source which, as always, was somewhere behind him.

The others started appearing in response to his summons.

Klinmerd was the first to arrive, followed closely by Wardlik. Both of them, Wardlik in particular, had been critical of Dhugalt's actions in the past and he experienced a feeling of unease, fearing as he did that he might be attacked for failing to report what he knew. The subsequent appearance of Barkeli, Sumethla and Fuormil, people with whom he had generally a good rapport, made him feel more comfortable and he relaxed slightly.

"What's this about then," asked Wardlik.

"I have news of the Failed Source in Eideann."

"Are you going to tell us something new? You've resisted telling us much about her for seventeen years. What's changed?"

"The worldline shift of course."

"And what has your pet Failed Source to do with that?"

"She was caught in it."

"Was! You're implying she survived the shift somehow?"

"Nonsense!" Wardlik stated.

"If she was in another world during the shift she'd be lost between the worlds, just like all the others we've heard of," said Klinmerd.

"How many is that?" asked Sumethla.

By the time Klinmerd responded to this question all of the Eleven were present, and each of them knew of at least one person who they described as lost; a total of nineteen.

"Well, Dhugalt," said Sumethla. "I suppose you can explain why, seventeen years after we first became aware of her, you've decided to tell us more about Trinafar Chiolet Fion Eideannach. And why you've been so protective of her for all those years."

"Is that who this infamous Failed Source is?" a goblin asked in a surprised tone.

"You mean you didn't work that out for yourself, Tredun? I thought we all knew that."

"I never bothered to try, Brangret. Since we didn't know anything about what causes a Failed Source, finding out who it was never seemed relevant."

"Well, now that you do know can you think of a good reason why Dhugalt should be so secretive?"

"No, I can't."

"It's quite simple," said Dhugalt. "We are quite closely related. Her mother is my father's sister's second daughter and her father was my older brother. He died in an accident a year before Trinafar was born. I merely wanted to protect her from the curious. I haven't tried to keep her a secret, but I have tried to minimise her significance.

"You're right, Dhugalt. It is simple. You're not the dithering, indecisive person some of us seem to regard you as."

"Thank you for that endorsement, Sumethla. Now I think we should move on to how Trinafar survived a worldline shift."

"You didn't make that up! She really did come through the shift safely?"

"Not only her but her three companions as well."

"How?"

Dhugalt described what he knew of the history of the NEbox and its functions and capabilities, including its association with Igrainid's premonition. For what seemed to him to be at least two hours he tried to anticipate and deflect any criticism directed against him by Wardlik and Klinmerd. He did get support from Sumethla, Tredun and Fuormil but the odds for and against him were, if he was right, about equal.

The hopeful, as usual, were paying close attention to the ongoing debate. The ambience of the halo made Dhugalt feel they were marginally on his side if that mattered, which it probably didn't.

From the point of view of Igrainid and the others in her study Dhugalt had been in a trance for only a few minutes when he opened his eyes and said, "I've told the Eleven the history of the NEbox as far as I know it. I hope it hasn't been as long a time for you as it has for me. They would like to see some of the images you have made with it. They want to see images of the other worlds you were in and, in particular they want to see what seems to be magic being used by someone with no magical ability."

As Dhugalt requested, Duncan showed how the NEbox responded to magic in action. This included images taken of places on the other side of a lacuna, using the box to modify spells and the iridescent appearance of how Dhugalt appeared on the screen. Eventually Dhugalt said, "Now we want to see a magnified image of the spot between Trinafar's eyes."

A long interval ensued before Dhugalt said, "Thank

you. You may put the box down now. Please wait in case we want to see more."

He closed his eyes again.

This time it was almost an hour before he came out of his trance. He stretched, asked for tea and, in response to the questions everyone had, said, "The Group believes that Lady Trinafar's inability to generate latency has been artificially produced. The most recent of us to join reports having been exposed to an idea of how to produce what we call a Failed Source, like Trinafar. He claimed not to have tried to put that idea into practice. But, of course, that can't be proved."

"Or refuted," commented Igrainid.

"True," replied Dhugalt. "The idea," he continued, "suggests that Trinafar may have been kept from exposure to latency by a shield during her childhood with the result of cutting her off from her heritage."

"What a mean, horrible thing to do to a child," said Igrainid.

"Now what?" asked Duncan.

"The Group suggests someone attempts to take apart the layer of shielding they think is surrounding Trinafar. If that is the cause then they want you to be aware that removing the shielding may have no beneficial effect because it has been in place for many years and she may be habituated to its presence."

"Will it have a detrimental effect?"

"I don't know, Cridhe. Nobody has any experience of this."

"Do it," said Trinafar.

Igrainid started to object but changed her mind. *It's her choice. I have to accept it if that's what she wants, whatever the result. May the Starmaker bless her.*

"Very well," said Dhugalt. "If you're sure that's what you want."

"Yes! No – Wait. Mother, what about your premonition. You said whatever caused it would mark something that will affect the Domain. Do you thnk this could be what provoked it?"

"I suppose so. But what could Duncan do to cause it?"

Trinafar turned to look at Duncan. "You could use one of the new tricks you've made for the NEbox and try to remove this shielding."

Duncan sounded incredulous as he said, "Me? You're not serious."

"Yes, I am. What do you think, Dhugalt? Doesn't that make sense?"

"Actually it does."

"And you could guide Duncan. Explain the structure of the spell and tell him how to take it apart."

There was silence in the room for a few minutes then Dhugalt said, "Yes, I think I could do that if that's what you want."

Duncan went pale and swallowed several times. He looked around the room wondering what would happen if he got it wrong.

"Aye, Lady Trinafar, Ah'll dae it if that's whit ye want."

"It is. Please do it."

Duncan picked up the NEbox, pointed it at Trinafar and studied the screen. Igrainid and Dhugalt were the only ones who could get into a position to watch what he did.

Trinafar appeared on the screen as a darkness, a featureless nothing with the glimmer of the iridescent patch visible just off centre.

"Right, Duncan. Let's see what happens when you touch the screen."

Tentatively he did that after taking a deep breath. A dull red dot appeared to one side of the patch.

"Good. Now draw a line across the screen to touch the edge of the patch."

The red dot elongated and where it touched the patch a twist appeared.

"I didnae mean tae do that."

"Don't worry. It doesn't surprise me."

The twist became a hook which caught on the edge of the patch.

"Do it again on the opposite side of the screen."

A second red dot appeared where another of Duncan's fingers touched the screen. Like the first it formed a hook and this caught on the opposite side of the patch.

Following Dhugalt's instructions Duncan spread his fingers and the two hooked lines separated pulling the patch into an oval. He used fingers from his other hand to add more hooked lines. Quite suddenly, the nothingness between his fingers thinned and tore like flimsy paper.

Iridescence, glowing like mother-of-pearl, flared in the space where the darkness had been. Gasps from the audience accompanied Trinafar's appearance on screen.

#

Dhugalt found himself in the place-that-doesn't-exist. It was in turmoil.

"What's going on?" he asked Sumethla.

"Wardlik. He's the one responsible for the Failed Source."

"What!"

"Almost unbelievable, isn't it. Whatever he's been doing has made him very strong. So far he's been able to resist all of us and there's something happening in the first world that's prevented us joining forces and tackling him."

"That 'something' is Trinafar Chiolet Fion Eideannach being released from the shield that prevented her becoming a Source."

"You mean that crazy idea worked!"

"It most definitely did. Eideann has a new Source."

"Does that mean the power Wardlik was generating from the Failed Source isn't available to him any more."

"I think you're right. Let's contact all the others, tell them the news and take him together."

"Don't forget the halo. We have Wardlik's place to offer to whoever emerges from that struggle."

It didn't take long for Wardlik to be overwhelmed. His despairing wail echoed through the non-space and faded into oblivion.

Dhugalt's awareness returned to Igrainid's study.

He was just in time to join in the celebrations that had erupted spontaneously as the people of Eideann realised they had a new Source. The rejoicing had both Trinafar and her mother in tears.

#

Dhugalt stayed another month in Eideann to help Trinafar settle into her new rôle. During that time he was approached by Wardlik's successor in the Group of Eleven for a one-to-one. The news she had to impart was, inevitably, quickly disseminated among the Group and the halo. She reported finding a record in the place-that-was-not which amounted to a confession by Wardlik. It also contained enough information to identify his other targets and free them from the little of his influence that remained.

#

"I am leaving tomorrow," announced Dhugalt at a farewell dinner Igrainid arranged for him.

"Of course I knew this was coming, but I will be sorry to see you go," she said. "I don't know if I can ever thank you enough for your part in freeing Trinafar."

"You don't need to thank me, because you're going to forget all about what I did and about the Group of Eleven as soon as I leave."

"I know. However, at the moment I can still feel gratitude so I will say it again, this time on behalf of the entire Domain."

"They can't know what I am either," he said with a laugh.

"Then how can I explain the gifts you have arranged for me to give to the others I need to thank?"

"Don't worry. They all come with amnesia spells built in."

Igrainid smiled as she looked around the table. "The first gift I asked Dhugalt to prepare is for Fergus Monteith."

Fergus sat up at this unexpected statement.

"I think I know what gift you would have asked for before you ever met my daughter. It would have been the ability to cross a lacuna. Am I right?"

It took several minutes of open-mouthed gawping before Fergus could answer.

"Good. I'm glad you agree because Dhugalt is going to cast a spell on you which will let you do just that."

"I don't know what to say. I just hope that proximity to a lacuna feels a bit nicer than it did when I first experienced it on our journeys."

"Fergus, I too have a gift for you," said Trinafar. "I hope you will find it acceptable. Tell him what it is, Dhugalt."

"Pick your favourite animal, Fergus. I've been able to use your shapechanging heritage to give you that ability. Only one animal's shape I'm afraid, so choose carefully."

"I haven't forgotten you, Duncan," said Igrainid. "Saefan tells me you've always wanted to be able to do magic."

"Aye, Cridhe. True enough, but Ah've kept it tae mysel' and pretended it didnae matter tae me. Ah never even telt my faither aboot it."

"With your invention of the NEbox you've found your own way to do it."

"Aye, but it's no as satisfying as I think it would be doing it myself."

"I hear you trapped Rulidh quite successfully with spells you developed yourself."

"Aye! Thae spells worked just fine. Now Saefan and I control NorEast and my faither cannae bully me ony mair."

"Well done. I asked Dhugalt to give you some magic as a gift."

"And I have done that. You'll need to find out what abilities you have for yourself. I've also made you immune to amnesia spells, so you will not be forced to forget what you have learned. The only restriction placed on you is being unable to discuss anything about the events you have experienced with anyone who doesn't already know about them."

Fergus received a reply to the letter he had sent his mother. In it she wished him the blessings of the Starmaker, but gave no indication that she wanted to meet him.

He was saddened, but couldn't say he was surprised. He wondered if he should become a Lutran like her, but decided to wait until he had a better reason for picking any particular form. He didn't feel any particular urgency about choosing which form to adopt.

His long term ambition had been to be able to use the lacunae and, now that he could use the NEbox as a guide, he started exploring the many paths available.

Duncan and Saefan formed a partnership to run NorEast and successfully resisted Rulidh's attempts to take over the business. Together, they sought out new ways the NEbox could interact with magic, but only once they'd managed to successfully track down Duncan's mother and sequester her away from Rulidh's ire.

Trinafar spent her year and a day in Edinburgh and then begged Igrainid's permission to stay there longer. Whenever she was in Eideann she had to suffer the endless apologies she got from those who had blamed her for failing to be a source. Eventually these died down and she returned to Eideann to assist her mother with the running of the Domain. That pleased all her siblings; she even became friends with Rhiannis.

Five months later Maedron and Volissen emerged from their breeding seclusion and heard the news. Trinafar and Volissen became very close, particularly after Trinafar asked Maedron to father her first child. Volissen tried to apologise to Trinafar for her previous attitude, but she wouldn't hear of it saying that friends didn't need to apologise to each other.

acknowledgements

With many thanks for Elsewhen Press and for Sandra, Sue and the other members of the Middleoak Group who have been so helpful in encouraging me with their comments and making it possible to bring this work to fruition.

David M Allan
February 2024

Elsewhen Press
delivering outstanding new talents in speculative fiction

Visit the Elsewhen Press website at elsewhen.press for the latest
information on all of our titles, authors and events; to read our blog;
find out where to buy our books and ebooks; or to place an order.

Sign up for the Elsewhen Press InFlight Newsletter at
elsewhen.press/newsletter

THE EMPTY THRONE

Three thrones, one of metal, one of wood and one of stone, stand in the Citadel. Between them shimmers a gateway to a new world, created four hundred years ago by the three magicians who made the thrones. When hostile incorporeal creatures came through the gateway, the magicians attempted to close it but failed. Since that time the creatures have tried to come through the gateway at irregular intervals, but the throne room is guarded by the Company of Tectors, established to defend against them. To try to stop the creatures, expeditions have been sent through the gateway, but none has ever returned.

On each throne appears an image of one of the Custoda, heroes who have led the expeditions through the gateway. While the Custoda occupy the thrones the gateway remains quiet and there are no incursions. Today, Dhanay, the newest knight admitted to the Company, is guarding the throne room. Like all the Tectors, Dhanay looks to the images of the Custoda for guidance.

But the Throne of Stone is empty. The latest incursion has started; a kulun escaping into the world, capable of possessing and controlling humans.

The provincial rulers, the oldest and most powerful families, ignore the gateway and the Tectors, concentrating on playing politics and pursuing their own petty aims. Some even question the need for the Company, as incursions have been successfully contained within the Citadel for years. Family feuds, border disputes, deep-rooted rivalries and bigotry make for a potentially unstable world, and a perfect environment for a kulun looking to create havoc…

ISBN: 9781911409359 (epub, kindle) / ISBN: 9781911409250 (304pp paperback)

Visit bit.ly/TheEmptyThrone

QUAESTOR

When you're searching, you don't always find what you expect

In Carrhen some people have a magic power – they may be telekinetic, clairvoyant, stealthy, or able to manipulate the elements. Anarya is a Sponger, she can absorb and use anyone else's magic without them even being aware, but she has to keep it a secret as it provokes jealousy and hostility especially among those with no magic powers at all.

When Anarya sees Yisyena, a Sitrelker refugee, being assaulted by three drunken men, she helps her to escape. Anarya is trying to establish herself as an investigator, a quaestor, in the city of Carregis. Yisyena is a clairvoyant, a skill that would be a useful asset for a quaestor, so Anarya offers her a place to stay and suggests they become business partners. Before long they are also lovers.

But business is still hard to find, so when an opportunity arises to work for Count Graumedel who rules over the city, they can't afford to turn it down, even though the outcome may not be to their liking.

Soon they are embroiled in state secrets and the personal vendettas of a murdered champion, a cabal, a puppet king, and a false god looking for one who has defied him.

ISBN: 9781911409571 (epub, kindle) / 9781911409472 (304pp paperback)
Visit bit.ly/Quaestor-Allan

THIEVER

Change is not always as good as a rest

After the events in Jotuk at the end of *Quaestor*, Anarya is no longer a Sponger but is now a Thiever – when she takes someone's magic talent they lose it until she can no longer hold on to it. Worryingly, the power also brings a desperate hunger to take others' talents, just as the false god did. As Anarya struggles to control the compulsion, Yisul is fraught with worry and seeks help for her lover. But Jotuk is in upheaval; the Twenty-Three families are in disarray, divided over how the city should be governed.

In Carregis, the king seeks to establish himself as an effective ruler. First, though, he must work out whom he can trust.

Meanwhile, the priestesses of Quarenna and the priests of Huler are having disturbing dreams…

Thiever is the much anticipated sequel to David M Allan's *Quaestor*.

ISBN: 9781911409977 (epub, kindle) / 9781911409878 (386pp paperback)
Visit bit.ly/Thiever

Sooty Feathers series by David Craig

A supernatural war for control of late 19th century Glasgow.

1: *Resurrection Men*

Glasgow 1893.

Wilton Hunt, a student, and Tam Foley, a laudanum-addicted pharmacist, are pursuing extra-curricular careers as body snatchers, or 'resurrection men', under cover of darkness. They exhume a girl's corpse, only for it to disappear while their backs are turned. Confused and in need of the money the body would have earnt them, they investigate the corpse's disappearance. They discover that bodies have started to turn up in the area with ripped-out throats and severe loss of blood, although not the one they lost. The police are being encouraged by powerful people to look the other way, and the deaths are going unreported by the press. As Hunt and Foley delve beneath the veneer of respectable society, they find themselves entangled in a dangerous underworld that is protected from scrutiny by the rich and powerful members of the elite but secretive Sooty Feathers Club.

Meanwhile, a mysterious circus arrives in the middle of the night, summoned to help avenge a betrayal two centuries old…

ISBN: 9781911409366 (epub, kindle) / ISBN: 9781911409267 (400pp paperback)

Visit bit.ly/ResurrectionMen

2: *Lord of the Hunt*

June 1893.

Undead prowl the streets of Glasgow at night hunting for blood. They, in turn, are hunted by the formidable Lady Delaney and her apprentice Kerry Knox, whose fight against the secret society ruling Glasgow will lead them into the city's industrial heart where the poor toil in miserable conditions. Children have been exploited in mills and factories for decades, but the Sooty Feather Society has refined its cruel disregard in service to the undead.

Delaney and Knox are not the society's only problem. The elusive demon Arakiel employs murder and necromancy in his campaign to seize control of Glasgow, avenging betrayal and reclaiming what was once his.

Wilton Hunt and Tam Foley are lying low in the Highlands where Hunt's father has recently inherited title and estate. The blue skies and clear waters of Loch Aline may seem a tranquil sanctuary to the city men, but its forbidding forests and shadowed glens conceal dark secrets pertaining to Hunt's family, and a diabolical revelation will change Wilton's life forever.

Demons walk the crowded, cobbled streets of Glasgow, and a necromancer's debt is called in. Knox will learn what joining this war might cost her; Hunt and Foley will learn they can't escape it. Their diverged paths will meet again when dark magic unleashes a horror not everyone will survive…

ISBN: 9781911409762 (epub, kindle) / ISBN: 9781911409663 (416pp paperback)

Visit bit.ly/LordOfTheHunt

3: *Lucifer & Son*

Coming Soon

SIMON KEWIN'S WITCHFINDER SERIES
"Think *Dirk Gently* meets *Good Omens*!"

THE EYE COLLECTORS
A STORY OF
HER MAJESTY'S OFFICE OF THE WITCHFINDER GENERAL
PROTECTING THE PUBLIC FROM THE UNNATURAL SINCE 1645

When Danesh Shahzan gets called to a crime scene, it's usually because the police suspect not just foul play but unnatural forces at play.

Danesh Shahzan, an Acolyte in Her Majesty's Office of the Witchfinder General – a shadowy arm of the British government fighting supernatural threats to the realm – is called in to investigate a murder in Cardiff. The victim had been placed inside a runic circle and their eyes carefully removed from their head. But there are wider implications…
  ISBN: 9781911409748 (epub, kindle) / 9781911409649 (288pp paperback)

THE SEVEN SUCCUBI
THE SECOND STORY OF
HER MAJESTY'S OFFICE OF THE WITCHFINDER GENERAL

Of all the denizens of the circles of Hell, perhaps none is more feared among those of a high-minded sensibility than the succubi.

The Office of the Witchfinder General may employ 'demonic powers' so long as their use is 'reasonable' and 'to defeat some greater supernatural threat'. After recent events Acolyte Danesh Shahzan had been struggling to define 'reasonable'. Then an unexpected evening visit from his boss to discuss his succubi thesis presaged another investigation.
  ISBN: 9781915304117 (epub, kindle) / 9781915304018 (334pp paperback)

HEAD FULL OF DARK
THE THIRD STORY OF
HIS MAJESTY'S OFFICE OF THE WITCHFINDER GENERAL

Quis custodiet ipsos custodes?

There is clearly someone in the Office of the Witchfinder General who is working for or with English Wizardry, and Danesh and the Crow are determined to track them down. It might even be one of the Lord High Witchfinders. Who can they trust? Can Danesh even trust the Crow?
  To ensure the traitor is not alerted, Danesh conducts an off-the-books investigation under cover of an inquiry into a cold case. But not all cold cases stay cold; not all dead witches stay dead; and not all traitors stay hidden…
  … and what is the significance of the goat's skull?
  ISBN: 9781915304384 (epub, kindle) / 9781915304285 (338pp paperback)
Visit bit.ly/WitchfinderSeries

King Street Run

V.R. Ling

To Thomas, archaeology was time travel... little did he know how literal that would turn out to be.

King Street Run is a satirical fantasy thriller set among the iconic buildings of contemporary Cambridge.

Thomas Wharton, an archaeology graduate, becomes drawn into the problems of a series of anachronistic characters who exist in the fractions of a second behind our own time. These characters turn out to be personi cations of the Cambridge Colleges; they have the amalgamated foibles, history, and temperament of their Fellows and students and, together with Thomas, must enter into a race against time to prevent their world being destroyed by an unknown assailant.

At the age of six V.R. Ling (Victoria) watched the TV adaptation of *The Hitchhiker's Guide To The Galaxy* and it sparked a life-long love for science fiction and fantasy (she therefore considers the first five years of her life to have been a waste). Science and fiction have separately shaped her life; the science part came in the form of a degree in archaeology, a Masters in biological anthropology, and then a PhD in biological anthropology from King's College, Cambridge. On the fiction front, Victoria is influenced by the likes of H.G Wells, Jules Verne, M.R James, Charles Dickens, Wilkie Collins, and many others. Victoria by name, Victorian by nature. She is a huge animal lover, vegan, loves sixties music, adores classic *Doctor Who*, and has an antique book collection that smells as good as it looks.

ISBN: 9781915304513 (epub, kindle) / 97819153041414 (304pp paperback)

Visit bit.ly/KingStreetRun

The Vanished Mage

Penelope Hill and J. A. Mortimore

A vanished mage…
A missing diamond…
The game is afoot.

"From Broderick, Prince of Asconar, Earl of Carlshore and Thorn, Duke of Wicksborough, Baron of Highbury and Warden of Dershanmoor, to My Lady Parisan, King's Investigator, greetings. It has been brought to my attention that a certain Reinwald, Master Historian, noted Archmagus and tutor to our court in this city of Nemithia, has this day failed to report to the duties awaiting him. I do ask you, as my father's most loyal servant, to seek the cause of this laxity and bring word of the mage to me, so that my concerns as to his safety be allayed."

The herald delivered the message word-perfect to The Lady Parisan, Baroness of Orandy, Knight of the Diamond Circle and Sworn Paladin to Our Lady of the Sighs. Parisan's companion, Foorourow Miar Raar Ramoura, Prince of Ilsfacar, (Foo to his friends) thought it a rather mundane assignment, but nevertheless together they ventured to the Archmagus' imposing home to seek him. It turned out to be the start of an adventure to solve a mystery wrapped in an enigma bound by a conundrum and secured by a puzzle. All because of a missing diamond with a solar system at its core.

Authors Penelope Hill and J. A. Mortimore have effortlessly melded a Holmesian investigative duo, a richly detailed city where they encounter both nobility and seedier denizens, swashbuckling action, and magic that is palpable and, at times, awesome.

ISBN: 9781915304186 (epub, kindle) / 97819153041087 (212pp paperback)

Visit bit.ly/TheVanishedMage

about david m allan

David M Allan got hooked on reading at a young age by borrowing to the max – 3 books, twice a week – from the public library. He was caught up and transported to fabulous other worlds by the likes of Wells, Verne and Burroughs (and later by Asimov, Bradbury, Clarke, Heinlein, Le Guin, Wyndham…). Alas, the journeys were temporary and he had to return to Earth.

His love affair with science fiction and fantasy had him thinking vaguely about writing but he didn't follow through until after retirement and his relocation, with wife and cat, to a houseboat on the Thames. It was reading one book which he didn't think was very good that led him to say "I could do better than that" and then setting out to prove it. David has since had a number of short stories published in online magazines, and his debut novel *The Empty Throne* published by Elsewhen Press. *Quaestor,* his second novel, and *Thiever*, its sequel have also been published by Elsewhen Press.

Unlike his previous novels, *The Magic is always with us* is set in the land of his birth… well, sort of!